DARKNESS BETWEEN THE STARS

THE FATELESS TRILOGY
BOOK TWO

LINDSEY SPARKS

RUBUS PRESS

DARKNESS BETWEEN THE STARS

THE FATELESS TRILOGY
BOOK TWO

LINDSEY SPARKS

RUBUS PRESS

Editing by Fresh as a Daisy Editing

www.freshasadaisyediting.com

Cover by We Got You Covered

www.wegotyoucoveredbookdesign.com

9781949485301

Also by
Lindsey Sparks

ECHO WORLD
ECHO TRILOGY
Echo in Time
Resonance
Time Anomaly
Dissonance
Ricochet Through Time

KAT DUBOIS CHRONICLES
Ink Witch
Outcast
Underground
Soul Eater
Judgement
Afterlife

THE NIK CHRONICLES
(Patreon exclusive serial)

FATELESS TRILOGY
Song of Scarabs and Fallen Stars
Darkness Between the Stars
Uncross the Stars

LEGACIES OF OLYMPUS
ATLANTIS LEGACY
Sacrifice of the Sinners
Legacy of the Lost
Fate of the Fallen
Dreams of the Damned
Song of the Soulless
Blood of the Broken
Rise of the Revenants

Allworld Online: Looking Glass
(Patreon exclusive serial)

ALLWORLD ONLINE
AO: Pride & Prejudice
AO: The Wonderful Wizard of Oz
Vertigo

THE LAST VAMPIRE QUEEN
(Patreon exclusive serial)

THE ENDING WORLD
THE ENDING SERIES
(writing as Lindsey Fairleigh)
The Ending Beginnings: Omnibus Edition
After The Ending
Into The Fire
Out Of The Ashes
Before The Dawn
World Before

THE ENDING LEGACY
World After
The Raven Queen
The Ghost King

For more information on Lindsey and her books:
www.authorlindseysparks.com

Signed books and exclusive merch:
lindseysparksbookshop.com

Join Lindsey's mailing list to stay up to date on releases
AND to get access to her FREE subscriber library, including
Ink Witch, *Echo in Time*, and *Legacy of the Lost*
in ebook AND audiobook.
https://www.authorlindseysparks.com/join-newsletter

Check out Lindsey's Patreon for bonus scenes and exclusive serials:
https://www.patreon.com/lindseysparks

AUTHOR'S NOTE

Dear reader,

Once again, this series is pushing my boundaries as an author – and I love it! This is definitely the steamiest book I've put out into the world, which I don't think should come as too much of a shock after all the silent promises I made in Song of Scarabs and Fallen Stars. *I hope you enjoy continuing Tarset's journey of self-discovery. She has most certainly enjoyed it!*

As with the first book in this series, there are some content warnings: depression, suicidal thoughts, self-harm, explicit sex scenes, mature language.

THE PLAYLIST

Listen to the playlist on Spotify: spoti.fi/3uzAINA

Island - SVRCINA

Midnight Oil – Tommee Profitt, Fleurie

Masochist - Sophie Ann

Somebody Else - Ruelle

Whispers - Halsey

The Enemy - MXMS

RX - MXMS

I Scare Myself - Beth Crowley

Hurricane - Tommee Profitt, Fleurie

Bad Dream - Ruelle

Long Suffering - Eliza Grace

Find You - Ruelle

Way Down we Go - Unions
Hurts Like Hell - Tommee Profitt, Fleurie
Without You - Ursine Vulpine, Annaca
Empires - Ruelle
Last Goodbye - The Hot Damns, Smokey Jones
Down - Simon, Trella
I Hope You Cry - Meg Myers, Morgxn
Heart of The Darkness - Tommee Profitt, Sam Tinnesz
Nothing Is As It Seems - Hidden Citizens, Ruelle
Glass Heart - Tommee Profitt, Sam Tinnesz
In My Blood - Tommee Profit, Fleurie
The Fear of Letting Go - Ruelle
Don't Let Me Go - RAIGN
Breathe - Tommee Profitt, Fleurie
Too Far Gone - Hidden Citizens, SVRCINA
Breathe Me - Sia
Carry You - Ruelle, Fleurie
Immortalized - Hidden Citizens, Keeley Bumford
The Other Side - Ruelle
Run Baby Run - The Rigs
Play With Fire - Sam Tinnesz, Ruelle, Violents
Closer - J2, Keeley Bumford
Casualty - Hidden Citizens, Tash
Never Surrender - Liv Ash
Stay - Rihanna, Mikky Ekko

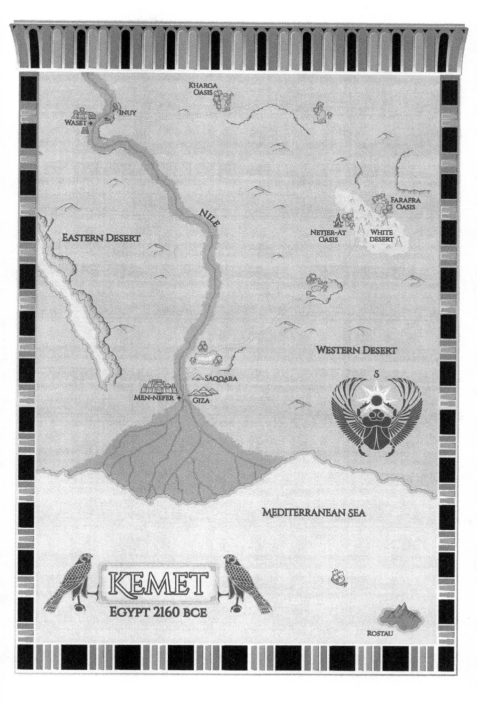

ANCIENT TIMES

TARSET

A TUM ASKED ME A question, his voice a velvety caress behind me.

I closed my eyes, basking in the heat from the glowing *At* logs in the faux campfire Atum had created to warm the cavern. Even if I had never seen the man—the god—with my own two eyes, I would have found him irresistible based on his voice alone. So deep and rich, with the perfect gentle rumble.

"Tarset?" Atum touched my shoulder, a mere skim of his fingertips, but even that faint contact sent pleasure zinging through me.

My eyelids snapped open, and I craned my neck to peer up at him. His shadow appeared enormous on the pearlescent *At* wall behind him. His dark features were sculpted to perfection, and his eyes were pools of midnight swirling with stars, threatening to swallow me whole.

In the weeks since we left Men-nefer, jumping south to his hidden cavern across the river from Waset, any doubts that we were potential bond-mates had long since vanished from my mind. The gravity between us was too strong. If I closed my eyes and walked blindly in any direction, he would be where I ended up. His soul called to me, a siren song I couldn't ignore. Resist, perhaps. For a time. But never ignore.

I licked my lips, unintentionally drawing his attention to my mouth. "I'm sorry—what?" I had absolutely zero clue what he had said.

Atum clenched his jaw, his nostrils flaring. He pulled his hand away from me and raised his chin, taking a deep, steadying breath. At least I wasn't alone in this attraction. He felt the lure just as strongly as I did. The only problem was that he *wasn't* resisting. I was alone in the desire to maintain my soul's independence. Atum wouldn't push the matter until I had decided; he had made that very clear. He was respecting my wishes far better than I would have been doing were I in his shoes and *he* was the one resisting *me*.

"Are you cold?" he asked.

"Oh." I shook my head, tearing my stare away from his to look at the imitation campfire glowing in the sunken pit in the middle of the cavern. Wood was scarce in the Nile Valley, and with Atum's ability to pull *At* into the physical realm and imbue it with properties like heat or a gentle glow, it just made sense not to fuss over an actual fire. Besides, we were in a sealed cavern, and we weren't interested in killing ourselves via smoke inhalation.

"No, I'm perfect," I said, smiling in his direction but not quite looking at him—to prevent myself from being ensnared by his gaze once more. "Thanks."

The sand that had blown into the cavern on the hot summer winds crunched under Atum's sandals as he made his way to the far side of the sunken fire pit. "Tefnut will reach Waset tomorrow," he said, crouching near the edge of the faux campfire.

We had been waiting for his daughter's return after her seafaring trip of delivering my mom and Kiya to the mysterious island of Rostau. I would have asked why we were waiting for her and not simply crossing the river ourselves, except I wasn't remotely eager to return to that place—that palace of nightmares. And despite Atum's notable ability to travel through time, we couldn't simply hop forward to the moment Tefnut would arrive. Apparently Atum and his children could only shift between eras via Rostau, like the island was their own personal time travel hub.

Atum settled on the ground, his elbow resting on his one upraised knee. The position stretched the white linen of his schenti, affording me a tantalizing peekaboo view of the smooth, dark skin running the length of his inner thigh.

I narrowed my eyes at him. Was he doing this on purpose? Was he taunting me with his body, showing me what I was missing out on? I pursed my lips. Maybe he *wasn't* respecting my wishes quite as well as I had thought. He was just being extremely subtle with his seduction.

"When we return to Waset, I will be wearing a disguise," Atum said, a note of wariness in his tone.

A mental image of him wearing a pair of those plastic joke glasses with the ridiculous attached fake mustache flashed through my mind's eye, and I choked on a giggle. I cleared my throat and suppressed my amusement. "Will you be Temu again?" I asked. The muted, human version of himself was the only disguise I had ever seen him wear. Well, I had seen him cloaked in shadows deep enough to make himself invisible, as well, but I preferred not to think of those dark days.

When I did, I was forced to recall that Atum hadn't stepped in to put a stop to my torture *for weeks*, giving voice to insidious thoughts that spread doubt through my mind. What did it mean that he *let* Inyotef torture me? How could he have let it go on if he truly cared about me? Would it be a mistake to choose him over my family when he hadn't chosen *me* over the timeline?

Atum shook his head, his expression serious, his stare locked on me. He inhaled, and his reticence made my muscles bunch with tension. "When we enter Waset," he said, "I will look like Inyotef."

My heart lurched, and my stomach twisted. I swallowed audibly and shook my head. Inyotef, my tormentor, was dead, killed by Atum's hands right in front of me. I wasn't supposed to ever have to see him again, to look into his cruel, calculating eyes.

Even the thought of hearing that psychopath's voice again sent a shiver down my spine. My rib cage seemed to constrict around my lungs, making it harder to draw in a full breath. Tears welled on the brims of my eyelids, and my chin trembled as I fought to control my breathing.

I sensed Atum's stare on me, but my focus drifted inward until I was back in that dungeon beneath the Waset palace. Alone. In pain. Not only waiting for death but hoping for it. I could feel the cool, dry air, smell the earth and urine and smoke from the torches, hear the screams—my own screams and those from strangers in other cells. My shoulder joints throbbed with a memory of the agony of being strung up by my wrists.

I recalled how Inyotef's pet priest had spent hours upon hours *experimenting* upon me, exploring the boundaries of my Nejeret healing abilities and jotting down everything he learned about the inner workings of a living body on his papyrus scrolls. Atum *must* have been aware of what was happening to me, but he had let it happen anyway—for the sake of the timeline. To guarantee I wouldn't cave under enough pressure and put the timeline at risk in order to save myself. To test my commitment to preserving *what must be.*

We hadn't spoken about my imprisonment since my recovery time in this very cavern. Atum had apologized for the part he played in my suffering, but he *had* let the suffering happen. A not-so-small part of me still resented him for not stopping it sooner. He wanted me—desperately—that much was apparent. But how deeply could he truly *care* for me, the person I was on the inside, if he wasn't plagued by guilt over what he had let happen to me? Maybe he thought about it all the time, but there was no way for me to know without asking him.

"If there were any other way," Atum started but trailed off. He let out a heavy sigh. "But there is not, and this is the cost of ending Inyotef's life prematurely. The timeline demands it. There was much left for him to do, and now I must step in and finish his life's work for him."

I swallowed, but there was no saliva in my mouth. There was only glue. I cleared my throat, and when I spoke again, my voice was weak and thready. "How closely will you resemble him?" I asked, blinking back to the here and now, focusing on Atum rather than my memory of Inyotef. "Will it be just your appearance? Or will you sound like him?" My throat convulsed with the threat of a gag. "Will you smell like him?"

Atum studied me for a long moment from across the firepit. "Let me show you," he said gently. "Just for a moment, so you will know what you must prepare yourself to endure during the coming weeks." His stare searched mine, an apology written across his features. "And then, when our work here is done and we leave Waset, I swear to you I will never resurrect him again."

I squeezed my eyelids shut and nodded. "Do it," I whispered. "Do it now. I don't want to see you become him." I couldn't have that image forever linking the two of them in my head, waiting to haunt me every time I closed my eyes.

A faint, electric crackle touched my ears, and the tingle of otherworldly energy sizzled over my skin, more intense than when Atum pulled solidified *At* into the physical realm, but not so bad as when he jumped me from one place to another.

"It is done," Atum said, except it wasn't *his* voice that uttered those words. It was a voice dragged from the worst of my nightmares, and I had plenty of awful dreams vying for the role.

I inhaled shakily and braced myself for what I was about to encounter, and then I forced my eyelids open.

The shock of seeing Inyotef again stole my breath. I stared at him—at Atum, I consciously reminded myself—for long seconds without moving. Without breathing. Between one heartbeat and the next, I became prey, caught in the sights of a predator.

Atum stood, wearing Inyotef's lighter skin and smaller frame. Slowly, he made his way around the firepit and knelt beside me. I watched him out of the corner of my eye, but I couldn't bring myself to actually look at him.

"Tarset," Inyotef—Atum—said softly. "I am not him."

A quake racked my body. His voice. His smooth, deep, horrible voice. It was spot on. Absolutely perfect. I *knew* this wasn't Inyotef, but my mind couldn't make sense of what was happening, and I began to lose my grasp on reality. The knowledge of who was truly beside me conflicted with what I was seeing and hearing. My body remembered what those hands had done to me, and it refused to believe they weren't still a threat.

My breaths came shallower, quicker. Truth and reality twisted up inside me until I couldn't tell what was real.

I am not him, he had said.

I shook my head, panicked and confused. Who was the *him* he referred to—Inyotef or Atum? Which man was he really? And which was he *not*?

"Look at me, Tarset," he—whoever he was—commanded. "You must be able to face me looking like this and keep a clear head."

Tears streamed down my cheeks as I forced my head to turn. As I forced myself to look at the visage of the man who had taken joy in tormenting me, in torturing me. Everything about the man beside me *was* Inyotef. Everything except for his eyes.

Atum's midnight eyes stared out from that handsome, hated face. "Inyotef is dead," he told me. "I killed him so he would never hurt you again." He reached for me, and I was too stunned to move away. He took my hand, clasping it tight in both of his. "I will never let anyone hurt you ever again."

My nostrils flared, and my chin quivered. My next blink set a fresh stream of tears free.

Atum's stolen features softened until he wore an expression I had never seen on the real Inyotef's face—genuine concern. "Close your eyes," he murmured. "I wish to show you something else." The corner of his mouth tensed, Inyotef's thin lips hinting at a smile. "Something you will enjoy." He tilted his head to the side. "I think."

I stared at him a moment longer, taking refuge in his familiar eyes. And then I let my eyelids drift shut, hoping he was returning to his true appearance, because I certainly enjoyed that.

"All right," he said, his voice having changed again, becoming somehow both softer and rougher than Inyotef's. Something about the unique timbre tickled my memory. "Open your eyes."

Curious about the familiarity of the voice, I lifted my lids. And when I saw who sat beside me, my mouth fell open.

Atum had become the friendly boatman who had ferried me back and forth across the Nile, his lips spread into a cautious smile that revealed the slightly crooked white teeth I remembered. His sun-kissed skin was darker than Inyotef's but still far lighter than the skin tone I had expected. His eyes glittered with amusement, now a hint of brown in his irises to temper their divine inky shade.

I shook my head, my eyes opened wide, at a complete loss for words.

"Perhaps this was a mistake," Atum said under his—the boatman's—breath.

"I—" I searched his face, his friendly gaze. "I don't understand."

Atum withdrew the hand that was atop mine and reached into the folds of his linen kilt. When he pulled his hand out again, his fingers were curled into a loose fist. He turned his hand over and extended it in front of me, and when he uncurled his fingers, a gold cone-shaped senet piece about the size of my thumbnail rested on his palm. It was a perfect replica of the one I had given the boatman as payment for his services.

Except, I didn't think it was a replica. Just as I didn't think Atum merely *looked* like the boatman.

Brows bunching together, I looked from the gold game piece on Atum's disguised hand to the mask he currently wore, of the man who had befriended me and helped me when I had first arrived in Waset possessing little more than the clothing on my back.

"It was you?" I puzzled aloud. "You were him? You don't just look like him, do you? You were—*are*—the boatman?"

Atum nodded, a single dip and rise of the boatman's chin.

"You helped me," I said, my voice wavering as I processed what this meant. I glanced down at the gold token. "And you've been carrying that around with you ever since?"

When I looked up at his face again, the boatman was gone. He was Atum once more, in all his dark glory, the only spots of light on his body the golden scars he cut into his skin at sunrise every morning to help him honor the thousands of lives he had ended in service to his sworn duty to protect the one true timeline. Twenty-six new, long scars ran the length of his forearms.

Atum's thumb traced slow circles over the back of my hand, and he curled his fingers around the senet piece. "You can't have it back," he said, the corners of his mouth tilting upward. "I earned it."

The absurdity of that statement cut through the tension in the air between us, and laughter bubbled up from my chest. Suddenly, I felt a thousand pounds lighter.

"Keep it," I told him and fluttered my lashes dramatically. "A token of our love."

I regretted the words as soon as they were out of my mouth, but I held my easy smile, hoping Atum would take them as a joke and not as something more. I wasn't quite sure which they were.

His gaze heated, and his focus dropped to my lips. "It could be," he said, continuing to graze the pad of this thumb over the back of my hand. His stare returned to mine. "If you let it."

Well, shit. I was in trouble. Atum definitely *wasn't* happy to sit back and wait for me to decide whether or not to give in to temptation and bind my soul to his. He just had far subtler, sneakier game than anyone I had encountered in the past.

"I, um . . ." I pulled my hand from his and stood. "I need to pee," I said, blurting the first thing that came to mind. I approached the shimmering barrier of *At* blocking the cavern entrance shielding us from the rest of the world. "Will you let me out?"

I heard Atum approaching behind me before I felt his heat against my back. "Of course," he said, reaching an arm over my shoulder and pressing his palm flat against the impenetrable barrier. He leaned in closer, and when he spoke next, his breath caressed my ear. "I would let you do almost anything."

I inhaled sharply, and a jolt of need shot to my core.

A tingle of otherworldly energy tickled my skin, and the *At* barrier melted into a rainbow mist before evaporating completely. Below, beyond the ledge of the cliff, the floodwaters from the Nile gleamed atop the submerged barley fields.

Atum's fingertips skimmed over my collarbone and shoulder as he pulled back his arm. "I'll get dinner started," he said, as if his words hadn't just instantly flicked the on switch for my libido. "Let me know when you're done, and I'll join you on the path."

But that was the problem. I wasn't sure I would ever be done with him. It would be so easy to just give in. To let him become my whole world. To give up everything for him, including the chance to ever go home to the future.

I wanted to do it—to seal our fates together, forever, despite my doubts. I had only known Atum for a couple of months, but I wanted him more than anything.

And *that* scared the hell out of me.

I COULDN'T GET COMFORTABLE on my cushy *At* bedroll, and I tossed and turned in a fruitless search for sleep. Atum and I had been waiting in the cavern for weeks, just the two of us, so I should have been used to sleeping in an enclosed space with him by now. I *had* been used to it. The last week or so, I slept soundly, comforted by the knowledge that with Atum nearby, nobody could get close enough to hurt me. That Inyotef was no longer *alive* to hurt me.

But pain and fear were the furthest things from my mind as I stared up at the curved cavern ceiling, the smooth *At* gleaming as it reflected the glow from the faux logs in the firepit. I couldn't stop thinking about Atum and that senet game piece of gleaming gold on his dark palm.

Atum *was* the boatman. The boatman was *him*. The layers of significance concealed within that revelation boggled my mind. Every time I learned something new about Atum, the puzzle pieces of him in my mind had to rearrange, ceaselessly shifting until I figured out how to fit them back together.

I had known he had been watching me before we met at the market, but I never would have guessed we had *already* met. That he had helped me, back when he was still deciding whether or not he needed to kill me—a time anomaly, an unknown threat to the one true timeline. Back when logic and duty dictated that he *should* have killed me. What did that mean—that he had stayed his hand? That he had preserved my life at notable risk to the integrity of the time tapestry? Was it the potential to bond? Had he been able to sense it, even then? Did his sparing my life *then* negate all the suffering I experienced *after*?

Glancing at Atum lying beside me on his own bedroll, but just out of reach, I pushed the layered linen blanket off me, letting the cool night air kiss my bare legs. All my rolling around had bunched the hem of my shift high on my thighs, and I didn't bother pulling it down. Atum's back was to me anyway, so I hardly needed to worry about sending him mixed signals with my show of skin.

I inhaled deeply, releasing the breath in a sigh. Why was I even trying to prevent the bond? It wasn't like I had any way to travel thousands of years into the future to get home anyway. I wasn't even sure if Aramei, the only time traveling Nejeret I knew of who had lived in Egypt during this general era, could or would transport me back to my family in the future. She wasn't even alive yet to ask. In all likelihood, I was doomed to take the long, slow road home, living each and every day between this moment and the one I had left behind four thousand years in the future.

Which meant I could either stand at Atum's side for *four millennia*, fighting the urge to jump his bones, until I finally reached the time I had abandoned. Or, I could get it over with already. Do the deed. Ride the stallion. Seal the bond.

True, consummating our relationship and igniting the bond would bind our souls together *for eternity*. Our bodies would become addicted to one another's bonding pheromones. I wouldn't simply crave him; I would require him to continue living. I would *die* without him, as he would without me. If I bound my *ba* to Atum's, I would never go home, not even if I took the slow, four-thousand-year road.

But would I even want to return to the life I had left behind after being Atum's companion for four thousand years? Would I be able to find any joy or fulfillment in my vapid existence as a pop star?

Oh, who was I kidding? I wasn't delusional enough to believe I could resist Atum for even four thousand hours, let alone four thousand *years*. I had never been known for my self-restraint. Self-indulgence was more my thing. I would have bet my life that I would give in to the urge to bond with Atum *long* before I even reached the time of Aramei's birth, let alone my family and fans in the distant future.

Again, I glanced at Atum, studying the strong, smooth lines of his back exposed above the edge of his blanket. The gold scars from his sunrise ritual peeked over his shoulders, but the rest of his back was pristine, unblemished skin, looking like gleaming onyx in the gentle glow from the firepit.

I should just do it, I thought. *Right here. Right now.*

As I thought of finally, intentionally putting my hands on Atum—of exploring every inch of that glorious body—my breaths came faster, and my suddenly racing heart thudded in my chest. A tsunami of arousal surged within me. My blood felt electrified, making my entire body sizzle with anticipation. A needy ache blossomed in my core, and my pulse throbbed insistently between my legs.

Holy hell, if just *thinking* about being with Atum had me this turned on, what would it be like to truly *be* with him? I was more than ready to find out.

"Atum?" I whispered, rolling onto my side toward him. "Are you awake?"

When he remained still, saying nothing, I sat up and crawled closer to him. I craned my neck to peer down at his face. His eyes were closed, and his features were relaxed, but the pulse jumping along the side of his neck told me he wasn't truly asleep. He was faking it.

"Atum?"

Still, he didn't respond.

I narrowed my eyes at him. I didn't know what game he was playing, pretending to be asleep, but after his taunting promises earlier, I wasn't about to let him play hard to get now.

"*Atum*," I sang softly, tracing my fingertips over the fluttering pulse point on his neck. "I know you're awake."

He inhaled, then held his breath for a few seconds. "Get some rest, Tarset," he said without opening his eyes. "We have a trying day tomorrow."

I leaned over him until I was so close that I drowned in his honey and spice scent. "I can't sleep," I whispered. "I'm too anxious." I trailed my fingertips over his shoulder and started down the length of his muscular arm. "Maybe you can help me relax?" I suggested, leaning closer to graze my lips over the skin of his throat.

A low, rough noise rumbled in Atum's chest, and he caught my wrist in one large hand.

My breath caught, and I raised my head enough that I could see his face. His eyes were still closed, but his jaw was clenched, his features tensed.

"Atum, I—"

The words died on my tongue as his eyelids lifted, and he peered at me sidelong. "I don't believe you are thinking clearly."

"My thoughts have never been more singularly focused," I countered, twisting my wrist free of his loose grasp. I slipped my hand under his blanket, brushing my fingertips over the ridges of muscle on his abdomen. "Of that, I can assure you."

"Oh, I believe that," Atum said, his nostrils flaring as he inhaled deeply. He made a rough, pleased sound and rolled onto his back, then sat up, forcing me upright as well. "But *focus* and *clarity* are not one and the same." He stared at me for long seconds, his gaze shifting back and forth as he searched mine, apparently weighing my conviction. He leaned in until his lips were a hairsbreadth from mine. "Perhaps I could help you clear your mind," he murmured. "I would hate for you to make such a significant decision in haste."

I licked my lips, swallowing roughly as I knelt beside him. "What did you have in mind?" I asked breathily, squeezing my thighs together in anticipation.

Atum made that rough sound again, like a cross between a laugh and a groan, and it lit my kindled insides on fire. "Nothing too strenuous," he murmured, his hand settling lightly on my knee.

"Right," I breathed. "Big day tomorrow."

"And nothing too permanent." His fingers inched up my thigh between my closed legs, the movement slow but deliberate, filled with promise. "Lie back, Tarset," he murmured. "And I will thoroughly clear your mind." The tip of his fingers skimmed the crease of my bare sex, already damp with arousal. Bless this sweet, ancient time period for being oblivious to underclothes.

I sucked in a shuddering breath. "That's not where my mind is located," I said, my voice shaky. But despite my words, I eased backward onto my bedroll, stretching out my legs and resting back on my elbows.

"Is it not?" he said, nudging my legs apart as he traced up and down my slit. He was teasing me, never quite reaching high enough to touch the swollen bundle of nerves that ached for his attention. His gaze remained locked with mine, his voice a low purr. "Is this not currently the focal point of your every thought?"

I tilted my pelvis, seeking a very specific point of contact, but he anticipated the movement and slid his fingers lower again.

Atum chuckled. "I know what you want, Tarset," he said. "But I'm not ready to give it to you."

I whimpered as he dipped his fingers deeper between my lips, teasing my entrance. "Atum," I pleaded.

He moved closer, kneeling beside me, and reached out with his other arm to push my knees farther apart, exposing me to him completely. Even in my lust-fueled delirium, it was not lost on me that we were in essentially the same position as we had been on that hillside in Waset, only this time Atum's hands were on me in place of my own.

"What if I told you there was a way for you to go home?" he said, pushing a fingertip inside me. "Would you still want to do this?"

"Yes," I breathed, not fully comprehending his words, only that *yes* was the word I needed to say to keep his hands on me.

He sank his finger further in. "Would you still want me inside you?"

"Yes," I hissed, drawing out the *s*.

"Would you still want me to claim your body?" He added a second finger, pushing both into me. "To claim your soul?"

"Oh dear gods, yes," I said, letting my elbows slide out from under me and falling back onto the bedroll. Pleasure mounted in the core of my being, and the tension spooled tighter within me. My inner muscles fluttered, teasing what promised to be an epic climax.

"Would you still want to bind your *ba* to mine," he said, pumping his fingers into me, "knowing it would seal your fate with mine?"

"Atum," I panted, my hips lifting with each thrust of his hand. My fists clenched in the bedroll. If he would just touch that throbbing point at the apex of my sex, I would be done for. Just one brief brush of his thumb. Just a flick of his nail. Gods, if he simply blew on me there, I would likely fly over the edge into blissful oblivion.

"Knowing it would mean you could never go home?" he said, the velvet gravel of his voice like another form of caress.

"Yes!" I proclaimed, not hearing his words at all, just the sound of his voice. "Yes, Atum. Anything. Just finish it, please," I begged. "*Please.*"

"Would you give up your family for me?"

I closed my eyes, sinking into that tantalizing rumble. "*Please...*"

"Say it," he demanded. "Tell me you would give up everything for me, and I'll give you your release."

"Yes," I sobbed, thrashing my head back and forth as he continued to thrust his fingers into me, keeping me expertly teetering on the brink of ecstasy. "Everything. Anything. Take it. Take it all. I just need you. I just need you to—"

He buried his fingers inside me and swept the pad of his thumb over my aching bud.

My words died in a choked groan as pleasure exploded from my core. My back bowed, my shoulders lifting off the bedroll, and my mouth opened in a silent scream. Wave after wave of ecstasy pulsed through me, and for a brief eternity, I lost myself to the pleasure.

I melted back onto the bedroll as the climax waned, and I let my eyelids drift shut. My muscles felt like Jell-O, and the featherlight caress of Atum's thumb sent tiny aftershocks of pleasure shooting out from my core.

"Mmm," I purred. "That was—" My eyelids snapped open as my mind finally—*finally*—processed Atum's words. I lifted my head, propping myself on my elbows once more. "Did you say there's a way for me to go home?"

"See?" he said, withdrawing his hand. "Clarity." He flashed me a tight smile and angled his head to the side, raising his eyebrows pointedly. "Not the same as focus."

"But how—" I shook my head. "Why didn't you tell me about this before?"

Atum stood, smooth and graceful as a panther, and stalked to the shimmering *At* barrier blocking the cavern mouth, his back to me. "Because I wanted you," he snapped. His shoulders rose and fell with a deep breath, and when he spoke again, his voice was even, calm. "Because I wanted *your help*," he amended. "I was never going to kill you—not once I came to know you. Not once I understood your conviction to protect the timeline was just as strong as mine. If you didn't want to help me, I would have sent you home."

My emotions were a tangled ball of confusion. Brow furrowing, I sat up and adjusted the skirt of my shift to cover my lower body. "How?" I asked softly. "*How* would you send me home?"

"Rostau," he said, still facing the *At* barrier. "The same way I am able to travel through time. From Rostau, I can create temporary portals to any era, even one-way portals to times outside the boundaries of the timeline to which I am bound. I can send you there, but I cannot follow." He was quiet for a moment. "That is what I will do when we reach Rostau, if it is your wish. I will create a portal to your home in the future." His shoulders rose and fell with another of those deep breaths, and he turned his head, peering back at me. "But first we must clean up the mess in Waset. The dissonance we—I—created by killing Inyotef is the most extreme disturbance of the timeline I have ever encountered. I will need your unique effect on the lifethreads if I am to have any hope of correcting it."

I laughed bitterly under my breath. "One chaos bomb, at your service." I stood, my legs still a little wobbly, and approached Atum. "And when we're finished in Waset, we'll travel to Rostau?" I asked, coming to stand beside him.

Atum's eyes searched mine, and he bowed his head. "You wish to return home, then."

"I didn't say that," I corrected him, slipping my hand into his.

Atum's brows drew together, his expression turning puzzled. "You wish to stay?" he asked. "With me?"

I gave his hand a squeeze. "I don't know," I said truthfully, flashing him an apologetic smile. "I wish to get to know you better, so I can make a decision based on more than, well..." I glanced down at my bedroll, my cheeks heating. I cleared my throat. "In my time—in the future, I mean," I said, "people usually spend time together before they commit to forever."

The corner of Atum's mouth tensed, then quirked upward. "You wish me to court you."

My smile widened, and I nodded. "But only if *you* wish to court me."

His eyes narrowed. "I wish to do many things to you," he said, leaning in and letting his gaze skim down the length of my body. "Many, many things." He pulled away, once again facing forward. "I have never courted anyone before," he said. "At least, not as myself."

A deep loneliness resonated from that last statement, and I leaned into him, resting my head on his broad shoulder. "I have every confidence in your ability to sweep me off my feet."

He pressed a kiss to the top of my head. "You are a remarkable woman, Tarset."

I wrapped my arms around his middle, wishing I could soak up some of his loneliness. I wasn't the remarkable one. After all he had done to protect the timeline—and through it, the entire universe—and with all the ghosts he lived beside every day, he was the most incredible, determined, resilient person I had ever met. But I knew from experience that he wouldn't appreciate me mentioning the burden of his duty. He would not welcome my sympathy for all he had been forced to do.

So instead, I held him, reassuring him that, at least for right now, he wasn't alone.

A TUM CHANGED HIS APPEARANCE first thing in the morning so I had a chance to grow accustomed to seeing him look like the man who had taken such glee in having someone literally flay the skin off my body. Thankfully, he left his eyes unchanged. He intended them to be a subtle reminder of who he really was in the moments when the instinctive panic within me from the remembered trauma threatened to wash away all reason.

My own transformation was purely internal. I was to be Inyotef's pet Nejeret, broken and obedient after my escape and recapture in Men-nefer. It wasn't a difficult role to play.

Being Inyotef's captive had changed me. I wasn't the same woman I had been when I first arrived in this ancient time nearly four months ago. Since then, I had been stripped down and cut open, my essential self dragged out of me to be poked and prodded. It was easy enough to awaken that wounded creature slumbering within me. To become her, spine bowed and shoulders slumped, because in so many ways, I *was* her.

We packed up what little belongings we had traveled with from Men-nefer, returning our water and foodstuffs to one large reed basket, our spare clothing, bedrolls, and blankets to another, and trekked down the path cut into the cliff toward the valley. Atum claimed altering his appearance so drastically sapped his power, making it unwise to jump directly to the grounds of the Waset palace. Besides, he wanted the people to see us arrive—their leader risen from his rumored death, his cowed slave in tow.

Atum had concocted a story about a bandit attack to explain away the slaughter he himself had dealt out in Men-nefer and why "Inyotef" was returning alone with me as his only companion. Apparently, he had also left a forged note for Nitocris in her Men-nefer palace—from Inyotef—letting her know their impending marriage was off and blaming the unrest in her region when he expressed his doubts that their alliance would do anything but weaken their two lands. I thought the first of his "fixes" might work to appease the curious people of Waset, but I doubted the latter would do anything but aggravate the northern queen.

When we reached the valley floor, we crossed through the dirt fields, barren above the level of the flooded Nile, and waded through the shallow floodwaters to the boat awaiting us at the deeper riverbank.

I stood in murky water nearly up to my knees, holding the baskets as I watched Atum raise the sunken riverboat from the river's depths, the vessel safe and dry within a bubble of shimmering, solidified *At*. Even this relatively minor use of his *sheut* seemed to strain his abilities, and I understood why teleporting across the river was out of the question.

It was so unsettling to see him using his *sheut* like Atum but *looking* like Inyotef. I shivered, horrified by the idea of Inyotef having that kind of power.

He's not Inyotef, I reminded myself, as I'd had to do many times already.

Once the boat was floating atop the water, I passed the baskets to Atum one at a time. He tucked them into a storage chest near the stern, then returned to me, standing with one foot on the river bank, the other on the boat's shallow deck, a hand out to help me board.

I hesitated, staring at the duplicate of a hand that had caused me so much agony that the ghosts of the pain still echoed through my body.

He's not Inyotef, I repeated silently. And with conscious effort, I placed my hand in Atum's and stepped onto the boat.

"Tarset," Atum said, Inyotef's voice grating on my nerves. He gripped my hand tight, refusing to let go. "Look at me."

I closed my eyes and drew in a deep, steadying breath, and then I obeyed, like a good pet Nejeret. Except it wasn't Inyotef's face I saw when I looked at him, but Atum's eyes. It was becoming easier to look past those hated features, to see the man gazing out from within that deceptive shell.

Where Inyotef had been like a beautiful, unblemished apple, secretly rotten in the core, Atum's purity of purpose shone out through those midnight eyes. He was a *good* man. A *noble* man, who took no pleasure in hurting innocents. Who never enjoyed bending another's will to his purpose, even when he had to do it. Who respected the desires of others, despite his grim duty.

I relaxed a little as I stared into his guarded gaze, my fingers tightening around his. "I see you, Atum."

Some of the tension left his stolen features. "I must wear this visage in public, but when we are alone, I will appear as myself."

My lips curled into a small but genuine smile. "What a relief." I moved farther onto the flat-bottomed boat, and Atum released my hand as I settled on the central bench. "Is it difficult to maintain the disguise?" I asked as Atum settled on the bench opposite mine.

He placed his hands on his knees and pushed his shoulders back, stretching his neck first one way, then the other. "It is tiring and exhausts my *sheut*, but it is not difficult."

Atum raised his hands, holding them out in front of himself like he was pressing his palms against an invisible wall. I couldn't see what he was doing, drawing on his *sheut* to direct the *At* laced through the river boat's hull, but a tingle of otherworldly energy washed over my skin, telling me the magic was happening. Right on cue, the boat lurched into motion, gliding away from the riverbank and cutting through the water as we started up the river, heading for the Waset harbor.

I settled in for the last leg of our journey, watching the palm trees and flooded grain fields as we drifted past. Men and women worked along the outer edges of the fields, some scooping out muddy silt and carting the rich dirt with its valuable nutrients further inland and others digging new irrigation channels to spread the gifts of the Nile beyond the reach of yet another lackluster inundation.

I watched the workers on board another, larger riverboat as we crossed paths. They were silt harvesters, their skin caked with mud from dredging the bottom of the Nile, likely since first light.

My focus shifted past them, to the western riverbank and the submerged fields. Even *I* could tell that the floodwaters weren't reaching high enough. The existing fields stretched well beyond the reach of the water.

"How many more years of this drought?" I asked Atum, not taking my attention off the disheartening landscape. I may have spent most of my lifetime in the distant future, but this was still my homeland, my native time, and it hurt my heart to see it suffering so.

"Three," Atum said. "But it will take much longer for the people to recover and for the nomarchs to stop squabbling. Only then, when the land is unified under Mentuhotep, will prosperity return."

"How long until that happens?" I asked, glancing at him.

Atum squinted, thinking. "About one hundred and twenty years," he said. "Mentuhotep is our main reason for returning to Waset."

I frowned. "But, if he doesn't reunite the lands for well over another century, aren't we a little early?"

"Mentuhotep's great-great-grandfather would have been taken under Inyotef's wing and raised to be his successor, paving the way for Mentuhotep's rise to power," Atum explained. "Now that Inyotef is gone, he cannot fulfill that essential role."

My eyebrows bunched together, and I shook my head. "So, we're really here to adopt and raise Mentuhotep's ancestor?"

"And to cultivate Mentuhotep's family line."

I scoffed. "But that's going to take *years*."

"A century, in fact," Atum corrected me. I gaped at him, my mouth hanging open and my mind floundering for words. "But we need only to pave the way for the course correction. Tefnut and Shu can step in and take over as the shepherds of this flock once we've laid the groundwork."

"Shu?" I asked. I had met Tefnut, Atum's striking dark-skinned daughter twice, but only in passing. I had heard Shu's name mentioned, but that was all.

"My son," Atum said.

Again, I shook my head, attempting to rein in my scattered, stumbling thoughts. "How will they be able to replace us here? Don't you need to stay in Waset and *be* Inyotef?" I asked.

"Not at all," Atum said. "Tefnut is quite skilled at crafting personal illusions. She will step in as Inyotef, allowing us to depart for Rostau once your anomalous presence has softened up the lifethreads enough that the pattern can be more easily corrected."

"But—" Whatever I had been about to say stuck in my throat as understanding dawned. He was saying she could disguise herself like he could. "Tefnut has a *sheut*?" I clarified.

"She does," Atum said. "As does Shu, though his gifts predominantly lie elsewhere."

"Oh." I chewed on the inside of my cheek and stared out at the flooded fields.

It was impossible not to wonder about the mother of Atum's children. Was it the same woman for both? Someone Atum had loved enough to father two Nejeret children with? And if two of his offspring had manifested as Nejerets, he likely had more children—human offspring were the far more common outcome among children sired by a Nejeret father. Though, maybe that was different when the father had a *sheut*.

Obviously I had known Atum had been with other women—likely *loved* many women in his long lifetime. I had seen him with Nitocris, and I had experienced his expert touch firsthand. A man didn't instinctively know how to please a woman like that.

"Does their mother still live?" I asked, the words spilling out of my mouth before I could stop myself from asking the intrusive question.

"Their mother?" Atum repeated, looking genuinely puzzled.

"Yeah, Tefnut and Shu's mother." I lifted one shoulder. "Or *mothers*?"

Atum shook his head. "They have no mother," he said, and I stared at him, dumbfounded. "I created them, just as my father created me, by tearing off a sliver of my *sheut* and nurturing it into a child."

I gaped at him, forgetting about Tefnut and Shu for the moment, at a complete and utter loss for words. Atum didn't have a *mother*?

I couldn't imagine such an existence. My mom had been such a central, formational figure in my life, even after she was no longer a part of it. Possibly even more so, then.

Atum studied me. "You are familiar with the legends surrounding me," he said, his tone faintly defensive. "I thought you knew this, too."

I laughed under my breath. "The legends surrounding you aren't about your origins, or about your kids' origins—at least, not in my time," I told him. "You're, ah, kind of like the *boogeyman* . . . That's a monster parents use to frighten their kids into behaving properly."

Atum's expression blanked. "A monster," he said hollowly. "Yes, well, I suppose the Nejerets of your time aren't wrong."

"Atum . . ." I raised a hand but let it drop back into my lap. "I didn't mean it like that. You're *not* a monster. You're a sentinel. A guardian. You protect us all, and I will make sure everyone knows it."

"When you return home," he said, his flat tone eerily reminiscent of Inyotef's inflection when he wasn't attempting to sound friendly.

"*If* I return home," I corrected.

He looked at me but quickly returned to staring upriver. "I would appreciate that," he said quietly. "Though I would rather the world believe me a monster, if it meant I would have you by my side."

The breath whooshed from my lungs, and my heart sank. "Why?" I asked softly. "You don't even know me—not really." I dropped my focus to my hands, fidgeting on my lap, and gave a slight shake of my head. "Not who I was before I came here. Not what I was like. I don't think you would have liked me much." I let out a breathy laugh. "I don't think *I* liked me much."

Atum was quiet for a long moment, but I could feel his stare on me. "We all have stories we tell ourselves—about who we've been, about who we are, about who we should be. But they're just stories." He leaned forward, letting the boat drift on its own as he rested his elbows on his thighs. "I have seen inside you, Tarset, past the stories you tell yourself. I have seen your soul, and it is truly wondrous."

I swallowed around the swell of emotion choking my airway. I had never met anyone so capable of using their words to leave me so unbalanced, and I had been blasted and shamed by the best of the best—or the worst of the worst, depending on your point of view.

"Do you need a moment?" Atum asked gently.

Flustered, I looked at him. "A moment?"

"Before we dock." He glanced past me, pointing with his borrowed chin. "We're approaching the harbor."

Eyes widening, I twisted on my bench. And sure enough, there was the familiar limestone quay cutting a T-shaped harbor through the water. River crafts of all sizes bordered the quay, and men in white linen kilts bustled around on the boats. Gulls cried out, soaring and swooping overhead, and the sun shone high in the sky, glowing cheerfully.

My stomach knotted. I hated this place, the setting of some of my worst nightmares. It was my own personal hell.

I inhaled deeply and turned back to Atum, my savior, wearing the skin of my own personal devil. "No," I said hollowly, then slowly released the breath. "I'm ready."

A TUM ROWED US INTO the harbor, having switched to the more mundane mode of propelling the boat now that we were within view of so many humans.

"Won't it seem strange," I wondered aloud, "Inyotef rowing himself? Didn't he usually have servants do that sort of thing for him?" I reached out, placing my hands on Atum's to stop him mid-pull on the oars.

He looked at my hands gripping his, then met my eyes.

"I should be the one rowing," I said. "Inyotef would have enjoyed that, having the people of Waset watch his pet Netjer-At serve him in such a public, menial way." I glanced over my shoulder at the bustling quay some two hundred yards away. "We're still far enough out. Nobody will notice the switch."

Atum looked at me for a long moment, considering my words. "Inyotef would have taken great pleasure in that," he admitted begrudgingly. "Do you know how to row?"

I nodded and said, "I grew up on the water." I may have had more experience with *motorized* boats, but I had manned the oars of my fair share of dinghies.

Atum's focus dropped back down to my hands. "You'll blister," he said, genuine concern warping his features into an expression that looked out of place on Inyotef's face. It struck me that he was so concerned about my physical wellbeing *now*.

"I'll heal," I countered, withdrawing my hands.

Atum clenched and unclenched his jaw several times. "Fine," he finally said, pulling the oars into the boat one at a time so we didn't lose them in the river during the switch. He stood with that slow, balanced grace he had first displayed as the boatman, and I couldn't help but envy his steady sea legs. I may have grown up on the Puget Sound waterfront, but I was no natural mariner.

Atum reached out to grip my elbow as I stood, steadying me. I eased down onto his bench and went about placing the oars in their notches and getting myself situated. At the sound of fabric tearing, I looked up to find Atum cutting a long, one-inch strip of linen from the hem of his schenti.

"What are you doing?" I asked, my brow furrowing.

Atum tore the strip free from his kilt and extended one hand toward me, holding it palm up. "Give me your hand."

Frowning, I shifted the oars so I hugged the ends of both somewhat awkwardly with one arm and reached out with the other, placing my hand on Atum's proffered palm.

Atum wound the long strip of white linen around my hand, being careful to ensure my palm was covered by several layers of the thin fabric before cutting the strip short and knotting the ends together. "Your other hand," he said, releasing the one he had already wrapped.

My eyes stung, my heart warmed by the care Atum was taking to prevent me from suffering further. It was so disconcerting to see him *looking* like the man who had caused me such agony while he was making every effort to protect me. How had this gentleness survived within Atum, when his duty had required him to do such unspeakably horrific things? And how unfair that the world considered him a monster when he was anything but.

"This isn't necessary," I told him. "If I get blisters, I'll heal quickly enough."

"I cannot abide unnecessary suffering," he said softly. He cast a pointed look at my other hand, and I swapped my hold on the oars to extend my bare palm for him to wrap in linen.

I couldn't help but think back to the first time Atum had taken care of me—during my first round of imprisonment. The moment Atum decided I had proven my dedication to preserving the timeline above all other things, he seemed to have appeared out of thin air to heal my flayed back. The pain as he coated my ravaged flesh with his potent, ancient blood had been shocking, but his touch had been so sure and gentle. In his eyes, my trial had ended, and he refused to let me suffer any longer.

And then I recalled our morning meal just a few hours earlier, and all the meals that had come before it. He never touched the jerky or the meat stews, though he always made sure they were there for me.

"Is that why you don't eat meat?" I asked Atum as he knotted the linen wrapping around my other hand.

He exhaled heavily and released my hand, raising his eyes to the seagulls circling overhead. "Ma'at dictates that there must be a balance in all things, including within ourselves." His focus shifted lower, to my face. "I only end a life when there is no other option." That he had plenty of other options where food was concerned was a statement left unsaid.

"Does it bother you when I eat meat?" I asked, adjusting the oars so I gripped one in each hand and settling in to row toward the harbor.

"It is not for me to determine what brings you inner balance," Atum said. "Only you can do that."

I pulled on the oars, propelling us through the water. "I don't think I've ever felt balanced," I admitted. One needed only to examine my pre-manifestation stints in and out of rehab to see evidence of *that* truth. I glanced over my shoulder at the quay, still relatively far away. "Will you let me know when we're close?"

"Of course," Atum said with a bow of his head. I watched him as I rowed. His mannerisms were still his, and it was almost like I could see an aura shining through his Inyotef disguise, revealing his true appearance to me.

"Do you think—" I hesitated, uncertain how to voice my thoughts. I was breathing harder, my heart beating faster from the exertion. "Have I been unable to find a balance in my life because I've been living in a time period where I don't belong? Where my *soul* doesn't belong?" I had been transported to that distant future as a child to save my life, but perhaps that temporal displacement had given rise to new, unforeseen issues within me.

Atum frowned thoughtfully, but mischief danced in his dark eyes. "If I said yes, would it convince you to stay here, where your soul belongs?"

My heart stumbled over its next beat. Did he mean that my soul belonged in this time period—or *with him*? I flashed him what I hoped came across as an easy smile, when everything about this situation was so difficult.

"But," Atum continued, "I think it is far more likely that coping with losing your mother is what left you so unsettled."

My eyebrows rose, and I laughed under my breath, pulling on the oars. I couldn't deny that she had been the principal topic of conversation in pretty much all my therapy sessions. "You're probably right," I said.

The oars cut through the water as I propelled us toward the quay. It struck me that there was an imbalance between us as well. Atum had been watching me before I even knew he existed, which meant that even if he didn't know much about my past in the distant future, he still knew far more about me than I knew about him, and I felt a surge in determination to remedy that, even if he was a book sealed shut with a lock and key. I would just have to make sure he understood that if he wanted to have any chance of wooing me into staying with him, he would have to open himself up to me.

"We'll moor near this end of the quay," Atum said, raising an arm to point off to my right. "I see Tefnut is already waiting for us."

"She is?" When I glanced over my shoulder, I found that the limestone platform was closer than I had expected. I dug one oar into the water to alter the trajectory of our boat, then continued on, easing the strength of my strokes to slow our approach.

I peeked over my shoulder again, quickly scanning the bare-chested male sailors and workers hustling about on the raised walkway and on the boats docked on this side of the quay. A lone, stationary woman stood at the very end, wearing a schenti like all the men hard at work around her, but a woven cuirass covered her torso, and the curved bronze blades of the two swords strapped to her weapons belt gleamed on her hips. Her skin wasn't Tefnut's striking ebony, but a warm bronze. Short black hair covered a head that had recently been shaved clean, and her face—

I did a double take, then looked again to make sure my eyes weren't deceiving me. "That's *Kiya*!" I looked at Atum. "She's back? She's *okay*?"

"That is not Kiya," Atum said. "Just as I am not Inyotef."

"That's *Tefnut*?" I said, digging the oars into the water and leaving them there to slow our approach over the last fifteen yards. I peeked back at the woman standing at the end of the quay, but I couldn't focus on her for long, as I was steering the boat and attempting *not* to crash into the side of the limestone platform.

"Indeed it is," Atum said, standing. He reached out to catch the edge of the quay and steady our docking.

I squinted up at the woman standing a few feet above us, silhouetted by the early afternoon sun. She looked identical to Kiya, the guard Inyotef had brutally maimed as punishment for befriending me. Her bronze skin was scarred in all the places it should have been after Inyotef's beatings, and she was thinner than she had been when we first met. I frowned, thinking Atum might have been mistaken about her true identity. Perhaps Tefnut had brought Kiya back here instead of taking her to Rostau on board Atum's massive *At* ship.

"I expected you earlier," she said, crossing her arms over her chest and peering down at us haughtily. That she could speak *at all* confirmed Atum's claim. This was Tefnut. Inyotef had cut out Kiya's tongue in Men-nefer. *She* would never speak again.

Atum crouched to grab a coiled line secured to a wooden notch on the inside of the hull and handed it up to his daughter. "How was the journey to Rostau?"

"Wet," she said, deftly wrapping the line around a stone cleat on the edge of the quay. "How there can be so much rain out at sea while it is so dry here is beyond me."

Atum lifted the stern line and started wrapping it around another cleat. "I cannot tell if you're complaining about the monsoons or the drought."

"Both," Tefnut said with a sniff. "This is a miserable era, and I can't wait to be done with it."

I snorted a laugh.

Tefnut gave me a dismissive glance, then returned her attention to her father. "We should get you to the palace." Her attention shifted to me, and though her expression remained one of bland annoyance, her eyes sparked with irritation. "There's much work to be done after the mess you made in Men-nefer." She refocused on her father in the middle of that statement, but it was clear she held me responsible for everything that had happened in Men-nefer and for her having to be here and now, in this *miserable era.*

"It was necessary," Atum said, returning to the bow of the boat.

He approached me, and before I realized what was happening, his hands were on my waist and he had lifted me onto the edge of the limestone platform. With a grunt, he hoisted himself up beside me and climbed to his feet on the quay, then held a hand out to me.

I placed my hand in his and let him pull me up to my feet. Atum released my hand, raising his to curl his fingers around the front of my neck.

I stiffened immediately, my eyes widening, and panic flitting through my chest.

Looking exactly like Inyotef, he leaned in close to whisper in my ear. "Any unkindness I show you during the walk to the palace is purely for show, and I swear to you I will atone for my actions in any way that you desire."

I stared at him sidelong, and again, it was as though I could see his true self shining through the unsettling disguise. "I understand," I murmured.

"Thank you," he whispered. When he spoke again, his voice was raised so others would hear him. "Such a good pet," he said with laughter in his booming voice. His hand slipped away from my neck, and he turned his back to me, striding up the quay. "Come along, *Bek*," he tossed over his shoulder, calling me by the name I had used publicly the last time I had been in Waset. "We have much work to do."

I gulped and followed on unsteady legs. All eyes were on us, and where being the object of such focused attention used to thrill me, it now made me feel uncomfortable in my own skin. I hugged my middle as I walked, keeping my eyes downcast and wishing I could disappear.

Tefnut strode past me to catch up with Atum.

"Kiya?" I said, using her assumed name.

She stopped mid-step, her posture stiff.

"How is she?" I asked quietly.

When I reached Tefnut, she fell in step beside me. "She is recovering well," Tefnut said, her voice pitched low, for my ears alone. "She will be fine—in time." After a prolonged silence, Tefnut added, "She thinks of you often and holds you in high regard. As does my father." Tefnut eyed me up and down, the curl of her lips telling me she remained unimpressed. "Don't let them down," she added.

Without another word, Tefnut strode ahead to join her father, leaving me to walk behind them, discarded and alone.

THE MILE-LONG STROLL FROM the harbor, through the town of Waset, and to the palace was mildly degrading but not overtly humiliating. Atum walked with Tefnut, speaking quietly about the dissonance and the specifics of how they might fix it. I trudged along behind them like a good, obedient pet, keeping my head down and saying nothing when Atum stopped to speak with the few people we passed along the eastern road near the edge of the desert, elevated above the height of the flood waters.

Acting as Inyotef, he expressed variations of the same thing to each person—how glad he was to be home, how disappointed he was about the broken alliance with Nitocris, and how devastated he was by the organized bandit attack that had resulted in his two ships, en route to Men-nefer, being destroyed and his troops slaughtered.

I tuned out Atum's and Tefnut's assumed voices, finding them unsettling, and hummed to myself. How long had it been since I actually sang a song? I stumbled over some of the melodies to my own songs, second-guessing notes that had been second nature only a few months earlier. But they didn't feel like *my* songs anymore. They had been written by someone else. Someone who cared about what others thought of her. Someone who would have been horrified by an entire region of people believing her to be a cowed captive. A slave.

But now, all I cared about was reaching the palace and sinking into the baths to wash away the dust of the last leg of this journey. We had been washing in the river, but the inundation left the water murky, and no matter how hard or long I scrubbed my skin, I emerged with a thin film of silt covering my body. I was desperate to feel clean for the first time in weeks.

We approached the palace along the same path that Atum and I used to walk together each morning after his sunrise ritual, before Inyotef had changed my status from honored guest to degraded prisoner. At the time, my life had felt so complicated, but looking back, it seemed so simple compared to now. Then, I had a singular purpose—to get home. Now I was torn, my thoughts and emotions tangled in an impossible knot.

I still wanted to go home, but I didn't want to leave Atum. The options were mutually exclusive. Atum was bound to his stretch of the timeline, which fell short of reaching my home in the distant future. Events from the past two decades of "my" time had forged something of an impenetrable barrier between Atum's part of the timeline and mine. I couldn't have both *him* and *home*, which meant I needed to figure out which I wanted *more*.

Tension coiled in my muscles as we approached the palace. I had been a prisoner within the tall limestone walls long before Inyotef had thrown me into his dungeon. I wasn't sure I could willingly pass through the open gate at the front of the massive structure. Within me, my resolve rebelled. Instinct told me to turn around and run away.

I was so lost to my mounting panic that I didn't notice Atum and Tefnut's conversation had ceased until Atum's fingers curled around my upper arm and he fell in step beside me. I blinked, looking first at him—at his stolen face—then at Tefnut's back as she strode purposely ahead toward the palace's open gate.

"We're almost done," Atum murmured, his grip on my arm keeping me moving forward. "We just need to let the courtiers and staff see us together like this, and then it will be over."

My chin bobbed. But even as I agreed, I knew, in my heart, that he was wrong. This was where I had been so beaten and broken that I had wished for death. So long as I was within those palace walls, the torment would continue. I would be a captive of this place, of the ghosts and memories that would forever haunt the corridors and chambers.

"Welcome home, pet," he said, raising his voice so the workers on the grounds surrounding the palace would hear him.

I kept my eyes downcast as we passed through the gate, my pounding heart and roaring blood muffling my ears. I was aware of Atum guiding me through the palace, speaking with various people, showing off his pet Nejeret, but it was as though I watched from above, outside of myself.

"No interruptions," I heard Inyotef say. *Not Inyotef*, I reminded myself, though it was more difficult to feel certain of that now that I was back here, in this wretched palace of nightmares. The traumatic memories were messing with my perception of reality.

A tingle of otherworldly energy touched my skin, shocking me back to full awareness. On my next inhale, I noted the faint scent of sulfur and earthy minerals. I blinked, looking around. Straight ahead, I saw the crystal-clear surface of the palace's communal baths reflecting the late afternoon sunlight that poured in through the opening in the ceiling onto the rough limestone walls. A thin, shimmering barrier covered the opening to the sky, making the light refract like it was passing through a thin slice of clear crystal.

"Tarset?" That voice. It didn't belong to Inyotef.

Tears welled in my eyes, and I spun around. Atum stood before me looking like himself, as tall, dark, and striking as ever. His scars gleamed gold in the filtered sunlight, and otherworldly power pulsed off him in waves. He was completely unshielded, his true, imposing, glorious self. Here was the man—the god—whose reputation had terrorized my people for millennia, and I had never beheld a more comforting sight. I wanted to wrap myself up in him, to brand him into my skin.

Atum approached slowly, cautiously. "Are you all right?"

"What if someone sees you?" I asked, voicing the question despite my soul-deep desire that Atum never alter his appearance again. That he always look like this. Like himself. Like *my* Atum.

Except he wasn't mine.

But he could be, whispered through my mind.

"Tefnut is guarding the doorway," Atum said, stopping directly in front of me, "and I've surrounded us within a shell of *At*. I couldn't stand to see you look at me with such fear and hatred for a moment longer." His eyes searched mine. "Are you all right?" he repeated.

I let my eyelids drift shut, soaking up the pleasant tingle of his latent power washing over me. "I'm fine," I said, a small smile curving my lips. "Now that I'm with you—with the real you."

"Tarset . . ." There was pain in his voice, a subtle, heartbreaking agony.

I opened my eyes and looked at him, studying the strong, angular lines of his beautiful face. There was a deep yearning in his midnight eyes, the quiet hope tempered by sorrow, like he was already mourning losing me. Like he knew, in his heart, that I would leave, even when I was less certain.

"I'm here now," I told him. "All you have to do is convince me to stay."

"How?" he asked, his voice hoarse.

"It's easy," I said, raising my hands to rest on his shoulders and standing on my toes. Skimming my thumbs over the raised scars, I pressed my lips to his, softly, gently. "Let me in," I whispered against his mouth, kissing him again. "Let me know you." Another kiss. "Let me know *all* of you."

"That's all?" he asked, settling his hands possessively on my hips and pulling me closer.

I curled my arms around the back of his neck, pressing myself against him. Desire raged through my veins as our lips parted and the kiss deepened. Atum's tongue swept into my mouth, and one of his hands glided up my spine to the back of my head, fisting in my hair. I could feel the hard length of his arousal pressing insistently against my belly, and need pulsed in my core.

Atum broke the kiss, breathing hard and resting his forehead against mine. "This is unwise," he rasped. "Unless you want me to take you now." He squeezed his eyelids shut, his arms trembling. "The lure is too strong, and I am at the limits of my restraint."

I nodded, unable to speak but understanding his meaning completely. The need to bond with him, to make him mine forever, came ever closer to overwhelming my coherent mind with each successive heartbeat.

With painfully deliberate movements, I stepped backward. My hands glided down over the intricate pattern of small, ridged scars on his muscular chest and abdomen, which really wasn't helpful in the battle of wills I was having with my libido. The man was as tactilely pleasing as he was stunning to look at. I curled my hands into fists and took another backward step, hating the sensation of his hands sliding from my hips but needing him to stop touching me so I could think clearly again.

We were both still breathing hard, our burning stares locked together. The force drawing us together seemed to strengthen with every touch, every close encounter, every near miss, and it took every ounce of my self-restraint to *not* throw myself back into Atum's arms.

I licked my lips, still swollen from his kiss. "I'd like to bathe, but I don't want you to leave," I said, my voice breathy.

I jutted out my jaw, images of the last time I soaked in the spring-fed pool flitting through my mind. Inyotef had interrupted my bath, invading my peace with his needy presence. It had been before my imprisonment, when he still believed he could charm me into getting what he wanted from me. When I had still believed I could string him along long enough to get what *I* needed from him. Gods, I had been such a fool.

"I don't want to be alone here," I explained. My chin trembled, and I hugged my middle. If Atum weren't nearby to anchor me to the present, I thought I might drown in the disturbing memories this place dredged up from the past. "Please don't leave me alone here."

Atum's legs swallowed up the distance between us in a single step, and his arms were around me, holding me close. Our bodies were pressed together, as before, but this was different. The resurfacing trauma muted the siren song resonating between us. I clung to him, soaking up his strength, and fought back the encroaching despair threatening to shatter me into a million pieces right there on the rough limestone floor.

"I'm sorry, Tarset," he murmured against my hair. "I'm so sorry. It was the only way to know your true intentions—to *truly* know you weren't a threat to the timeline." He paused, stroking my back. "I can dull the memories, if you wish, but one day, they will return..."

I shook my head. I had survived the doing of it. I could survive the memory. I *could*.

"Just stay with me," I said, my voice high and tight. "If it's not too difficult . . ."

Atum pressed a kiss to the top of my head. "I'll manage," he said roughly, like he, too, was barely controlling his own tsunami of emotions. He released me and stepped back, then turned away from me. "Let me know when you're in the water."

"Atum," I whispered. "If it's too hard—"

"Take off your dress, Tarset," Atum ordered, "or I will take it off for you, and I cannot guarantee the outcome of that course of action."

Just like that, my all-encompassing desire for this man beat away the darkness looming within me, and my pulse throbbed in my groin. "Okay," I said, clutching the sides of my skirt and drawing the dress up over my head. I dropped the linen shift on the stone floor and made my way on silent feet to the rough-hewn steps that sank into the pool. "I'm in," I told him, once my breasts were submerged in the luke-warm water.

Atum turned only his head my way as I waded backward to the shadows at the far side of the pool. He stared—hard—clenching and unclenching his jaw. He could still see my nudity, of course, but the rippling water obscured his view. Was that enough?

"Are you going to join me?" I asked, knowing I was playing with fire. Part of me hoped to get burned. Hoped he would lose control. Hoped *I* wouldn't have to choose between a life with him and the one I had left behind in the future, but that he would choose for me.

Atum blew out a breath and tore his stare away from me, looking up at the ceiling instead. Shaking his head, he unfastened his weapons belt with jerking motions and set it on the floor, then worked on untying the complex knot holding his schenti in place.

I told myself to look away. To close my eyes. To do anything else besides watch him as he undressed. But I couldn't stop myself.

I had seen him in the nude once before, and only once—when I had stumbled in on him when he was with Nitocris. The utter perfection of his bare backside was burned into my mind's eye. Of his powerful thighs, glutes, and back, all working together in that seductive, primal motion. But even then, I hadn't seen all of him. It was hardly fair, considering he had seen all of me many times over.

This was my secret price, my reward to myself for letting him parade me through town and across the countryside. I would see him. *All* of him.

I held my breath and pressed my back against the rough limestone wall, waiting as Atum worked on the knot. When the white linen finally fell away from his body, the air whooshed from my lungs. He belonged in a museum alongside all the beautiful classical Greek sculptures of the male physique. But then he faced me, full frontal, and my eyes bulged. Those poor statues couldn't hold a candle to Atum.

In some recessed part of my mind, I could hear my stepmom, Lex, holding in her amusement as she explained to me why the classical Greek statues in the British Museum displayed Greek men with smaller *packages*, while those the ancient Greeks had perceived to be heathens and barbarians, like the Egyptians, were portrayed as more well-endowed. It had something to do with the ancient Greeks' perception of civility and restraint, or some such nonsense. Apparently, a smaller penis meant more self-control, as if a man could will his junk to shrink.

By the time I *finally* dragged my focus up to his face, Atum wore the most unexpected smirk.

Flushed and flustered, I averted my gaze to the water.

"Don't do that," he said, approaching the edge of the baths. "Don't look away."

Choking on my sudden discomfort, I forced myself to look at him—at his face. "I didn't want to make you uncomfortable."

"I have felt the touch of many lustful gazes," Atum said, descending the stairs and sinking into the water. "But none belonged to anyone who knew who I really was, who saw me as I truly am." He waded off to the side and eased back against the wall of the pool, facing me. "I like the way you look at me," he said. "Because you're looking at *me*."

My heart broke for him for about the thousandth time. If we hadn't been alone and naked in a communal bath, fighting the urge to fulfill our soul bond, I would have glided across the dozen feet separating us and held him, assuring him he was deserving of love as much as the next person. More so, in my opinion. Hell, there was a good chance that I was already falling in love with him, but I couldn't tell him that, not when I still wasn't sure if I was going to leave him.

"Are you ready to atone?" I asked, changing the subject to something lighter. I smirked at him, only slightly forced. "I was a good little pet out there, wasn't I?"

Atum's stare darkened with desire. "What did you have in mind?"

"A game," I said, smiling slyly.

Atum's eyebrows rose. Clearly, he hadn't been expecting me to say that. "What kind of game?"

"Two truths and a lie," I told him, slowly waving my arms through the water. "You tell me three things about yourself—two that are true and one that's made up—and then I get to guess which is the lie."

Atum narrowed his eyes thoughtfully. "And if you guess correctly?"

"Then you have to go again," I said. "But if I'm wrong, *I* have to tell *you* three things about myself."

"One of which will be a lie," he deduced.

"Precisely," I said, grinning. "And the three things have to be significant."

"Very well." Atum settled back against the wall of the pool, stretching out his toned arms along the ledge on either side of him. "I have a fear of cats," he said, then paused thoughtfully. "I was on board the Titanic when it crashed into the iceberg," he said and paused again. "And I never had a childhood, because I was never a child."

I guffawed. "I don't believe any of those!" I exclaimed.

Atum chuckled. "Two are true, I swear it."

I narrowed my eyes, thinking through his answers. Tons of people had irrational phobias, so he easily could be afraid of cats. Besides, some cats *were* genuinely terrifying. The Titanic—he knew it had crashed into an iceberg, or that it had existed at all, so maybe that was true. I supposed it was contained within the bookends of the millennia of time he was bound to and duty-sworn to watch over, so why the hell not?

But the childhood thing—that one was too heartbreaking. I wanted it to be the lie. But he *had* said he didn't have a mother, that Nuin had *made* him rather than *fathering* him the natural way.

"It's the childhood one," I ventured, crossing my fingers under the water, more for his sake than for the game.

Atum bowed his head, acknowledging my win.

"Oh thank the gods," I said on my exhale. "Then I would have pitied you, and I know how much you despise that."

Atum's eyes glittered with amusement. "You are not wrong."

I grinned, comforted by his good humor. "I won," I told him. "Go again." I held up one hand, splashing water. "But first, you have to tell me why you're afraid of cats."

His expression sobered. "They can sense me—what I am," he explained. "Even when I suppress my essence, they somehow know I am not human."

I raised my eyebrows, not expecting *that*.

"They are a factor I cannot control," he said. "And *that* is what frightens me."

I fought a frown, not wanting to ruin the mood, but I couldn't help but wonder if the same sentiment applied to me. *I* was a factor he couldn't control. I was a factor even *I* couldn't control, but I hated the idea that Atum might also fear me.

Even if he should.

I GASPED AWAKE, SOAKED with a cold sweat, the excruciating sensation of my skin being peeled off my body in narrow strips lingering from the nightmare. The pain wasn't so much imagined as remembered.

Opening my eyes, I sat up and blinked into the darkness. I wasn't in a dungeon cell; I was in a moonlit sleeping chamber. And I wasn't tied up by my wrists, left to doze awkwardly on my knees; I was unrestrained on a bed platform. I curled up my legs and hugged my knees to my chest, taking shuddering breaths. Tears streamed down my cheeks, and the linen of my shift stuck to my sweat-soaked skin.

But I could still feel it. The pain. The fear. The desperation.

I buried my face between my knees, muffling my frustrated scream. The nightmares had been happening every night since Atum rescued me in Men-nefer, but this had been the most vivid, by far. Being back here, in the place where it all began, fleshed out the memories, giving them new life.

A tingle of otherworldly energy tickled my skin, and I raised my head.

Atum appeared in a burst of iridescent mist in the middle of the long, narrow room, already striding toward me before he had fully formed. He scanned me, searching for evidence of harm, then sat and pulled me into his arms.

I clung to his bare torso, burying my face against the crook of his shoulder and releasing a sob. He had awakened me from the nightmares many times before, but it had been different opening my eyes to see him. That instant confirmation that I was safe always banished the horror to the far reaches of my mind. But this time, I had awakened alone, and that made it so much worse.

"You will sleep in my chamber," Atum said, tucking his chin over my head and stroking my back through my sweat-soaked shift with slow hands.

"Won't that seem strange to the servants?" I asked, breathing in his intoxicating scent, like spiced wine sweetened with honey. "Inyotef sharing his room with a slave?"

Atum let out a harsh laugh. "Not at all," he said. "Inyotef coveted you for many reasons. He would have viewed it as a significant accomplishment to have his pet Nejeret warming his bed every night." Atum sighed. "By sharing a room, the closest thing to letting him take you publicly, the people of Waset will *know* you are not merely his obedient Nejeret, but also his whore."

I laughed bitterly. "Whores are paid," I corrected him.

Atum inhaled and exhaled audibly. "As you say," he said. "I merely wished to let you keep that piece of your dignity."

"My dignity?" I snorted. "Do you know who I was—what I did—back home?" I lifted my head and pulled back enough that I could see his face. "I was a singer. An entertainer." I posed, fluttering my lashes. "One of the most famous people in the entire world."

Atum was quiet for a long moment. "I knew it had to be something like that," he finally admitted.

My brows rose. "You did?"

Atum nodded. "You're confident when you walk into a room, and then there's the way you soak up attention, like it fuels you. I knew you were used to being in the public eye as some sort of entertainer."

I blushed, unsure how I felt about his assessment of me.

"Perhaps, someday, you will sing for me," he said, his inflection rising to turn the statement into a question.

"Sure," I said, my lips spreading into an uncertain grin as I felt shy about singing for the first time in as long as I could remember. "I can do that." I cleared my throat. "But, um, *my point* is that the whole world was all up in my business, and I've been called every demeaning name imaginable by people who believed the absolute worst about me with their whole hearts." I laughed bitterly. "This won't be the first time—or even the thousandth time—that I've been called a whore."

Atum opened his eyes again, studying my face as I spoke.

"It took me a while, but I learned that dignity isn't something someone else can take away. It has to be given. Surrendered." I offered Atum a tight smile. "My dignity may have taken a beating while I was in that dungeon, but it's resilient." I leaned into Atum, resting my head on his shoulder once more and wrapping my arms around his middle. "Let the people call me a whore. My dignity knows the truth." I gave him a squeeze. "Now, take me to your chamber, *my lord*."

Atum's hold tightened around me, and goosebumps erupted on my skin as he drew on his powers. A moment later, my stomach dropped like I was on a roller coaster, and the world fell away.

I KNELT ATOP THE rooftop patio above the servant's wing and stared out at the Eastern Desert, its sand turned pink by the rising sun. Atum was out there, hidden beyond the dunes, carrying out his sunrise ritual.

I had slept like the dead in his arms, surrounded by his scent, but I had awakened at dawn, when he carefully attempted to disentangle our limbs. Atum offered to take me out to the desert with him, but I was determined to prove to myself that I could survive on my own for a short while. That I was still capable of being alone without dissolving into a puddle of quivering, blubbering flesh. I had never been dependent on another person before, let alone a man, and I wasn't about to start right now, not even for someone who was more god than man.

A scuffing sound drew my attention to the open hatch leading down to the palace's ground floor. Someone was climbing up the ladder. Kiya's shaved head appeared through the opening, and my heart soared momentarily before dropping like a stone when reason butted in. This wasn't Kiya. It was Tefnut.

"There you are," Tefnut said with only a cursory glance at me and none of Kiya's trademark wry humor. She climbed the rest of the way onto the rooftop and crossed to the raised edge, standing with her hands planted firmly on her hips. She said nothing more. Just, *there you are*.

"Here I am," I said lightly, hoping to prompt her into sharing why she had apparently been looking for me.

Tefnut continued to stand with her back to me, her sickle-shaped sword blades gleaming in the morning sunlight. Each successive inter-action with Atum's daughter gave me an increasing certainty that she didn't like me.

"Can I help you with something?" I asked, providing a more direct nudge to get this conversation started.

"You can leave," she said coolly, still not looking at me.

"Excuse me?" I choked on a laugh. "I was here first," I said, though it came out as more of a question.

Tefnut glanced at me over her shoulder, her dislike clear in the down-ward curve of her lips. "Leave this timeline," she said and returned to staring out at the Eastern Desert. "I know my father told you he can create a portal from Rostau to your home. Accept his offer. Tell him you wish to go—now." She delivered the words matter-of-factly, directions to be followed, orders to be obeyed. "Shu and I can manage here. Your anomalous presence has surely had the desired effect on the time tapestry by now, making the lifethreads more malleable." She sniffed dismissively. "We don't need you here anymore."

My jaw dropped further with each new statement, and for long sec-onds, I gawked at her back, at a complete loss for words. "Atum needs me," I finally managed to say, defiance ringing in my voice.

Tefnut scoffed. "My father *wants* you, but he does not *need* you. He will survive without you in his life, but he may not live much longer if you remain a part of it."

"I would never hurt him," I declared.

Tefnut made that rough, ugly sound again and turned to face me, crossing her arms over her chest and looking down at me. "You already have," she said, her words a sucker punch. "You will be his downfall."

I shook my head. "I want to help him. The timeline—"

"*You* are the greatest threat to the timeline we have ever faced," Tefnut cut in before I could finish. "Because *you* are the only person—the only *thing*—my father has ever put before his duty." She glared at me. "Are you truly this selfish? You already nearly killed him once. How long until it happens again?"

I opened and shut my mouth, my brow furrowing as I searched for the right words. "That was an accident."

"Precisely my point," Tefnut said. "Which means you can't control it. You can't *prevent* it."

I shook my head, refusing to accept the truth even as she shoved my face in it.

Tefnut's expression softened minutely. "Do you love him?"

"What?" I blurted, thrown off by the personal question.

She snorted a laugh. "You must. You know who and what he is, and you're still here. You have *seen* him at his worst—you've seen him *do* his worst—and *you're still here*. If that's not love . . ." She shook her head, letting out another soft, humorless laugh. "If you love him *at all*, then you must leave him," she said. "Ask him to take you to Rostau and to create the portal to send you home. Leave, now. Before you destroy him." She looked past me, toward Waset, the town bustling now that the sun was up. "Before you destroy us all."

"I can't," I said without thinking.

Tefnut narrowed her eyes, her glare returning. "The bond has been fulfilled?" she said. "I did not think—"

"No," I said, shaking my head, unsure of my meaning beyond the fact that thinking about leaving Atum—about never seeing him again—caused a sharp pain in my chest. Thinking about leaving him, about the actual act of leaving, felt abhorrent to me, like cutting off my own arm to save my life. Like killing someone I loved.

The pain swelled, growing into an unbearable agony, and I clutched at my chest. I *couldn't* leave him.

A sizzle tickled my skin, making the small hairs stand on end. It was the telltale touch of otherworldly energy, pulled into this reality by a *sheut*. Atum was returning.

Tefnut's eyes widened. "Your skin!" she gasped, flinging a hand out toward me. "It's glowing!"

Taking heaving breaths, I pulled my hands away from my chest and stared at them, horrified by what I saw. Ribbons of slithering golden light wreathed my hands and arms, pulsing brighter with every beat of my heart.

The otherworldly sizzle hadn't come from Atum teleporting back to the palace.

It had come from me.

"Get out of here," I croaked.

Tefnut was right. I couldn't control whatever was happening to me. I had almost killed Atum once. Eventually, I *would* kill him.

Which meant I *had* to leave. I groaned at the next pulse of agony within my chest and curled in on myself. I had to leave him before I killed him.

Tefnut sidestepped toward the open hatch on the floor, her movements cautious, slow.

"Leave now!" I shrieked. I hugged my middle, attempting to hold in the impending explosion.

I couldn't stay here. I *couldn't*. I was a danger to Atum. To *everyone*.

The next beat of my heart sent out flares of golden energy lashing around me. "Get away from me!" I yelled.

Tefnut scrambled down through the hatch and slammed it shut.

I held my breath, attempting to slow my thudding heart. The next beat sent out more of those golden flares. And the next made the rooftop tremble. The one following turned my blood to acid, burning through me from the inside.

Time slowed, the next beat of my heart taking forever to come.

Finally, it pulsed, and light exploded out of me, golden and burning. My spine arched, and I threw my head back, screaming as energy whipped around me. The floor beneath me bucked, then gave way, but I didn't fall.

I hovered where the rooftop patio had been, a supernova that had once been a woman, my golden light destroying everything it touched.

Chunks of limestone and mudbrick were sucked into my personal whirlwind, then flung out to fly across the parts of the palace that remained untouched by my explosion. People ran from the palace, their screams muted by the roaring filling my ears.

"NO!" I shrieked, watching the destruction I had caused—*was* causing. But I couldn't stop it.

It seemed to go on forever, a nightmare that wouldn't end, but eventually, with a *whoosh*, the light sucked back into my body, and I dropped to the rubble below. My foot lodged between two large chunks of limestone, wrenching painfully as my body fell in the other direction. A *crack* of breaking bone whited out my vision, and I cried out, crumpling onto the fresh ruins.

I listened to the muffled cries of people all around me as the darkness of unconsciousness crept in, swallowing me whole.

I RETURNED TO CONSCIOUSNESS feeling like a bell that had been rung. My senses were muted, taking eons to register any sights or sounds or smells. I seemed to be floating, and I had the strangest sensation that my brain was vibrating inside my skull.

Groaning, I lifted my eyelids, but my view of the world was hazy and indistinct. Muffled crying tickled my ears, and my ankle throbbed with blinding agony. As my nerve endings awakened further, I no longer felt like I was floating, but lying on a bed of jagged boulders. I raised my head and attempted to shift my aching ankle.

I gasped, the pain quadrupling, shooting through my body like bolts of lightning and making me see stars.

"Don't move," a man said, his voice injecting panic into my veins. Inyotef.

My heart pounded, and the spike of adrenaline sharpened my senses. I struggled to tug my foot free, crying out when the pain overwhelmed me once more. I sagged back onto the rocks, sobbing through each heaving breath and building up the nerve to try again.

"It's me, Tarset. Atum, not Inyotef," that hated voice said as powerful hands settled on my shoulders, holding me down. Inyotef leaned over me, his face filling my vision. "Inyotef is dead, Tarset. He's dead."

With wide-open eyes, I stared up at him, my heart beating so hard it seemed to be trying to burst out of my chest. I looked past Inyotef's face, finding Atum's eyes, indigo-black and swirling with silver stars.

"Atum?" I whimpered, struggling to piece together the hows and whys of what was happening. I attempted to reconcile his true identity with the input from my addled senses, which were screaming for me to run. My chin trembled. "What's going on?"

Atum relaxed visibly and let up the pressure on my shoulders. "Go ahead," he said, glancing at someone near my feet—a man with the same incandescent ebony skin as Atum and Tefnut when they were in their true forms—before refocusing on me. "This will hurt, Tarset, but we can't do anything for your injured ankle until your foot is free."

I heard the grind of stone against stone, and then agony pushed the breath from my lungs. I twisted to the side, retching.

Atum slid his arms under me, one at my thighs, the other at my shoulders, and lifted me off the ground. "Go on," he said, his borrowed voice grating on my frayed nerves. "Help the others. I've got her from here."

"Is that Shu?" I asked, the agony in my ankle fading as though the influx of pain had charred the sensory pathways, numbing them. Feeling woozy, I rested my head on Atum's shoulder.

"It is," Atum said. "He arrived early this morning."

Despondent wails caught my attention, and I peeked over Atum's shoulder. This portion of the palace had been demolished, and through the dust clouds, I could see people milling around beyond the place where the tall exterior wall should have been. More people lay on the ground in a neat row.

My heart turned leaden and sank into my roiling gut. Those weren't just people *lying* on the ground. Those were bodies. Dead people.

"I did this," I whispered, snippets of my conversation with Tefnut flashing through my mind, along with the explosion of energy that followed. My breaths came faster, pain worse than that of my injured ankle sprouting in my chest. "I—" I sucked in a shuddering breath. "I *killed* them."

"Shhh . . ." Atum pressed his lips to my forehead. "I'm taking you home," he breathed. "Rest now."

Darkness closed in around me, and the world—and the agony of living in it—faded away.

A GENTLE ROCKING MOTION lulled me back to consciousness. Lying on my back, I opened my eyes, feeling well rested and absolutely famished. And so far as I could tell, I was on a boat.

I examined my surroundings from my supine position. Everything from the boards making up the walls and the low ceiling to the bedframe appeared to be made of *At*. Small pieces of thin, transparent *At* even took the place of traditional glass in a broad, diamond pane window a few feet beyond the end of the bed.

So, not just any ship. I was on Atum's sloop.

The only other furniture in the compact cabin besides the narrow bed was a dresser situated against the wall to my right, also constructed of *At* in a simple, mission-style design. Just those two pieces of furniture paired with the low ceiling and cramped floor space made the cabin feel claustrophobic.

I sat up and searched for a door, finding it to the immediate right of the headboard, directly opposite the window. A quick glance down at myself revealed I was wearing the usual white linen shift.

My groaning stomach drove me to my bare feet, and my left ankle throbbed, dredging up memories of pain and destruction and death. Images of parts of the Waset palace in ruins flashed through my mind, of bodies lined up on the ground beyond the demolished wall, of grief-stricken mourners on their knees, wailing for the dead.

I stumbled against the door, my knees suddenly weak.

All that destruction—I did that. I killed those people. Innocent people. Not bandits or psychopaths or some other villainous type, and not to protect myself or anyone else. Harmless, hardworking palace servants. And they were dead. Because of me.

I was the villain in their stories, the one they had needed protecting from.

I stifled a sob as agony knotted in my gut, twisting around and around. I was starving, having gone through a round of regenerative sleep to heal my ankle and likely in need of another round, but the grief- and guilt-fueled nausea roiling in my stomach banished my appetite. I *needed* to eat. But I wasn't sure I *could*.

Someone knocked on the door from the outside, and I jumped, scrambling backward on shaky legs until I bumped into the side of the bed. "Who's there?" I asked, clutching my neck with one hand while I gripped my side tightly with the fingers of the other.

The door opened inward on silent hinges, and Atum's towering figure appeared, blocking the doorway, a tray of fragrant food balanced on one hand. The aroma coaxed my appetite back to life, and I started salivating immediately.

Atum ducked to enter the room, turning to shut the door. The ceiling was a few inches too low for him to stand up straight, and he remained crouched as he took the single step to the dresser and set the tray atop it.

Still crouched, because what other choice did he have other than to drop to his knees and crawl, Atum crossed to the bed—two steps, this time—and sat.

The entire scene was slightly ridiculous, and a semi-hysterical laugh bubbled up my throat. I slapped my hand over my mouth, my eyes bulging with embarrassment.

Atum peered up at me, his forearms resting on his thighs and his eyebrows raised in question.

"I'm sorry," I squeaked, lowering my hand. "I just—" I suppressed another inappropriate laugh, but it forced its way out as a snort. "Didn't you *make* this ship?"

"Obviously," Atum said dryly.

"Well, why didn't you make it *taller*?" I glanced up. The ceiling even felt low to me, and I wasn't even close to Atum's height.

"Ah." Atum threaded his fingers together between his spread knees. "The added height makes the ship too top heavy for the modified hull required for shallower river travel," he explained. "The ceiling in my quarters is higher, but if I constructed the entire ship that way, it would be more prone to capsizing. When we reach the sea, I have more leeway to make the cabins roomier."

"Oh," I said, my brow furrowing. "Right. That makes sense." Or, at least, I felt certain it would have made sense if I knew anything about the physics of boats.

I turned toward the window and wandered closer, peering out at the glittering Nile, the river stretching out until it snaked around a bend in the distance. Far beyond the right bank, the sun hung low in the sky.

Assuming that was the setting sun and we were heading north toward the Mediterranean Sea, that put this cabin at the stern of the ship. I vaguely recalled Atum telling me he was taking me home.

"Are we going to Rostau?" I asked as I gazed out the window. Was that *home* to him?

"We are," he said, his tone solemn. "We should arrive in about a couple weeks, weather depending."

My chin trembled and I hugged my middle as I thought of *why* we were on a boat sailing to Rostau instead of managing the dissonance in Waset. Tears welled and spilled over the brims of my eyelids in record time. "I'm sorry," I whimpered. "I didn't mean to hurt anyone."

Atum sighed. "I know," he said, his voice telling me he still sat on the edge of the bed. For once, I was glad he didn't approach. I didn't want him any closer to me than he already was, not when I had zero understanding of what might set me off. Not when, at any moment, I was a heartbeat away from obliterating him, however unintentionally.

I cleared my throat. "And the dissonance—" I choked on the question, fearing the answer. But I had to know. "How much worse did I make it?" I could only imagine the damage I had dealt to the pattern.

"Not worse at all, actually," Atum said, and I spun around to face him. "Your unique presence combined with the results of the explosion seems to have disturbed the time tapestry enough that the lifethreads have completely reoriented." He frowned, looking oddly impressed. "The dissonance is far more manageable now. I have complete confidence that Tefnut and Shu can handle the situation on their own."

I gaped at him. "You're kidding." His words didn't make me feel any better, but they also didn't make me feel worse, which kind of felt like a win at this point.

"I am not," he said.

I blew out a breath and shook my head. "Wow. That's just—wow."

"Indeed." Atum nodded toward the tray of food. "You should eat, then rest," he said. "Regain your strength. We can discuss how to handle the new situation when you've recovered fully."

The new situation. It was such an innocuous way of referring to the fact that I was a walking, talking miniature nuke.

Seeming to sense my desire to keep my distance, Atum stood as much as he could with the low ceiling and moved to the door, placing his hand on the doorknob. He pulled the door part of the way open and glanced back at me over his shoulder. "What happened back there wasn't your fault, Tarset," he said, conviction shining in his dark stare. "I hope you know that."

"I killed those people," I countered, my cheeks wet with tears. "If it weren't for me, they would still be alive. Intentional or not, it *is* my fault that they're dead."

Atum let out a displeased grunt that let me know he disagreed, but he didn't argue the matter further. "Eat," he said, glancing at the food atop the dresser. "Rest. I'll return when you wake."

And with that, he stepped out of the cabin and shut the door.

WHEN NEXT I WOKE, the luscious aroma of chocolate filled my nostrils, making my mouth water. Of course, the cacao tree didn't exist in Egypt in this era—or anywhere else outside of South America, so far as I knew. But then, I supposed limitations like the *current* time period or *availability* didn't really apply to someone who could easily step into and out of *any* era within the portion of the timeline he guarded.

I luxuriated in the scent, my mind filling with images of frosted layer cakes and French pastries, of boxes of truffles and chocolates, of card houses built of chocolate bars, and even of a glorious chocolate fountain. When I opened my eyes, reality was less dramatic, but not remotely disappointing: hot cocoa.

The tray on the dresser held only a large, steaming ceramic mug—what I assumed to be the source of the delectable smell—an earthenware pitcher with a fitted lid, and a basket of what appeared to be scones. There were also three small bowls holding condiments for the scones, including what appeared to be clotted cream, a dark-red jam, and what I assumed was lemon curd.

Despite the hunger groaning in my belly and the saliva pooling in my mouth, I only studied the tray of promised deliciousness for a moment. Atum stood near the window, away from me, one hand clasping his wrist behind his back. He no longer crouched to avoid the low ceiling. I couldn't help but wonder if he had added more headroom to the cabin permanently, or just for his visit.

The back view of Atum was just as nice as the front, and I took my time in admiring him. He no longer wore the white linen kilt I was so used to seeing him in, having traded his schenti for a pair of fitted black trousers and a dark and loose-fitting shirt that had been tucked into his waistband. He still wore a weapons belt with wicked-looking khepesh swords, but the curved blades were no longer bronze. Now, they gleamed with razor-sharp, iridescent *At*. He had rolled the sleeves of his shirt up nearly to his elbows, revealing the thick leather cuffs bearing a gold and onyx winged scarab adorning each of his wrists. He looked delightfully roguish, the image of a Caribbean pirate.

I pushed up onto my elbows. "Hey," I said, my voice raspy from sleep. I cleared my throat.

Atum turned, releasing his wrist and taking a step toward my bed, but he stopped short of coming any closer. Now that he faced me, I could see another winged scarab decorated his belt buckle. How *on brand* of him.

I couldn't help but wonder at his hesitation. Was it because he was afraid of me? I wouldn't have blamed him if he was. After the death and destruction I had caused back in Waset, *I* was afraid of myself.

"How do you feel?" he asked, his focus shifting to my feet, hidden under the blankets. "How's the ankle?"

Frowning, I rolled my injured foot, then shook my head. "All better. No pain." I offered him a tight smile. It seemed so unfair that I was fully healed while those people I had killed were still dead. "Thanks for asking."

Atum's brows bunched together, and again, he clenched his jaw. His gaze roved over my face, searching for something—I wasn't sure what.

Sensing a serious topic of conversation was about to be broached, I lurched up and scooted to the edge of the bed. "I'll be right back," I blurted, standing and hurrying to the door to flee like an absolute coward. I yanked the door open and retreated into the bathroom across the narrow passageway, which I had discovered during my previous—however brief—moment of wakefulness.

Once the bathroom door was locked and I was alone, I exhaled heavily and fell back against the slab of *At*. The bathroom—or *head*, I supposed, since I was on a boat—was another of those out-of-time oddities I was learning to expect from Atum. I now had access to a modern flushing toilet and an actual shower that was obscenely spacious for a ship bathroom, plumbed with blissfully hot water. I had only used the water from the tap, not actually bathed the last time I was awake, and I was really looking forward to spending some quality time in that shower. Now, however, was not the time for that.

I relieved myself on the toilet, splashed some cold water onto my face from the faucet at the sink, and studied my dripping reflection in the mirror hanging on the wall. Nejerets didn't age physically once we manifested our immortal traits, but I would have sworn I looked older. Maybe it was the regeneration taking its toll. My face definitely had a distinctively gaunt appearance.

Sighing, I pulled the hand towel from the hanger on the wall beside the mirror and dried my face, then replaced it and turned around. A couple of doors were all that stood between Atum and me, and what was bound to be an uncomfortable conversation. Would he continue to attest that the disaster at the palace wasn't my fault? Would he declare that he wasn't afraid of me? I wasn't sure I could stand hearing him utter lies, even if he believed them.

I took a deep breath, bolstering my courage, and opened the door. I strode across the passageway and burst into my cabin, prepared for an emotional battle.

Except, Atum wasn't there.

I stood just inside the doorway, momentarily frozen by the shock of finding the cabin empty. The tray of what qualified as rare delicacies nowabouts remained, along with the still tantalizing aroma of hot chocolate, but Atum was gone.

Leaning backward, I peered up and down the passageway. I shouldn't have begrudged Atum for leaving after I had already done that same thing. But I did. I had never claimed *not* to be a hypocrite.

Shoulders slumping, I shut the door and trudged over to the dresser to grip the outer edges of the tray. I carefully shifted the tray to the bed and sat, ready to drown my misery in an oversized mug of hot cocoa.

I lifted the lid on the pitcher, and my eyes widened. "Wowzers," I murmured. Make that a *pitcher* of hot chocolate to drown my sorrows.

The scones were delicious, still warm from the oven and so soft and fluffy that they practically dissolved in my mouth, and the hot chocolate was positively sinful. I ate and drank until my stomach groaned in protest and I was desperate for a glass of water to cleanse my overstimulated taste buds.

With a satisfied sigh, I moved the tray back to the dresser, then headed for the door with the drained mug to retrieve some water from the bathroom. When I opened the door, I found Atum standing in the corridor, his fist raised to knock.

"Oh," I said, blinking stupidly and hugging the mug to my chest. "Hey."

"Apologies for vanishing like that," Atum said, bowing his head. "We encountered another vessel, and I had to take extra precautions to ensure we weren't noticed."

"Um, that's all right."

He glanced down at the empty mug in my hand. "You didn't care for the hot chocolate?"

I snorted a laugh, thinking back to the barely quarter-full pitcher sitting on the tray. "It's delicious," I said, averting my gaze as my cheeks heated. I had guzzled down three mugfuls, after all. "I'm just thirsty."

I looked up at Atum, our eyes meeting only for a moment, but long enough to make my heart stumble. We hadn't been this close since *before*, and his gaze grew exponentially more penetrating the nearer I drew.

"For water," I added, returning my attention to the empty mug hugged against my chest and refusing to let the lure of our potential bond sink its hooks into me yet again.

I couldn't. Not now. Not ever. Not when I posed such a threat to him.

"Ah, I see," Atum said, and stepped off to the side, making room for me to pass.

I hurried across the passageway to the bathroom, rinsed the mug, and gulped down some cold water, then refilled the mug and returned to my cabin.

Atum remained in the passageway, his hands braced on either side of the doorway, like he was holding himself back from following me inside.

I set the mug of water on the tray atop the dresser and retreated to the window at the far end of the room, putting as much distance as was possible between Atum and my volatile self in this small space. It was an effort not to hug my middle, but I kept my arms relaxed at my sides.

"I thought I might shower, if that's all right?" I asked over my shoulder, not quite looking at Atum.

"Of course," he said, his voice tight, restrained. "I had the dresser stocked with clothing from your time." When I looked at him, my brow furrowed in question, he amended his statement. "Well, *almost* from your time. While Shu was in Rostau, he used the portals there to retrieve the items from the future edge of the timeline, as none can travel beyond the boundary and return."

I nodded, shifting my attention to the dresser.

I generally found the logic and mechanics of the time tapestry and related limitations confusing, but when thinking of the timeline itself, and the clear division between his part and mine, it helped me to picture an audio clip. The barrier was like a cut in the clip, creating two separate tracks. The first still flowed fluidly into the second, but they were separate things. Adjustments to the first didn't alter the second. Of course, that interpretation might very well be complete trash, but it helped me to wrap *my* mind around the way things worked. Or, at least, the way things *seemed* to work.

"He also retrieved some things I thought might make your stay on board the *Bennu* more comfortable," he said, and I assumed *Bennu* was the name of the ship carrying us north. "A music player, some books and notebooks . . . that kind of thing."

"Thank you," I said, facing Atum fully. "For everything. I really appreciate it."

Again, Atum bowed his head. "Would you dine with me tonight?"

My brows rose. This new formality from him caught me off guard, and I wondered if I was meeting the real Atum for the first time, or if his changed manner resulted from *me* distancing myself from *him*. I had grown so used to thinking of Atum as an ancient Egyptian that I hadn't considered he actually belonged to *all* eras contained within the time tapestry, from as far back as the Stone Age, for all I knew, up to the moment Lex absorbed Nuin's power some twenty years before I died and journeyed backward in time.

"Yes," I said automatically. "Of course. I would love that." My chin trembled, but I forced a smile.

It would be a last supper for what could have been a beautiful relationship. After the meal, I would keep my distance from him—to protect him. Whatever we might have been could never be.

"I look forward to it," Atum said, bowing more deeply, then turning and striding away. By the time I reached the door and peeked into the passageway, he was gone.

Heart aching, I shut the door and turned to the dresser. A quick examination of the drawers and their contents revealed clothing that appeared fashionable but dated—for me. The fabrics were all luxurious, though, and the labels assured me each item would have cost a small fortune had I actually purchased it. I pulled out a pair of the softest black leggings I had ever felt and a long, dove-gray cashmere sweater. I added a black pair of panties that were both lacy and soft, and a comfy looking black T-shirt bra, also lacy and soft, and headed for the door.

The shower was calling my name, and while I doubted even fully functional plumbing could ease my breaking heart, at least I would be squeaky clean while I spent the rest of the day wallowing in self pity. When my life was falling apart all around me, it was important to appreciate the little things. The small wins. And right now, a shower was definitely a win.

"HOW MANY LANGUAGES DO you speak?" I asked Atum, my belly full from the deliciously modern dinner and my heart warmed by being in his company. The contents of my dresser were not the only items Shu had gathered from a distant era. The ship was apparently stocked with relative luxury items and non-perishables from the twentieth century.

We had dined on pizza and salad, and my tongue delighted at my first taste of tomatoes in months. And, thankfully, the formality of our last few interactions had been worn away by comfortable conversation and laughter.

We sat across from one another at the small table in his cabin, which I discovered neighbored mine—and truly did have more headroom, courtesy of a sunken floor. I couldn't help but wonder what was below us. Hopefully storage and not some crew member's sleeping quarters. Atum was dressed the same as before in his pirate-esque attire, and I wore a pair of dark jeans—such a novelty—a pretty, flowy silk blouse, and the softest slouchy suede booties I had ever encountered.

Atum slumped back in his chair, leaning on his left armrest, his *At* wine goblet in hand, half-full of the robust red he had chosen for tonight's meal. I was guessing the wine was yet another item plucked from the future, as it didn't taste anything like the wines I had grown used to in this era.

Elbows resting on the table and head tilted to the side, I slowly spun my wineglass on the table and studied Atum through narrowed eyes. He had to be proficient in many languages, considering all the time periods and locales he monitored on the time tapestry. "A dozen?" I guessed.

The corners of his full lips tugged upward with the faintest hint of a smile, and without lifting his hand from the armrest, he raised his index finger, pointing up toward the ceiling.

"Two dozen?" I guessed, my eyebrows climbing higher.

Again, he raised his index finger.

"A hundred?"

That index finger made another appearance.

I guffawed. "A *thousand*?"

Chuckling, Atum shook his head. "Not quite that many," he said, amusement curving his lips.

My eyes narrowed again, this time with suspicion. "Do you speak English?"

All our interactions had been carried out in Old Egyptian, the language of the current place and time, of which I had decent mastery but a truly horrific accent. I had never considered that we might be able to communicate in a language with which I was more comfortable.

Atum responded in a language that wasn't Old Egyptian but also wasn't English. It sounded like a cross between Scots and German and tickled the edges of my comprehension but was still gibberish to me.

I frowned and shook my head. "I don't understand."

"That language is what the people of your time commonly call 'Old English'," he explained in perfectly understandable *Modern* English, his faint accent eerily similar to my dad's. "I speak Middle English as well," he added.

"Like Shakespeare?" I asked, also switching to Modern English, though the shapes of the unique phonemes felt strange to my tongue after going unused for months.

Atum laughed softly and shook his head again. "Not quite. The works of Shakespeare are written in an early version of Modern English. Had they been written in Middle English, they would be far less popular in your time because so few people would understand them. For example . . ." He cleared his throat. "'Whan that Aprill with his shoures soote the droghte of March hath perced to the roote, and bathed every veyne in swich licour of which vertu engendred is the flour.'" When he finished, he watched me from under raised eyebrows.

"What was that?" I asked, my eyes narrowed.

"Did you understand any of it?"

"Um . . ." I laughed awkwardly. "Something about bathing in flowers?"

"Not quite," he said. He raised his wineglass and took a sip. "When the sweet showers of April have pierced the drought of March, and pierced it to the root, and every vein is bathed in that moisture whose quickening force will engender the flower." He took another sip of wine when he finished his translation, then set his glass on the table. "It's the opening of Chaucer's *Canterbury Tales*, written at the end of the fourteenth century. You would be able to read the printed text better than you can understand it spoken," he explained. "There was a shift in vowel sounds that transformed the English language shortly after, starting in the 1400s."

"Huh," I said, releasing the stem of my wineglass and relaxing back into my chair. "I had no idea you were so scholarly." I may not have spoken English in months, but I was settling back into the language easily enough, like donning a favorite pair of old, worn jeans.

"I hide it well behind all the brutish savagery required of me in these more ancient times," Atum commented dryly.

I scoffed. "You're neither a brute nor a savage."

"What am I then?" he asked, straightening and leaning forward to rest one forearm on the table. "How do *you* see me?"

I studied his striking features, taking in his stunning beauty. I recalled how he had looked, taking Nitocris on the floor of his sleeping chamber. Atum's stare heated, and a flush crept up my neck, warming my cheeks. I averted my gaze, focusing instead on my wineglass, and smiled to myself. "Maybe a little savage."

"Tarset . . ." His raw tone drew my attention back up to his face, to his sorrowful eyes. "You're going to leave me, aren't you?"

My lips parted, and I sucked in a breath, caught off guard by his question. "I don't know." My brow furrowed, and I shook my head. "This afternoon, I think I would have said yes," I admitted. "But now . . ." Again, I shook my head. In my mind's eye, I saw the destruction I had wrought at the palace in Waset, followed by Atum slumped against a mastaba, his body broken and blood staining his lips.

I knew what I needed to do. I *should* tell him I was leaving, that we would never bond, because as soon as we reached Rostau, I was marching straight through the portal to my far future home, and I was never coming back. But I couldn't bring myself to actually do it. To say the words. To commit to leaving. Part of me grasped onto the hope that we could find a way to make this work. That *I* could learn to control whatever was happening to me.

I inhaled deeply, preparing to voice my inner conflict. "I'm afraid I'm too dangerous to be around you," I told him. "You're too important to *everything*, and I'm not sure I can live with the constant fear that I'm accidentally going to kill you."

I leaned forward, resting my elbows on the table once more. Honestly, I wasn't sure I could live with the same fear that I would harm my family either, were I to return home. There was no safe place for me.

"I *want* to stay," I said, speaking my heart. "I know that now, but my being here, near you, threatens the entire universe."

For a dozen heartbeats, we simply stared at one another. Finally, Atum spoke, his voice hushed. "I have never asked for anything for myself—not from anyone. I have never had anything that was mine alone. I have never had the privilege of being selfish—" Breathing deeply, he leaned forward and set his goblet on the table, seeming to need a moment to collect himself. "But I have to be selfish right now, with you. I have to try."

My heart lodged in my throat. This was so unfair. Here I was, trying to convince myself to do the right thing. Trying to put the needs of others before myself. Trying *not* to be selfish for once in my self-centered life.

"I will ask you just this once," Atum said, his words impassioned. "Stay with me, Tarset. Be my companion. My partner. My fallen star. Be *mine*."

The breath whooshed from my lungs. "Those aren't questions," I whispered, then added, "I might *kill* you."

"Not if you learn to control the power within you."

I opened and closed my mouth, but no sound came out.

"At least consider it?" he asked, definitely a question this time.

I stared at him, my eyes stinging with the threat of tears. "Of course," I said quietly. It wasn't like I had thought about much else for weeks. Clearing my throat, I pushed back my chair. "I should go," I said, then feared he would misunderstand me and added, "to bed. I have a lot to think about."

Atum stood as I did. "I'll walk you to your door," he said, but his expression was uncertain, like he expected me to refuse his offer.

I gave him a small, almost shy smile. "I'd like that."

He followed close behind me, a palpable shadow, as I made my way out to the passageway and to the door of my cabin, neighboring his.

I turned to face him, leaning back against my door. "Thank you for tonight," I said. "Dinner was delicious."

"The company was better," Atum murmured, planting his palms on the door on either side of my head and smoldering down at me.

A wry grin touched my lips. "When you say things like that . . ."

He returned my grin with a roguish one of his own, but it was impossible not to notice the doubt shadowing his eyes. The fear. The grief. Like he was already mourning losing me.

I angled my face up toward his. Maybe I couldn't commit to giving him all of myself, but I could give him this. I could give him a kiss.

"You are temptation incarnate," Atum murmured, leaning in so his breath brushed over my lips. "I would make it worth your while if you stayed. You would want for nothing—not food, not comfort, not pleasure . . ."

"I know," I breathed, and then I closed the distance between our lips, sinking into that promised pleasure, if only for a moment.

Atum's hands moved to my head, cradling my jaw, his fingers tangling in my hair. He growled his approval as I gripped the sides of his belt and pulled his hips flush against mine. Desire raged through my veins, and I groaned into his mouth, savoring the scratch of his stubble and the sinful strokes of his tongue.

The kiss was bruising and intoxicating, and the longer it went on, the less certain I was of why I wasn't simply jumping into his bed right now. Or, considering where we were, dragging him into mine.

A flash of bodies lined up on their backs on the ground flitted through my mind. People beside them on their knees, some silent with grief, others wailing out their heartbreak. Atum, his body bloody and broken. Atum, showing me the time tapestry and all the lifethreads that depended on him. Atum, standing by while Inyotef tortured me. Atum, pushing me away, telling me he didn't deserve my pity. Atum, healing my back. Atum, slaughtering everyone who had hurt me. Atum, watching me with interest in the market. Atum, gazing at me with longing. Atum, pleading with his eyes. Atum . . .

I had to leave him. I *had* to leave him. It was the only way to save him from me—and from himself. My heart seemed to swell in my chest, pulsing not just with grief, but with mounting power. Not my heart, I thought, but my soul.

I gasped and broke the kiss, bowing my head and resting my forehead against his chest. "I'm sorry," I whispered, my chin trembling. "It's happening again, isn't it?" But I didn't need him to answer. I could see the golden glow from my skin reflected on his shirt.

Panicking, I reached behind me, found the door handle, turned it, and practically fell backward into my cabin.

I righted myself and faced Atum. We stared at one another for what felt like an eternity, both of us breathing hard, that deadly power throbbing in my chest. He clenched his hands into fists and hunched his shoulders, seeming to be physically fighting the urge to follow me into my cabin.

"Shut the door," he rasped. "Shut it now, Tarset, or . . ."

Or I might kill him.

I gulped, choking on fear, and reached out with one shaky arm. A gentle push was all it took to swing the door closed, the latch clicking, blocking Atum from view.

I turned, leaning back against the door, and slid down to the floor. "I don't want to leave you," I whispered, hugging my knees to my chest. I repeated the words over and over. Slowly, as my mantra became more fervent, the mounting power stalled, then waned.

I raised one hand, watching as the golden glow faded from my skin. Letting out a miserable sob, I rested my head back against the door. I touched a fingertip to my lips, still swollen from our kiss, and my eyelids drifted shut as I relived that stolen moment. The feel of Atum. The taste of him. The sounds he made when he touched me. The way he made my blood thrum with promise.

I was falling in love with him. Or maybe I had already fallen for him. Maybe if I hadn't cared so much, I would have invited him in. What a cruel twist of fate that the only thing strong enough to override my own selfish tendencies was love. That I finally cared enough about another person to consider what was best for them before I concerned myself with my own wants and needs.

At this point, my love for him was the only thing keeping me from bonding with him. If I listened to Tefnut and did end up leaving, it would be because I loved Atum too much, not because I didn't care enough.

And that was complete and utter bullshit.

F OR DAYS AFTER DINING with Atum, I only left the cabin to use the bathroom. The night we dined together had been a near miss, and I wouldn't risk his life like that again. Part of me had been in denial, but now I had accepted reality—both of what I had done, and of what I might do.

My body was fully healed, no longer requiring rounds of regenerative sleep, which left me with hours upon hours to stare out the window at the winding Nile or to pace the cramped room. Atum had impeccable timing and a near infallible knack for anticipating my needs, and he somehow always managed to deliver a tray of food to my door just as I realized I was hungry. But his visits grew shorter and shorter.

Not that I could blame him. I was the greatest danger he had ever faced, and I didn't want him near me any longer than was necessary. Besides, my souring mood made me increasingly poor company.

To pass my time in isolation, I read and listened to music and jotted down lyrics and melodies, but with each passing day, I sank deeper into a black hole of guilt and self-hate. The nightmares of Inyotef and my time as his prisoner had faded into the background, overshadowed by macabre reenactments of the disaster at the palace that had claimed the lives of innocents and of my explosion near the Sphinx that had nearly killed Atum. Often, my subconscious mind combined the two events into something that was exponentially more horrific.

I often startled awake, shaking and soaked with a cold sweat. But thankfully, I kept quiet. The last thing I wanted was to draw Atum to my bedside. How weak and pathetic I must have seemed to him, falling apart over causing a handful of deaths—over *almost* killing him—when he had to hold himself together while living with having killed thousands of people. Except, the blood on his hands had been purposeful—for the greater good—while the blood on mine was utterly pointless.

If I had only been stronger. If I had only been more in control of my emotions. If I had only accepted the truth in Tefnut's words, rather than fighting her from the depths of my soul. Dozens of *ifs* rattled around in my mind, all the different ways I was deficient. Inadequate. Not just useless, but dangerous.

Weeks passed, the gentle rocking of the ship barely perceptible as I perfected my ability to mope. I stopped going to the window. I read every book in the drawer, escaping into the pages, where I could pretend I was someone else. Not a murderer. Not doomed to kill the man I loved. When I finished the last book, I found I couldn't face my own depressing reality, so I dove back into the stories, rereading my favorites.

Sometimes the darkness was like quicksand, greedily sucking me under. Thoughts whispered through my mind, suggesting the world would be better off without me. Better to just end it now and save everyone from the walking nuke that was *me*. In those moments, I filled the notebooks with macabre and morose poetry and page after page of depressing music. When I couldn't even manage that, I laid on my back on my bed for hours at a time, staring up at the ceiling as I listened to music, skipping any song that was remotely hopeful or upbeat, and wished I could fall into an endless, dreamless sleep.

You can, whispered through my mind. *You can end your misery . . .*

Days passed. I ate, bathed, sat with Atum and responded when he asked me questions. I stopped writing in the notebooks, stopped reading, stopped listening to music. When I was alone, I laid in bed, thinking about the people I had killed. Wondering about their lives before me. Imagining their loved ones' lives now. Their parents. Their spouses. Their children. Their friends. Even their pets.

That single moment consumed my entire existence, erasing everything that I had been before. I was a murderer. A destroyer. Death. I couldn't see any place in this world for me, not in any time period. I couldn't stay here with Atum, but I also couldn't go home.

I drifted among those thoughts, vaguely aware of the *Bennu's* increased motion and my growing queasiness. Until the ship lurched hard enough to the side to nearly fling me from my mattress.

I clung to the side of the bed frame, one leg hanging over and my head swimming. My stomach somersaulted, and I scrambled from the bed. There was no avoiding it; I was going to vomit.

I careened into the door, barely holding in the nausea, and yanked it open. I lunged across the narrow passageway and into the bathroom, not even bothering to shut the bathroom door before dropping to my knees in front of the toilet and emptying what little I had bothered to eat during my last meal.

Cool hands slid along my shoulders and up my neck, gathering my loose, unkempt waves at the nape of my neck. "Come out to the deck,"

Atum said, his voice a low rumble. "The fresh air will help with the seasickness."

I raised my head from the toilet bowl and inhaled to tell him to get away from me before his presence triggered another detonation of my soul, but my stomach heaved, drowning the words in another round of vomiting.

Holding my hair with one hand, Atum pulled a washcloth from a drawer in the cabinet under the sink and soaked it with cool water from the faucet. With gentle hands, he helped me to raise my head and wiped my mouth and chin, then tossed the cloth aside. He claimed another, wet it, and draped it around my neck. Then, he reached over my shoulder to pull the lever that would flush my sick away.

"Better?" he asked, his gaze burning into the side of my face.

I still felt lightheaded, and my stomach was far from settled, but the feel of the cool, wet cloth seemed to reset something inside my brain. Tears borne of mortification and physical strain streaked down my cheeks. I nodded, unable to look at him.

My teeth started chattering, and Atum swept the cold washcloth from my neck. "Here," he said, shrugging out of his overcoat and settling it on my shoulders. He guided my arms through sleeves long enough to conceal my hands completely, then wrapped an arm around the back of my waist and hoisted me up to my feet. "Let's get you some fresh air. It will help with the nausea until you acclimate to the motion of the sea."

I was too woozy to argue, so I let him guide me out of the bathroom and up the passageway, leaning on him as the ship lurched and swayed. We paused at a shut door at the end of the corridor, and Atum reached for the knob and pushed the door open.

I raised my hand to shield my eyes from the bright morning sunlight as the scents and sounds of the sea assaulted my senses. Briny air and crashing waves. Shouting people and snapping sails. We stood in the doorway, staring out at the deck of the huge *At* ship, Atum seeming to know I needed a moment to adjust.

"Atum!" a man shouted from across the ship, starting toward us.

He was a compact and muscular Nejeret, his breeches, billowing shirt, cuffed boots, and low ponytail made him appear even more the pirate than Atum. How he could move so quickly and steadily on the rolling deck was beyond me.

"The storm is heading our way." He spoke English, but his accent was not one I had ever heard. "We should lower the sails and batten down the hatches."

Only then did I look beyond the approaching man to the raised deck at the bow of the ship and the dark, angry storm clouds roiling in the distant sky.

"It's still a ways out, Ode," Atum said, his voice raised to reach the other man. He stepped out onto the deck, leaving me alone in the doorway. "We may outrun it yet."

"We're not all gods like you, old man," Ode said, looking past Atum to wink at me. "So you'll have to forgive me if I don't share your optimism."

"I can still drown, just like anyone else," Atum countered.

Ode barked a laugh and shook his head. "That's a good one. I'll have to remember it to tell Pen." His trajectory carried him past us, and he hustled up a stairway to the upper deck at the stern of the ship. "Not yet!" he yelled. "Captain says to wait."

I glanced up at Atum's face as he turned back toward me. "He speaks English," I said, my voice husky as I stated the obvious.

"He does," Atum agreed unnecessarily. "Are you ready to come out onto the deck?"

"Do I have a choice?" Because what I really wanted to do was to crawl back into bed and to pretend my entire existence was all a bad dream. To just fade away.

"No," Atum said. "You don't."

He guided me out of the shelter of the corridor and into the annoyingly cheerful sunshine, so at odds with the angry storm clouds in the distance. Crisp, warm air kissed my skin, and I begrudgingly admitted—if only to myself—that it felt good.

Atum led me to the bow of the ship, and we climbed a narrow set of stairs to a raised deck that afforded us a breathtaking view of the sea. The full sails overhead propelled the ship onward, and we cut through the swells, sending sea spray flying. A rainbow mist clouded the air directly in front of us, clearing a moment later to reveal a simple park bench made of *At*. Atum walked me around the side of the bench, then helped me sit before lowering himself to sit beside me.

"Stare at the horizon," Atum instructed, pointing toward the place where the dark clouds met the raging sea far head. "It will help your brain make sense of the motion and may ease the nausea."

I did as he instructed, my eyebrows rising as lightning streaked through the sky, cutting across the dark backdrop. "I'm not sure this is helping," I told him. "Can this ship survive a storm like that?" I asked, more curious than afraid.

Atum chuckled. "You have nothing to fear aboard this ship," he assured me. "There is not a storm we cannot weather. If it gets bad enough that we're at risk of capsizing, all I have to do is surround us within a sphere of *At*, and then we wait for the storm to expend itself."

"Why not do that *before* it gets bad?" I asked, wondering if the water was growing rougher or if it was just my imagination.

"Because Ode enjoys the challenge," Atum said, amusement in his voice. When I glanced at him, genuine affection shone in his midnight eyes. "Look at the horizon," he reminded me, pointing with his chin.

I redirected my focus to the storm. "Ode is a unique name," I commented. "Where is he from?"

"In about twelve centuries, he will be born on an island called Kefalonia," Atum said. "But you may be more familiar with its fictional name—Ithaca."

"Ithaca," I said, and I narrowed my eyes, bits of information surfacing from the depressive funk clouding my mind long enough to spark some independent thoughts. "That's from the Homeric epics, isn't it? The *Iliad* or the *Odyssey*—"

My jaw dropped, and I twisted on the bench to stare across the length of the ship toward the raised stern deck, where Ode barked orders at other members of the crew.

"You've got to be kidding me. That's Odysseus, isn't it?" I looked at Atum. "Like *the* Odysseus."

"The horizon," Atum reminded me, only answering when I complied, facing forward once more. "Yes," he said, "that's Odysseus, though many of the legends surrounding him are *grossly* overblown."

"Huh," I said, still riding the endorphin rush from such a shocking discovery. I thought it may have done more to banish what ailed me—at least physically—than the fresh air or the view of the horizon.

"Many more legends await your acquaintance in Rostau," Atum promised. "You may find you fit in quite well there."

I pressed my lips together, wondering if he had orchestrated the meeting with Ode for the very purpose of luring me out of my inner darkness by letting me know what I had to look forward to. But the excitement of discovery was already fading, the depression eroding my anticipation until it sizzled away and all I could see was the futility of my situation and the storm looming on the horizon.

W E DID NOT, IN fact, outrun the storm. As night fell, I watched the storm clouds overtake the view from my window, turning the sea into a dark, angry mass of rolling hills with frothy peaks. Lightning cut through the sky, illuminating the full horror of the endless, churning sea. It promised oblivion to any with the bad luck of falling overboard, something I didn't think was all that unlikely, considering how violently the ship lurched and bucked.

I sat on the bed in sweats and a T-shirt, braced against the corner of the wall to prevent myself from being flung about. I had lost track of how many times I had fled to the bathroom to empty my stomach. At least now, there was nothing left to throw up but sour tasting bile.

How long until Atum surrounded the ship in a protective shell of *At*?

How long until I found myself trapped here on this ship? In this era? This place? This life? This worthless body?

The longer I stared out the window, the louder the oblivion of the raging sea called to me, promising the dreamless sleep I yearned for so desperately.

Compulsion drove me to my feet, and I lurched to the door on unsteady sea legs. I braced myself against the walls of the passageway and hauled myself toward the door to the deck. As soon as I turned the door handle, the slab of *At* slammed open, pushing me backward, and the roaring wind filled my ears. Icy rain pelted my face, seeming to be falling sideways. Atum had set the *At* deck boards to glow so the crew could see in the darkness, but the intermittent lightning was like a blinding strobe light.

I stumbled toward the deck's side rail, squeezing my eyes shut as frigid water sprayed over the side of the ship, soaking me. The crew was so busy manning the ship's rigging that not a single member took note of me standing at the railing. The churning water looked like ink, like liquefied obsidian. Like silence. Like peace.

Fingers gripping the sodden railing, I leaned forward. Just a little more, and I would fall into the void I so desperately sought.

Someone grabbed my arm, their grip like iron. "What the *hell* are you doing out here?" Atum shouted, jerking me backward and into his unyielding body.

His hold on my arm was painfully tight as he dragged me back toward the door to our cabins and through the doorway, seemingly unaffected by the bucking motion of the ship. In no time at all, I was back in my cabin, the roaring wind and sea silenced by the walls of *At*. As soon as Atum released me, the ship lurched, and I crashed into the wall by the dresser.

Atum flung his hand out, and the unsteady motion eased. He must have encased the ship in the protective bubble he had promised. I pictured it, the ship bobbing along in an impenetrable sphere of *At*, oblivious to the storm raging outside.

Atum loomed in the middle of the cramped cabin, the ceiling seeming higher than ever before to accommodate for his larger-than-life presence. His dark skin glistened, and his clothing, heavy with water, dripped on the floor.

My sodden hair stuck to my face and neck, and my sweatpants and T-shirt clung to my body like plastic wrap. I huddled back into the corner formed by the wall and the end of the dresser. My teeth chattered as I withered from Atum's damning stare.

"I will not let you kill yourself," he growled, his hands balling into fists. "I cannot—" He seemed to catch himself, his shoulders rising and falling with a deep breath. "Since you seem to care so little about your own life, I offer you a deal," he proposed. "My life for yours."

I hugged my middle, already shaking my head.

"So long as yours continues," Atum said. "Mine will as well."

"I don't accept that," I shot back, straightening from my huddled position. "I don't *agree* to that." The timeline needed him. The *universe* needed him. But it needed *me* to go away.

Atum's cheeks twitched with a faint, humorless smile. "You don't have to," he stated clearly. "Just know that if you end your life willingly, I will end mine as well."

"No," I said, my chin trembling. I hugged myself more tightly. "Please don't do this." Despair thickened my voice. "I can't continue like this. I see them—all the time. I don't even know their names, but I still see them. They're haunting me, Atum, and I can feel myself fading away." I dragged in my next breath, fighting back sobs. "When I'm alone, there is nothing in my head—" I slapped my chest as superheated tears seared down my cheeks—"in my heart, but those people I killed and the certainty that I *will* do the same to you." I was all but shouting now. "There is *nothing* left of me."

Atum took a small step toward me, the starlight in his eyes burning with conviction. "You are *never* alone," he declared, taking another small step. "Even in your darkest moments, you have never been alone."

One final step, and he was in front of me, a wall of flesh and bone caging me in against the end of the dresser. He raised his hands to my face and swept the sides of his thumbs across my cheeks, wiping away the combined sea spray and tears.

"You may not always be able to see me," he said, his voice softer, quieter, "but I am there. I am *always* there in the shadows." He cradled my jaw in his large hands, his hold gentle. "In the middle of the night, when you wake and scream into your pillow, I am there. When you cry in the shower until you can no longer stand, I am there. When you claw your arms with your own fingernails because the pain within you is too great, I am there." His eyes searched mine. "You are never alone, Tarset. I am always with you. I have always been with you."

I swallowed repeatedly, incapable of responding.

"I will do what I must to keep you alive," he swore. "If I have to, I *will* force the bond to link our lives together, so don't make me take that step." His focus dropped to my lips, and the corner of his mouth tensed, hinting at a wicked smirk. "Despite how much we would both enjoy it."

I squeezed my thighs together, suppressing a sudden swell of desire. How fucked up was I that I could feel lust right now?

Atum drew in a deep breath, his nostrils flaring, then released it with a groan. "I would do almost anything to protect your choice about bonding with me," he said, dragging his gaze back up to my eyes. "But I will *not* let you throw your life away. It is far too precious to me."

His hands fell away, and he took a step backward. Only then was I able to draw in a full breath.

"You will move into my quarters," he declared. "I tried giving you space to come to terms on your own with what happened in Waset, but that's not working. You will remain by my side for the rest of the journey."

"But I could hurt you!" I exclaimed, raising my hands beseechingly.

"So be it," he said. "When we reach Rostau, if you wish, you may pick another to be your guardian." His stare was hard, his determination unyielding. "But so long as this darkness lives within you, so long as you cannot see the value in your own life, I cannot let you be alone."

A TUM HADN'T BEEN JOKING when he said I wouldn't leave his side for the rest of the journey to Rostau. The bathroom was the only place I was afforded any privacy, and even there, I couldn't be sure he didn't have some way to keep an eye on me. The man could disappear into shadows, after all. There was no way for me to know for sure if he was or wasn't around.

I didn't try anything. There would have been no point, other than adding further strain to my withering relationship with Atum. The only part of the day that remained impervious to my inner darkness was the morning, when I inexplicably awoke in Atum's bed, wrapped in his protective embrace, despite having fallen asleep in the bed he had moved into his space from my old cabin. I never had any memory of actually getting into bed with him. It was as though, in sleep, my soul took over once the obstacle of my mind was out of the way.

On the fourth such morning, I roused slowly, lazily, surrounded by Atum's enticing, spicy scent. The feel of his shoulder under my head, of his bare chest beneath my hand, and of his arm wrapped around me, holding me close against him, sent my heart beating double time. Thankfully, his own heart beat the slow, steady rhythm of sleep. I had some time to enjoy his embrace before he awakened and caught me indulging in something I had deemed forbidden.

I closed my eyes and breathed him in. The sensory input overrode my thinking mind, holding my ghosts at bay. It was as though he alone repelled my troubled thoughts—even though the worst of them centered around him and the certainty that I *would* hurt him. So long as I was touching him, I was safe from the haunting memories and the sense of inevitable doom.

I lightly traced the raised scars on his chest and let myself imagine we were different people—that I wasn't the greatest threat to his life that had ever existed—and that we might spend every morning this way until the end of forever.

My fingers took on a mind of their own, trailing down the valley between his pectorals and grazing over the scars decorating the gentle ridges of his relaxed abdominal muscles. He slept in only thin linen pants, laced at the front. My fingertips grazed over the thin dusting of tightly curled black hair that trailed down from his belly button to the waistband of his sleep pants.

Remotely, I wondered why he had a belly button at all, considering he had no mother who had carried him within her womb. But the curious thought fled as I toyed with the loose ends of the knotted laces holding his breeches closed.

My breath caught when the side of my pinky skimmed along the edge of an unmistakable hard bulge. I froze, holding absolutely still, and focused on the sounds of Atum's slow heartbeat and relaxed breaths. So far as I could tell, he was still asleep.

A dangerous curiosity held me in its grip. Just once, I wanted to touch him. To *hold* him.

Unable to stop myself, I traced a single fingertip around the outline of his erection. I had felt it pressed against me several times before, and I had seen him naked in the baths that one time, so I knew he was impressive, but I hadn't realized he would be *that* impressive. His erection was angled upward and toward me, and it was easily the largest I had ever encountered. I pressed my hand against it, feeling its girth through the thin fabric of his pants.

My heart beat faster as I imagined what it would be like to feel him inside me, stretching me, filling me so completely. Desire throbbed in my core, and I squeezed my thighs together. My hand moved down his length to the base, then back up toward the tip. It pulsed under my touch, hardening further.

My heartbeat thundered in my chest, but another beat rapidly beneath my ear. Again, I froze, my eyelids snapping open. Atum was awake.

I watched his chest rise and fall with his sudden rapid breathing and waited for him to grab my wrist and move my hand away. But he didn't. He also didn't tell me to stop.

I sank into the delusion that we were different people, and my lips curved into a small smile as I continued to stroke him through the thin, soft fabric. When he still made no move to stop me, I slipped my hand into the waistband of his breeches and took him in hand.

Atum hissed in a breath but made no other sound.

I curled my fingers around his length and stroked him. He was so incredibly hard, with velvety skin.

His hand clutched my side, his fingers digging into the soft flesh at my waist. I closed my eyes again, imagining taking him into my mouth. As the pad of my thumb skimmed over the wetness seeping from his tip, I imagined it was my tongue. In my mind's eye, I knelt between his legs and gazed up at him as I parted my lips over his bulbous head. He stared down at me, an inferno burning in his dark eyes.

I turned my face against his shoulder and brushed my lips over the raised, gilded scars as I stroked him, my grip firm, my rhythm steady. I wanted to draw this stolen moment out for as long as possible. For blissful minutes, I noted every touch that caused a hitch in his breathing, savoring his reactions. But it was impossible to draw it out forever. It wasn't long before his breaths came faster, heralding his climax.

"Tarset," Atum gasped, his body tensing. I continued to stroke him as he spurted his release into his pants, then slowed my movements, lightening my touch until my hand stilled completely.

I held my breath, afraid to move or even to make a sound. I didn't want to spoil this moment of singular perfection.

With a rough growl, Atum rolled me onto my back and knelt between my legs, a dark angel looming over me. The inferno I had pictured burning in his gaze was a reality searing through me. Before I could even think about trying to stop him, he gripped the waistband of my sweats and jerked my pants and underwear down over my hips and off my legs, throwing them aside.

"Atum!" I gasped. "What are you—"

With firm hands, he pushed my knees apart, baring my sex to him completely. He didn't bother with teasing touches. His hands glided up the backs of my thighs to grip my rear and lift my lower half off the bed. Bowing forward, he hooked my legs over his shoulders and dragged his tongue along the length of my sex, seeking that singular part of my body that would set me on fire. His lips closed around my aching bud, and I could no longer think. I could barely breathe. The delicious sensations he elicited with each pulse of suction and flick of his tongue sent bolts of lightning straight to my core.

With one hand, he pushed my oversized T-shirt up over my breasts and covered one with his palm, kneading greedily.

I fisted my hands in the covers and arched into him as sizzling tension coiled deep inside me. A groan slid up my throat as the mounting pleasure crested, and I hovered on a peak of the purest bliss for three heartbeats. Waves of ecstasy exploded from my center, making my entire body spasm. My eyes rolled back, my vision whiting out, my mouth opened in a silent cry of nirvana.

Atum traced the lightest circles around that now hypersensitive bundle of nerves, coaxing every last drop of bliss from my body like he was a starving man and only my pleasure could sate him.

As the ecstasy of the release waned, coherent thought returned to my lust-riddled brain. The darkness followed, closing in around me. Atum pressed tender kisses to my inner thigh, his gentle touch sending fissures through my breaking heart. This was the most I could ever have of him. The closest we could ever be.

My chin trembled, tears welling in my eyes. I turned my face away, not wanting him to see my ridiculous reaction to what had easily been the most satisfying intimate interaction of my entire life. I wanted more. I wanted all of him, forever. But I couldn't have him because I was a time bomb, and the stupid universe needed him *not* to get blown up by me.

I accepted that truth.

As Atum lowered my bottom half to the mattress, I choked on a sob and curled up on my side, away from him. I *had* to leave him, and it fucking hurt. I felt like I was being ripped apart. Like I was being shredded from the inside out. Like my soul was shattering alongside my heart.

"Tarset," Atum said, his voice rough. He gathered me into his arms and pulled me close, cradling me against his chest. "Tell me what to do," he begged. "Tell me how to help you."

Horror widened my eyes as power swelled in my chest, and I watched a shimmering golden light play across my skin. "Let me go," I said, pushing against his arms to get him to release me.

"Tarset—"

The glow intensified, and panic constricted around my ribcage, making my breaths come faster. "Let me go *now*, Atum! It's happening, and I can't—" I gritted my teeth, barely holding the swelling power inside me. "I can't stop it!"

"You won't hurt me," Atum said, stubbornly holding on.

I shoved against him, but he might have been made of iron for how much he yielded. Cracks spider-webbed over my skin, letting out a brilliant golden light. I squeezed my eyes shut, pleading with the universe to show me mercy for once in my fucking life, begging for it to spare him.

The power within me coiled in a bizarre mimicry of the explosive release Atum had just given me. And as it crested and I floated in that moment between moments, Atum's arms fell away, and the world dropped out from beneath me.

My eyelids snapped open. I found myself hovering over the quiet, moonlit sea, stars sparkling overhead. Some fifty yards away, the ship bobbed on the surface of the placid water, the limp sails flapping in the still night air. I could see myself reflected in the glassy water, a being of pure, golden light.

All of a sudden, the power exploded out of me, forcing my arms out wide and sending golden ribbons of light lashing about me like downed power lines. I screamed out my rage at the unfairness of my situation. I hated it—this power. This curse. This part of me that I couldn't control.

I screamed and I screamed and I *screamed*, pouring all of my anger and self-loathing into the whipping flares, until I had gone hoarse. Until there was nothing left but bone-deep exhaustion.

With a *whoosh*, the golden light sucked back into me. I hovered several dozen feet above the water for another heartbeat, and then I was falling.

I hit the water, limbs flailing, and dove deep like a falling stone, reflexively inhaling a lungful of saltwater. I clawed at the cool water, fighting to find the surface, but I couldn't even tell which way was up. My lungs burned, but there was no air. There was only the dark sea. There was only the oblivion I had been so desperate for just a few days ago. But now that I faced it, I no longer wanted it.

I twisted and flailed, searching for the water's surface.

I wanted to live, to hurt, to pine for Atum and struggle and grieve. I wanted to suffer, because at least then Atum would know I still lived. Even if we couldn't be together, even if I went home, he would know that somewhere, in some*time*, I still existed.

But the water's surface evaded me, and my limbs grew heavy.

I want to live, I thought as darkness closed in around me. But it wasn't enough, and as my limbs grew heavy, I sank deeper into the sea's eternal embrace.

PRESENT DAY

NIK

I BUMPED THE OUTSIDE of Kat's thigh with my knee, and she tore her
stare from her phone screen for the first time in at least ten minutes to
peer at me. I sent a pointed look toward my mom and Neffe, who stood
on the other side of what had come to be known as the "gathering table"
in the makeshift lab on the ground floor of Nuin's former palace. They
were discussing the problem of the exploding Nejeret souls, the entire
reason Kat and I were here. The only other person present was Dom,
who had the most experience with being incorporeal of anyone in our
core group, save for Anapa, our most trusted Netjer ally.

The soul explosions had become an increasingly big deal, with more
than half of the resurrected Nejerets having unwillingly unleashed the
seemingly uncontrollable destructive force at least once. It had yet to
happen to my mom, Kat, or me, but Neffe exploded at least once a day,
and it was impossible not to suspect a link between her volatile personality and her explosive soul. Heru was prone to larger, less frequent
explosions, almost like it was tied to his repressed emotions.

I suspected there was a link between emotions and soul detonation. Kat's soul was still fucked up from everything that went down with the Mother-of-all—much to the disappointment of our people who still watched her with hope-filled expressions, like she was our only route to salvation. Whatever. Fuck those guys. Anyway, her wounded *ba* invalidated her as a data set in my armchair study, or my theory would get thrown out the window.

But *I* had long ago come to understand the need for emotional release, and my mom was practically a fucking Zen master, both of our cases lending validity to my theory. Plus, Lex, who had a far steadier, calmer disposition than Heru, also hadn't exploded, while Jenny, Lex's sister with a hair-trigger temper, was logging soul explosions every few days.

My gut told me I was onto something with my theory, and as soon as Neffe and my mom exhausted their ideas, I was going to throw in my far less scientific two cents.

Kat rolled her eyes and locked the phone's screen, blacking out the map she had been staring at. It was a satellite image captured during the few brief hours the mysterious vanishing island had been visible. Why she was so focused on this *now* was beyond me, as she hadn't seemed to care one bit when the island actually appeared well over a month ago. But that was Kat, ruled by impulse and instinct. Maybe she'd had a dream or seen something in the cards. I would have to ask her about it later.

". . . like an infection of the soul?" Neffe said, clarifying whatever my mom had just said. "A pathogen that inflames on a spiritual level?"

My mom nodded. "Perhaps something we picked up in *Duat* or *Aaru*?"

Both Kat and Dom shook their heads.

"You don't agree?" my mom asked them, looking from Dom to Kat.

Kat shrugged one shoulder and set her phone facedown on the work-table in front of us. "I visited *Duat* and *Aaru* long before anyone else, and I never had a problem with this," she said.

My mom's brow furrowed as she considered Kat's input, but Neffe waved a hand dismissively. "You don't count."

Kat scoffed. "Thanks, *Nef*."

My mom donned her trademark warm, motherly smile. "I think what Neffe means is that you're different, Kat," my mom said. "The *At* and *anti-At* laced throughout your soul make you an outlier. The data we gather from you is not equivalent to the data we gather from everyone else. It is apples and oranges, both fruit, but with different nutritional properties."

Kat huffed out a breath and muttered, "Whatever." With a jerky motion, she snatched her phone off the table and unlocked the screen. And just like that, we had lost her.

I stared at Neffe, waiting for her eyes to meet mine. When she finally looked my way, almost reluctantly, I unlinked my fingers and twisted my wrist, giving her the one-finger salute. A silent fuck-you for her purposely pushing Kat's buttons.

Dom cleared his throat and angled his face down, attempting to conceal the subtle twitch of his lips.

"What about you, Dom?" my mom asked, ignoring the silent exchange. "What do you think?"

Dom straightened and crossed his arms over his chest. "I think it's about control," he said, voicing his thoughts for the first time since we all gathered in here a half-hour ago.

My mom raised her eyebrows, but Neffe snorted derisively. "Nice of you to finally show up," she griped.

"What do you mean?" my mom asked, placing a calming hand on Neffe's forearm while she turned her attention to Dom.

"Dominance and submission," Dom said.

Intrigued by his response, I broke the silent staring contest with Neffe and sat back on my stool, threading my fingers together as I turned my full attention to Dom.

"I believe that what we are seeing results from a struggle between the *ba* and the body," Dom explained. "A discordance, so to speak." He drew in a deep breath. "Now that the *ba* has experienced autonomy, both parts of the Nejeret seek dominance—control over the self—but that cannot be. Such a relationship between the two parts of a Nejeret is doomed to cause friction and, in time, to fail."

"Huh," I grunted, thinking his theory wasn't too far off from mine. "And do you think it's in those moments of failure that Nejerets are exploding?"

"I do," Dom said, nodding. "It's as though—"

Kat gasped, then let out a groan of pain, and all eyes snapped to her. Her phone slipped from her fingers, clattering onto the *At* floor, and she clapped her hands over her ears as she doubled over. Soul-energy sizzled over the exposed skin on her arms and face, looking like her own personal aurora borealis.

I reached for her, gripping her arms and suppressing my own groan as the electric energy coursing through her singed my nerve endings. "Kat!" I said, ducking so I could see her face. She squeezed her eyes shut, her features twisted into an agonized grimace. "Kat? Can you hear me?" I sensed the others gathering around us, but I couldn't spare even a fraction of my attention for them.

"Tarset," she ground out, tears leaking from between her lashes. "She's—she's in *Duat*." Kat whimpered, her entire body shuddering.

I pulled her close, wrapping my arms around her and tucking her head under my chin, hoping to reassure her that I was there. That she wasn't alone.

"It's too loud," she whined. "I can't—" She stiffened in my hold, going completely rigid, every joint and muscle in her body locking. Her shaking transformed, becoming jerkier, more like spasms than tremors. The intensity of the energy coursing through her increased, and my muscles locked.

"She's seizing!" Neffe exclaimed. "No, Dom! Don't touch them!"

"Let her go, Nik," my mom commanded. "We can't help her like this. You have to release her so we can help her."

"I'm trying," I said through gritted teeth, unable to unclamp my jaw, let alone my arms. "I *can't.*"

"Dom," my mom said, her voice urgent. "Run upstairs and fetch Lex. She should be in the PT room."

"Of course," Dom said.

"Hold on, my son," my mom murmured.

I let out a harsh laugh. "That's pretty much all I can do right now."

"Oh my God!" someone said from farther away. A new voice. Lex. "What happened?"

"Can you separate them?" my mom asked. "The current of soul-energy seems to have locked Nik's muscles. He can't let go."

"I'll try," Lex said, her voice closer now.

A moment later, I felt ribbons of *At* wrap around my wrists, wedging between Kat and me as they coiled up my arms. Ever so slowly, my arms were pulled away from Kat. More ribbons wrapped around my middle, and the feet of my stool screeched on the floor as I was dragged backward. Finally, the last point of contact between Kat and me broke, and my entire body slumped. If not for Lex's *At* ribbons holding me up, I would have fallen onto the floor.

"Catch her!" I yelled as Kat keeled sideways, teetering off her stool.

More ribbons of *At* appeared, wrapping around Kat's stiff, seizing figure and lowering her gently to the floor. Her full-body spasms continued for another ten or fifteen seconds, and then she fell still, lying limp on the floor. Small lightning bolts of colorful energy crackled over Kat's skin in pulses in time with her heartbeat. They grew weaker and less frequent, until, finally, they stopped—along with her heart.

My mom dropped to her knees and pressed her fingers to Kat's neck. "No pulse," she said and immediately began chest compressions. "Neffe!"

"I'm on it," Neffe said, rushing toward them with a mobile defibrillator. While my mom continued compressions, Neffe placed the large sticky tabs on Kat—one on the upper part of her chest, the other on the opposite side but lower, on her ribcage.

"Pulse detected. Shock recommended," the machine said in an electronic voice.

Neffe pulled her hand away from Kat and flipped a switch on the defibrillator. "Clear."

My mom stopped compressions and sat back on her heels.

Slumped against the worktable, I shook my head. This couldn't be happening. Not to Kat. Not again. I couldn't lose her again. This time felt different. There was nothing I could do. This entire fucking situation was completely out of my control.

The panic gripping my heart heated, swelling. Pulsing. Growing.

"Nik..." It was Lex, and there was fear in her voice.

"Merde!" Dom exclaimed.

A strange, golden light caught my eye, and I glanced down at my hands. They were glowing.

"Nik..." The fear in Lex's voice drew my attention away from Kat as Neffe placed the defibrillator tabs. Lex was backing away from my son, inching closer to the rest of us.

Because Nik's skin was glowing. Not with luminous, colorful waves like Kat did when the soul-energy overwhelmed her, but a steady gold, just like every other Nejeret right before their soul exploded out of their body.

Logic told me to flee, but this was my son. My sweet boy with the softest, kindest heart hidden behind the camouflage he decorated his body with to scare people off. His anguish was palpable, his desperation sucking me in. Here was the boy who had suffered from terrible nightmares. Here was the young man who had nearly died of grief after losing his first love. And now he thought he was losing Kat. I couldn't let him give up. I *had* to go to him, reassure him he wasn't alone. That we would save her. He was *my son*. I *had* to.

I stood and took one lurching step toward him.

Dom lunged in front of me, gripping my upper arms and blocking my path to Nik. "We have to go!" Dom said, his face angled toward Neffe on the floor behind me with Kat.

"I can't move her," Neffe snapped, and I heard the *zap* of the defibrillator discharging.

Dom's attention shifted to Lex, who was within arm's reach of us now. "Can you shield us, Lex?"

"I can try," Lex said, raising her hands and extending them palm-out in front of her. A thick sheet of *At* formed in front of each hand, quickly merging together, then growing outward.

Dom's grip on me loosened, and I tore free, diving past the edge of the *At* barrier before I was completely cut off from my son. Ignoring the shouts from behind me, I flung myself at Nik, needing to hold him. It was my right as his mother—my duty—to protect him. To remind him I would always be there for him. He was mine, *my* child. I brought him into this world, and there was no way in hell I would let him leave this world without me.

I slammed into Nik, causing him to stumble backward just as the bright, golden light exploded out of his body. Except, it didn't surround me. It didn't burn me or tear me apart. We moved *past* the glow—through it—and fell into the cabinets lining the wall, sending a microscope and slide crashing to the floor. Nik's body was completely limp, and I held onto him as he collapsed, easing his landing.

"Mom?" Nik's voice quaked, but it hadn't come from his body, cradled on my lap on the floor.

I looked up and found him standing a few paces away, a being of solid gold light. He stared at me, huddled on the floor with his body, his features twisted by shock. Beyond him, Dom and Lex watched from behind their protective *At* barrier, their mouths hanging open. But they weren't looking at Nik—at his glowing soul. They were looking through him, past him, at me. At his body.

"Am I dead?" Nik asked.

Without looking away from his soul, I pressed my fingers to his body's neck, searching for a pulse. "I don't know," I admitted, shifting my fingers when I felt nothing. "Get Anapa," I ordered, speaking to the others but still unwilling to take my focus off Nik. Still finding no pulse, I extended my hand toward Nik–toward his *ba*. "Come here, my son," a plea in my voice. "You must return to your body. It cannot survive without you in it."

Nik turned, looking at Kat. "I can't feel her. She's not there." He grew fuzzy around the edges, like he was beginning to lose his form.

"She'll come back," I told him, tears welling in my eyes. I was losing him. "Please, Nik, come here. Return to your body." He refocused on me, his despondent expression breaking my heart. "Nik, please. I'll find her," I assured him. "I'll bring her back. You won't lose her. But if you don't return to your body *right now*, I'm not sure I'll be able to save her. She needs you to be *here* to anchor her. Stay, Nik. Please—*please*—don't leave me."

I was little more than a child when I had him. He had been with me nearly my whole life, and I didn't know how to live without him. My baby. My boy.

"*Please*, Nik," I said, my voice tremulous.

"Mom," he said, approaching. He crouched in front of me and raised one glowing hand, pressing it to my cheek. His touch tingled against my skin. "I don't know if I can," he said, peering down at his body.

"Try?" I asked. Begged. "*Please*."

Nik stared at me for a long moment, his eyes searching mine. Finally, he bowed his head. "I'll try."

17

NIK

"CURIOUS," ANAPA MURMURED, HUDDLING over Kat's body and seeming to look through her. She lay on a cushioned bed of *At* I had created in the corner of the lab, surrounded by all the beeping and whirring machines that were keeping her alive.

I leaned forward on my stool, clutching Kat's hand more tightly, and studied Anapa's alien features. Kat thought he looked like how fae were often described in fantasy books—slightly larger than humans, with more angular features and a strange, otherworldly beauty, minus the pointy ears—but all I saw was one of *them*. A Netjer. The beings from another universe who had attempted to wipe us out of existence. Who *would* have obliterated us, if not for Kat and Anapa.

"What do you mean—*curious*?" I asked, narrowing my eyes at Anapa.

My mom and Neffe stood at the foot of the bed, silent and watchful, while Dom and Lex huddled together on the far side of the lab.

Anapa finally tore his examining stare away from Kat and looked at me. "She is not entirely here," he said.

My brows rose. I could have told him that. When I had been outside myself and more in tune with the ethereal plane, I had sensed that Kat was somewhere else. "Not in her body, you mean," I clarified.

"Not in *this time*," he said, returning his stare to Kat's face. "If I had to guess, I would say that the soul-energy pulled her *ba* into *Duat* and dragged her to some*when* else."

"But Isfet sealed the timeline," my mom said. "Not even you or Mei have been able to travel through time. How could Kat possibly—"

"Tarset did it," I reminded my mom, glancing her way. "So clearly there's still a way to jump through time." I looked back at Anapa. "She said Tarset was in *Duat* right before . . ."

Anapa's brow furrowed as he considered this new information. "Did she? How fascinating." He turned his attention to my mom and Neffe. "Katarina is beyond my reach," he said. "All we can do now is wait for her to return on her own." His attentive stare returned to me. "I am most intrigued by your recent out-of-body experience, Nekure," he said. "I would love to hear more about that while we wait for Katarina's return."

I scoffed. "I couldn't tell you what happened," I said, glancing at my mom. "One second, I was about to detonate, the next, I was standing still while I watched my mom tackle, well, *me*."

Anapa looked at my mom, his eyebrows climbing as high as they would go. "You touched him while he was glowing, but he didn't burn you?"

My mom shook her head. "I thought, perhaps, because he's my son . . ."

"Perhaps," Anapa said. "There is something similar to a soul bond shared between parents and their offspring." He frowned, his attention shifting to Lex. "Except you were burned by Heru's soul, were you not?"

Lex shrugged, hunching slightly like the memories of her bond-mate nearly killing her were too heavy a burden for her to face, and Dom wrapped an arm protectively around her shoulders. "I don't remember," she said. "I'm sorry."

"She had second- and some third-degree burns along one side of her body," Neffe said. "I was here when she first arrived. We focused on her spinal injuries first, but the burns were fairly severe. Her bond with my father did not protect her."

"Hmmm . . ." Anapa returned his attention to my mom. "Strong though it is, especially between the two of you, I don't think the maternal bond is what protected you."

"Maybe it's your *sheut*," I offered, looking from my mom to Anapa. "She has a *sheut*. It was a gift from the twins for helping Lex. That's where Kat got hers, too. We've never figured out what she could do with it, though."

My mom lifted one shoulder. "I thought maybe it was a dud."

Anapa studied my mom closely, giving the impression that he wasn't merely looking at her, but *into* her. "How fascinating," he murmured. "I can see it now that I know to look for it. It's definitely active."

"Not a dud," I told my mom, flashing her a lopsided smile. "Told you so."

"Pfff," my mom said, eyeing me sideways. "What do *you* think happened?" she asked Anapa.

"I'm not sure," Anapa admitted. "Would you try something for me?" He looked from my mom to me. "Both of you?"

My mom nodded.

"Yeah, sure," I agreed.

"Come," Anapa said, backing away from the bed into the relatively open space between the counter and a worktable. "I'd like to recreate what happened, if possible."

My mom and I exchanged an uncertain glance. There was a plea in her eyes, and as much as I didn't want to let go of Kat's hand, I couldn't refuse my mom. She so rarely asked me for anything. I could give her this.

I kissed the back of Kat's hand, then released it and stood. I followed my mom around the foot of the bed, and we joined Anapa. "Do I need to—" I mimed an explosion by raising my hands and spreading my fingers wide. "Because I don't think I can control that."

"I don't think so," Anapa said, "but I could always try irritating your *ba* with an influx of energy. That might work." His lips curved into an eager grin, and he clasped his hands behind his back. "For now, let's focus on intent. Aset, what were you thinking about when you approached Nekure while he was aggravated?"

My mom's shoulders bunched, and she shook her head. "I don't know," she said. "I was desperate. I . . ." Again, she shook her head, tears shining in her eyes. "Kat was unresponsive, and Nik was so upset. He was spiraling. I could see it on his face—he thought he had lost her, and I wanted him to know he wasn't alone. I wanted him to see me, to feel me, and to know that I was still here with him. That I wouldn't leave him."

Anapa narrowed his eyes in thought. "Interesting," he murmured. "Think about this, Aset. If you can replicate what happened with Nekure, you will be able to save lives by preventing other Nejerets from detonating. Would you like to do that?"

"Very much so," my mom said, stepping forward while ringing her hands. "That is what we've been trying to do—to find a way to stop these soul explosions."

"Would you say you're *desperate* to find a solution?" Anapa asked.

"Yes," my mom said, nodding emphatically.

"Hold on to that feeling, that desperation," Anapa said, tapping his chest. He glanced at me. "And shove Nekure out of his body."

Brow furrowing, my mom shook her head. "But how?"

"Push him with the intent of separating his *ba* from his body," Anapa said. "If you can do it here, with him *on purpose*, think of the lives you can save."

My mom gulped. "All right," she said, turning toward me.

I faced her, spreading my feet and squaring my shoulders. "Go ahead, Mom."

Her brows bunched together, and she pursed her lips, like she was focusing her entire self on the task. She inhaled deeply, raised her hands, and shoved me. Hard.

I stumbled backward and caught myself on the edge of the counter, surprised by the force of her strike. My mom had been my main sparring partner for thousands of years, but she had never displayed such strength. I straightened, rubbing my sore chest, and froze.

Anapa and my mom stood exactly where they had been. And so did I.

Except I was *also* here, three paces back, leaning against the counter. "Holy shit," I muttered and slowly approached the trio. "You did it."

My body was completely unmoving, while my mom watched *me* approach with a wondrous expression. Anapa appeared perfectly smug. Their chests rose and fell with each breath, while my body appeared frozen. A quick glance around let me know that Lex and Dom were equally immobile, more like statues than living people.

"This is too fucking weird," I said. Kat had mentioned Anapa's ability to freeze time, and I assumed that was what was happening at this very moment.

"Do you feel the pull toward *Duat*?" Anapa asked. "Usually when a *ba* becomes untethered from its body, it is immediately drawn toward the spirit realm."

Frowning, I focused on what I was feeling. I touched my chest, feeling a deep ache there, along with a faint tugging sensation. When I looked down, I noticed a shimmering transparent cord sprouting from my chest and stretching through the wall, leading to somewhere beyond this room.

"Maybe?" I said.

"Ah," Anapa said, stepping around my body. "*That* is not *Duat*. What you are feeling is your bond with Katarina." He tilted his head to the side, scanning me. "Perhaps it *is* tugging you toward *Duat*, but that is only because Katarina is there, albeit in another time."

I frowned. "Huh."

"What about your body?" Anapa asked. "Do you feel discomfort at being outside of it, and is there a force pulling you back to it?"

I raised my eyebrows and studied my frozen figure. "It's fucking weird to see myself standing there, but I don't feel naked or exposed or anything like that."

Anapa considered my words for a long moment. "Look at yourself—not at your body, but at your *ba*," he directed me.

I glanced down at myself, my jaw dropping and my eyes opening wide. "Woah," I said, taking in the warm, golden glow of my *ba*. I looked like me, clothing, ink, and all, except everything was made of varying shades of gold, all with a subtle internal glow.

I raised one hand and held it close to my frozen body, comparing my soul's skin tone to my body's. Right before my eyes, the golden glow faded until *my* hand matched my body's.

My mom gasped. "You look normal," she exclaimed. "How did you do that?"

I shrugged and shook my head. "I don't know." I looked at Anapa. "How did I do that?"

Anapa looked as surprised as my mom. "You should not have been able to do that," he said. "To alter your appearance like that—" He cleared his throat, looking uncomfortable with his own ignorance. "Kat could always do it, but she is unique. No other Nejeret I have encountered in *ba* form has been able to alter their appearance like a pure energy being."

"Like a Netjer," my mom clarified.

I sucked in a breath, then hesitated. I had a gut feeling, but I didn't want to be the guinea pig that was used to test my theory.

"What?" my mom asked me. "You had a thought. What is it?"

I licked my lips. "We died," I said. "We existed as energy beings. What if we've been thinking about this all wrong?" I paused. "What if our souls aren't the problem? What if the problem is our bodies?"

My mom crossed her arms over chest. "What do you mean?"

I looked from her to Anapa and back. "What if we don't need our bodies at all?"

NIK

"I WOULD LIKE TO explore your theory further," Anapa said a few minutes after I had resettled in my physical body and returned to Kat's bedside.

He had been pensive since I first brought up the possibility that Nejerets might not need our bodies anymore, and he remained where he had been standing, like his feet had implanted in the floor. I wasn't sure if he thought the idea was complete trash or pure genius. Apparently, my mom found it intriguing as well, because she had retreated to a stool at the counter and had been writing furiously in a notebook ever since, filling a few pages with notes in as many minutes.

"I *would* suggest working with you in *ba* form to test your capabilities and limitations, however—" Anapa glanced at Kat's empty shell, alive only because of the machines keeping her heart beating and her lungs drawing in air. Concern lined his alien features. "I am unsure if Katarina's *ba* is ready to spend much time outside of her body. As we've already seen, the soul-energy has a dangerous hold on her."

I rubbed my thumb over the back of Kat's limp hand. "You mean something like this might happen again?"

Anapa nodded sagely. "Until we can break that hold, I am hesitant to encourage either of you to spend much time outside of the protection of your bodies."

"You can experiment on me," Lex said, stepping forward. "Heru, as well. If I ask him, he'll do it."

"But what about Reni and Bobby?" my mom said, her pen halting as she looked up. "What if something happens to you two?"

"That's why I want to do it," Lex said, her eyes shining with emotion. "My kids are as susceptible to these soul explosions as everyone else. If this can help us find a safer, more stable future for them, I *have* to do it."

"Very well," Anapa said, bowing his head to Lex. "But I would like to do some research first. I'll return first thing tomorrow morning to begin working with you and Heru." And with that, Anapa vanished.

My mom huffed out a breath and slammed her pen down on her open notebook.

"You okay, Mom?" I asked. The others in the room eyed her, surprised by her unusual display of irritation.

"I'm fine," she said, pressing her lips together into a flat line that told me she absolutely was not fine. If I had to guess, which apparently I did, she was annoyed with Anapa for vanishing when she wanted to discuss the situation further.

Kat's fingers spasmed in my hand, and my attention snapped to her face. She coughed, fighting to breathe on her own without the help of the machine.

My mom jumped from her stool, and Neffe was already pulling the breathing tube out of Kat's mouth by the time my mom reached the bed.

"Ugh," Kat groaned as my mom helped her to sit up while Neffe discarded the tube. Kat coughed a few more times, working to catch her breath.

I shifted from my stool to the edge of the bed and rubbed her back, comforted when she leaned into me.

"I saw her," Kat said, clutching the front of my T-shirt. "I saw Tarset."

ANCIENT TIMES

TARSET

M Y SECOND EXPERIENCE OF dying differed greatly from the first. There was no hint of the emotional distance I had felt when the Netjer stabbed me in the heart. There was only the confusion born of drowning, followed by a panicked desperation to live after the *pop* of passing through the barrier to *Duat* jolted me into a more coherent state of mind.

Even once I was in *Duat*, I remained under water with my body, watching from the other side of the filmy barrier separating the rainbow stream of soul-energy in the spirit realm from the inky sea in the physical world. My limbs and hair floated lazily in the sea water, illuminated by the golden rays of the rising sun, distorted by the disturbed water. My T-shirt clung to my body's curves, and my face displayed no hint of the horror I had felt while drowning. I looked relaxed, at peace. Things I hadn't felt since my first death. Things I most certainly *didn't* feel right now.

Behind me, the dark shell surrounding *Aaru* pulled at me, but where the ominous force had been irresistible last time, it was now merely a nagging annoyance.

A quick glance down at my hands, and then a scan of the rest of my *ba*, revealed a form that was very much like my body floating in the water on the other side of the barrier between realms, only now, I appeared to be made of golden light. There were no streaks of energy lashing around me, like when my soul exploded from my body, but the shade of gold was the same as when I had detonated before.

I returned my attention to my physical body, close enough to touch but an infinite distance away.

A dark streak cutting through the water drew my eye. Atum. He dove toward my drowned form and wrapped his arms around it, powerful kicks of his legs propelling him and his burden toward the surface of the sea.

I needed only to think about following him, and the barrier shifted, like I was in an invisible, insubstantial submarine that trailed behind him through the water. I broke through the surface mere moments after Atum, but he was already using ropes of *At* to haul both himself and my body out of the water.

I pressed my golden, glowing hands against the barrier separating me from the physical realm as I trailed unseen after Atum, following him onto the ship. His otherworldly vines gently laid my body on the ship's deck, and he dropped to his knees beside it. His crew formed a circle around him, breaths held, utter silence filling the otherwise tranquil morning.

Movements practiced and sure, Atum angled my body's head back and cleared my airway with a sweep of his finger. "Don't you leave me," he growled as he bowed over my body, pinching my nose and inhaling deeply before sealing his mouth over mine.

"I'm here," I breathed, then slapped my hands against the barrier between realms. "I'm here, Atum! I'm here!"

Atum breathed into my body, then straightened and started chest compressions. I rooted for him, for her—for *my body*—to cough and sputter up all the water I had inhaled, even though I knew it was impossible when I—my *ba*—was stuck in *Duat*.

My slaps against the barrier turned into banging fists. I screamed and shouted, throwing myself against the impenetrable barrier again and again. I clawed at it, begging the soul-energy to help me. Pleading with the souls of the dead to push me out of the spirit realm and back into the only reality that mattered—the one that included Atum.

On and on Atum's CPR efforts went, so long that I lost track of how many times he had alternated between breaths and compressions. Dozens, it seemed. Breaking through the barrier was proving to be impossible, so I fell still and resumed watching the morose scene.

The gathered crew members murmured to one another, and finally, Ode stepped forward. He rested a hand on Atum's shoulder. "She's gone, captain."

"She's not!" Atum shouted, sweeping his arm around to push Ode away between chest compressions.

"I'm here!" I cried. "I'm right here!"

"She's not gone," Atum said, pumping my body's chest with his hands. "I can feel her. She's *not* gone."

At the mention of him being able to feel me, a tugging sensation pulsed inside me where my heart would have been—had I still possessed a physical body.

I pressed a hand to my golden chest and peered down. "What the hell?" I breathed, seeing the wispy, nearly transparent thread that sprouted from my luminous "skin" and passed through the barrier, reaching all the way to Atum.

Brow furrowing, I plucked the thread like it was a guitar string. A resonant note rang out, and Atum froze.

"She's here," he muttered, sitting up from breathing into my body. "I can feel her." He angled his head to the side as he resumed compressions, like he could hear that resonant note as well.

"Use the connection," voices whispered, echoing and repeating all around me.

I froze and peered from side to side without actually moving my head.

The multicolored strands of soul-energy beside me shifted, forming into a humanoid shape. I turned, watching it form, both horrified and fascinated as the figure gained definition, gradually becoming recognizable.

"Kat?" I balked. It looked like my aunt Kat, except she appeared to be made entirely of soul-energy.

"Hey, Tarsi," Kat said, her voice echoing but distinctly her own. Veins of onyx and moonstone spider-webbed through her rainbow features, giving her a fractured appearance. "We miss you."

I reached for her, but my golden hands passed through and scattered the gathered soul-energy making up her arms like it was no more substantial than water.

Kat flashed me an apologetic smile.

"How are you here?" I asked her.

"I—" She shook her head, dislodging some of the multicolored soul-energy to blur her features. "I'm not entirely sure," she said. "I was in the Oasis, and I heard you, and then I was here."

"Can you bring me home?" I asked.

"I don't know," Kat said, her rainbow features turning thoughtful. "Maybe?" She eyed the thread protruding from my chest and passing through the barrier to my body on the ship below, where Atum continued his relentless attempt to resuscitate me. "But is that really what you want?" She floated closer to the barrier. "Is that him—Atum?" She eyed me sidelong. "He's not at all what I imagined."

I smiled to myself. "No, definitely not the monster we paint him to be," I said. "He's not a monster at all."

"You're in love with him," she said, not a question but a statement of a perceived fact.

I nodded. If I had still been in possession of a heart, it would have been lodged in my throat.

"Do you want to stay with him?" she asked.

"It's not that simple," I told her. "He is *essential* to the continued existence of everything we care about, and I am . . ."

"Explosive?" Kat offered.

I looked at her sharply. "How did you know that?"

"Let's just say it's been going around since the big resurrection," she said. "We're working on figuring out the problem, and I'm waiting for Isfet to get back to me with more information, but all we know right now is that most Nejeret souls seem to prefer freedom over the constraints of a physical body. There are things a *ba* can do that a body cannot, powers a *ba* has access to, and it *seems* like our souls grow frustrated when their ability to act is hindered by the limitations of our physical bodies. In those moments, the *ba* attempts to break free, and . . ." She pressed her hands together, then spread her fingers wide. "Boom."

"My dad?" I asked, my eyebrows rising.

Kat repeated the explosion motion, only mouthing the sound this time. "One of the first to blow, actually."

"Is he all right?"

Kat nodded. "He is now. He's helping us—letting Aset and Neffe study him." Kat returned her attention to Atum, relentlessly performing chest compressions on my body. "You should get back there before your body is *dead* dead."

"I tried," I said, pressing my hands against the barrier. "I couldn't get through."

Kat looked pointedly at the translucent thread. "Use the connection."

I tapped the thread, making it hum. "Is it a soul bond?"

"Not yet," Kat said. "But it could be. You need to strengthen it. To make it resonate with the vibrations of your two souls so loudly that it weakens the barrier between realms, just for a moment. Just long enough for you to pass through. The bond still won't be fully activated." She smirked knowingly. "There's only one way to do that."

"But—" I shook my head. "How?"

Her eyebrows shot up her forehead, and she held up her hands, the thumb and fingers of one forming a circle into which she poked the index finger of her other hand, miming sexual intercourse. "I thought that was common knowledge," she drawled.

"Not that!" I squeaked, my eyes bulging as I stifled a giggle. Only Kat's immature sense of humor would have been able to coax a laugh from me in a situation as dire as this. "How do I strengthen *this*?" I asked, gesturing to the delicate thread.

"Oh, duh," she said. "Feed it. Pour yourself into it. Call on whatever emotions or memories make your *ba* swell with power and channel all of that into the connection." She looked at me. "What is it that sets you off?"

I gazed out at Atum. "Thinking about leaving him," I admitted. "Knowing that's what I have to do."

"Well, it's already done," Kat said matter-of-factly. "You left him. You're gone. Whatever you could have had together is over."

Pain swirled in my chest, agony at losing what had never been. My choice had been stolen from me by my own ineptitude, and I only had myself to blame.

The soul-energy around me churned, and I felt charged, electrified.

"Take everything you're feeling," Kat said urgently, "and channel it into the connection. Now, Tarsi!" Her voice was a whip crack. "Do it now, or you *will* lose him forever!"

With a hoarse cry, I poured my pain and desperation into the thread. My fear of losing him—of hurting him. My need to be here with him despite the danger I posed. The most beautiful chord of music I had ever heard thrummed all around me, and the thread thickened and brightened.

"More, Tarsi!" Kat urged. "You must give it everything you have. Surrender yourself to the connection. *Become* the song!"

I howled, agonized by the effort, my voice ringing in harmony with the chord. A golden haze slowly took over my vision until it was all I could see.

"I'll find you again," Kat said, her voice distant.

When the golden light receded, I was no longer surrounded by the rainbow stream of soul-energy, but I stood on the ship deck, directly behind Atum. Murmuring voices surrounded me as men and women backed away, shielding their eyes from my blinding, golden glow.

They could *see* me.

"Atum," I said, my voice sounding richer and more layered than usual.

Atom froze, his stacked hands resting on my body's chest.

I placed one shimmering, golden hand on his shoulder. "I'm here," I told him, and he slowly turned his head to peer up at me, squinting even as wonder filled his gaze.

I grazed the pad of my gilded thumb up his cheek, absorbing his tears. An iridescent glow streaked under his skin, his *ba* rising to meet mine.

"Thank you for refusing to let me go," I whispered, then floated around him to hover above my body.

Atum tracked me, his breath held, his focus unwavering.

I sank down, feeling the lure of the familiar vessel. I slipped into my body easily, like pulling on a favorite pair of sneakers, and closed my eyes.

Pain crashed into me. My chest was on fire.

I coughed, spewing water, and rolled onto my side. My lungs and throat burned with each attempted breath, and a sharp pain stabbed into my chest on either side, making stars dance along the edges of my vision. I hurt all over, my muscles fatigued to the point of cramps and spasms, but I refused to pass out from the pain.

Teeth chattering, I whimpered, laugh-crying. I was alive. In incredible pain, but alive, and *that* was all that mattered.

A TUM'S PERSISTENCE TO RESUSCITATE me had a cost: three broken ribs, a cracked sternum, and a punctured lung. Pneumonia set in after my first round of regenerative sleep, when my body had been focused on healing the larger skeletal injuries and repairing the structural damage to my lung. Were I not Nejeret with enhanced healing abilities, the pneumonia very well could have killed me. The fire in my lungs certainly made me *feel* like I was dying.

I went through the increasingly familiar gorge-rest cycles that dominated the Nejeret regenerative process, alternating between stuffing my face with everything Atum could spare from the ship's larder and passing out in a coma-like sleep. It took five cycles to wake up feeling rested and restored—and *not* famished.

I roused gradually, first noting the lack of a yawning void in my stomach, then drew in a delightful, pain-free breath, filling my lungs completely. I exhaled, a contented smile curving my lips, and raised my eyelids.

The pure golden light of dawn glittered off the water's surface and filtered in through the floor-to-ceiling windows at the back of Atum's cabin. A quick glance around confirmed what my nose already suspected—Atum wasn't in the cabin with me. His scent was too faint.

I glanced at the window again, then up at the ceiling. He was probably directly above me, carrying out his morning ritual. As soon as he finished, he would return here with a tray overflowing with food. I could only imagine the dent I had already put in the ship's limited resources. There were a lot of mouths to feed on the crew. I didn't want to make matters worse by slurping down another huge chunk of their rations, so I hurried into the bathroom across the corridor to quickly wash up and change before heading up to the quarterdeck to forestall the preparation of a relative feast.

When I opened the door to the main deck, a chilly gust drove me back to the cabin to add an extra layer over my jeans, loose blouse, and cozy long sweater. I found a smaller, slimmer version of Atum's famed knee-length leather coat, and I swapped the wool-lined moccasins I had been wearing since boarding this ship a couple weeks ago for the matching mid-shin cuffed leather boots. There was no mirror in the cabin, but a quick glance down at myself told me I was looking very chic lady-pirate, especially with my tight jeans and loose blouse under the long, fitted leather coat.

I was on my way to the door when I spotted the notebook on the bedside table. It was open to a page with a short list written by a hand that definitely wasn't mine.

Curiosity piqued, I headed back to my bed and picked up the notebook. It took my brain a moment to catch up with what I was reading. A list of names, spelled phonetically using Modern English characters, but clearly Egyptian in sound. There were six names.

An image flashed through my mind's eye. Six bodies, laid out on the ground in a line, barely visible through the billowing dust.

Shaken down to my soul, I sank onto the edge of the bed and stared at the list of names. These were the people I had killed. My eyes stung, tears welling and spilling over in a matter of seconds. In a moment of panic fueled anger, I had told Atum I didn't even know their names. And now, here they were, a macabre gift from the man who deserved my whole heart, regardless of whether our situation would allow me to give it to him.

Pulse racing, I wiped the tears from under my eyes and tore the page from the notebook. I folded it quickly and tucked it into my coat pocket, then rushed from the cabin. The chilly sea air felt welcome when I reemerged. I hurried to the stairs to the upper deck, offering brief smiles to Ode and the other crew members as I passed, and raced up the steps, only slowing when I crested the top and finally saw him.

Atum knelt facing the stern of the ship, his back and shoulder muscles bunching and flexing rhythmically as he nicked the skin of his left arm with the end of his black dagger's blade. I still wasn't sure if the dagger was obsidian, onyx, or *anti-At*, the otherworldly counterpart to *At*, which was poison to any Nejeret who touched it except for those who could wield it themselves.

I stood at the top of the stairs and watched Atum, listening to the indistinct murmur of his voice as he recited the names of his dead and wondering at the purpose of the ritual. Was it merely to honor and remember those he had killed in the line of duty, or was it more than that? Was it an outlet? A pressure valve? Did the physical pain dull the emotional turmoil?

I fingered the folded sheet of paper in my coat pocket. Would it do that for me?

Atum paused after about thirty seconds and set down his dagger, then reached into the pouch of gold dust and removed a pinch, rubbing it over the small open wounds.

He picked up the dagger once more and dragged it along his forearms, reopening the new, longer scars stretching from wrist to elbow. He hadn't had those when he had been Temu, but I recalled seeing them when he appeared in the corner of my cell and prevented Inyotef from violating my body with his blade in a new and truly horrifying way. These were always the last cuts he made during his sunrise ritual, and they were never accompanied by any names.

I stood at the top of the stairs, waiting until he finished. When he rubbed the last pinch of gold dust into his open cuts, I finally stepped forward.

Atum glanced over his shoulder as he smoothed his hand along his forearm. Upon seeing me, concern flashed through his eyes, there and gone in a blink. His face brightened, but something about the expression looked forced.

"You're up earlier than I expected," he said, sheathing his dagger and tucking away the pouch of gold dust before standing. His blood and gold smeared upper body gleamed in the morning light. Strides sure, he retrieved his shirt from a nearby barrel and pulled it on over his head as he made his way toward me. "How do you feel?"

"Fine," I said and shrugged one shoulder, unsure how to *be* around him.

We hadn't spoken more than a few words in passing when he delivered my food between rounds of regenerative sleep. Did he have any idea how I had come back to life? Did he suspect I had used our potential to bond to return to the land of the living? Did he think that meant I was here to stay? *Did* it mean I was here to stay?

Don't get me wrong—I wanted to stay with him. I wanted it more than I had ever wanted anything. I wanted it enough to rise from the dead just so I would have the chance to spend eternity with him. But I didn't know what to do.

"No more chest pain?" Atum asked, stopping in front of me.

He felt *more*. His presence had always been potent, even when he had been posing as a human, but now, the sense of *him* was more intense. If I closed my eyes, and he moved away, I thought I could have pointed to his exact location without looking.

I rubbed my sternum, remembering the lingering bone-deep ache that had remained the last time I woke, and I shook my head. "I feel fine, really," I told him. "Thank you . . . for not giving up on me."

"Never," Atum said, his voice lower and rougher than before. He inhaled, then hesitated for a moment before speaking, his eyes searching mine. "I felt—" His brow furrowed, and he pressed a hand to his own chest. "Right before you returned, I felt a tug *in here*." His throat bobbed, and he licked his full lips. "Are we bound?"

"No," I said, my cheeks flushing as I thought of Kat and her ridiculously childish hand gesture miming sex. "There's still only one way to seal a soul bond." I sighed. "I think our connection is more than it was before, but it's still not permanent." In other words, I could still leave, though I couldn't bring myself to voice the thought.

"I see," Atum said. His focus shifted past me, and he stepped to the side, angling his body to let me step off the stairs and join him on the elevated quarterdeck. He gripped my elbow and gently pulled me forward. "Will you tell me what happened?" he asked as we approached the railing at the back of the ship. "While you were gone, I mean."

"I—" I gripped the railing and peered down at the water, watching our wake spread out in a V behind the ship as we cut through the sea. "It's hard to explain," I finally said. I could feel Atum's attention on the side of my face, but it was easier for me to focus my thoughts when I wasn't looking at him. It was too easy to fall into the midnight pools of his gaze and drown all coherent thought.

"I—my *ba*—went into *Duat*," I told him, then shook my head. The memories were slippery and ephemeral, like they were from a dream. "I watched you," I said remotely. "I tried to get back here, but I couldn't, so I just watched you."

"But you *did* come back," Atum reminded me.

My brow furrowed, and I squeezed my eyes shut, picturing Kat as she had appeared in *Duat*, formed entirely out of soul-energy. "I had help," I admitted. "Someone from my future—my aunt Kat."

"Nekure's bond-mate," Atum said. "The one connected to Isfet."

I nodded. I had told him all about Kat and the rest of my family from the future, along with the Netjer war. It was nice to know he had truly listened.

"It was like she was both *there* and *not there* at the same time." Again, I shook my head and laughed under my breath, opening my eyes to stare down at the water. "Like I said, it's hard to explain."

"But she was able to help you break through the barrier between realms," Atum surmised. "For that, I shall forever be in her debt."

The conviction in his deep, rich voice drew my gaze up to his face. "I still don't know what I'm going to do," I told him. My gut knotted at just thinking he believed this meant I would stay. "I *want* to stay," I added in a rush.

"But you feel it is your duty to leave," he said and covered my hand with his on the railing. "This I understand well."

I closed my eyes, setting a string of tears free to glide down my cheek.

"I left you something on your nightstand," he said. "Did you see it?"

I pictured the list of names now folded up in my pocket and nodded, not trusting my voice.

"Perhaps tomorrow, if you like, you could join me at sunrise," he offered.

The bodies of my victims filled my mind's eye, and my chin trembled. I turned my hand over, curling my fingers around Atum's. "I think I would like that," I said, my voice breaking. My chest convulsed, and I bowed my head as the first sob clawed its way up my throat.

Atum turned toward me and pulled me close, wrapping his arms around me and tucking my head under his chin. "It will get easier," he promised.

"Time heals all wounds?" I murmured against his chest.

"Some," he said. "Most." He tightened his hold on me. "But not *all* wounds."

A TUM AND I SAT quietly on a bench he had magicked out of *At* on the quarterdeck near the stern of the ship and watched the sea together while we munched on a breakfast of protein bars he had snatched from the distant end of the timeline. With all the amenities he had borrowed from the future, it was easy to forget that we were still technically sailing across the sea in ancient times.

"You don't have to sit with me," I said after the silence grew heavy with expectation. I glanced at him sideways. "I promise not to swan dive off the railing." I broke off a piece of my protein bar—*Lemon Zing*, according to the label—and popped it into my mouth.

The corners of Atum's lips tensed at my gallows humor, and just looking at him, it was impossible to tell whether he was holding in a smile or a frown. But my gut—or maybe our strengthened connection—made me think it was a smile.

"I'm not sitting here out of a sense of duty," he said, his voice a gentle rumble.

Our eyes met for the briefest moment, sparking an electric jolt within me. Not desire, but something stronger, deeper. Longing or maybe even love.

I returned to staring out at the sea. "Do you remember your first?"

"My first kills?" Atum said and nodded slowly. "Yes." He held up his left hand in front of us, showing me the back, where a series of four one-inch scars followed the lines of his fingers. "When I made these first marks, I didn't realize how many more would follow." He glanced at his arm, then down at his torso, most of the scars hidden under his shirt. "The pattern has changed over the years." He made a fist with his raised hand. "But these four have remained the same."

"Do you think about them often?" I asked, looking at his profile.

"Every day," he said without hesitation and rested his open hand palm-down on his thigh. At sunrise during his ritual, obviously, but I wondered if memories of his dead visited him throughout the day, or in his dreams as well.

My gaze returned to the four raised lines on the back of his hand. Each question that popped into my mind was more personal than the last, and I grew more and more reticent to ask. "Do you picture them when you speak their names?"

Atum nodded. "As they are before I enter their lives," he said, and I noted the tense he used—not past, but present, as though they were still alive. But then, I supposed to someone who could move relatively freely throughout his assigned portion of the timeline, there was no future or past; there was only present. "That is how everyone deserves to be remembered," he added.

I pulled the folded list from my pocket and turned it around and around in my hands. "I didn't know them," I said, staring at the folded paper, my voice sounding remote. "I've made up stories—thousands of stories about what their lives were like—but when I see them in my mind, they're just bodies lined up on the ground."

Atum inhaled like he was going to respond, but he held his breath for so long that I thought he had changed his mind. "I didn't know any of them well, but I knew something about each of them that might give you a more vibrant image of them to hold on to." He reached over and plucked the folded paper from my pinched fingers. He quickly unfolded it and read the first name. "Djau is a butcher and a tanner." *Is*, not *was*. Atum frowned thoughtfully. "Older, maybe sixty at the end. His life is full, with many children and grandchildren who often help him with his work." He leaned his shoulder into mine. "Though none were there that day."

Emotion swelled in my throat, tightening my airway. My chin trembled, and my eyes stung. I cried silently as Atum introduced me to *my* dead. He spoke of each in the present tense, as though they still lived.

When he finished, I raised my hands to wipe away my tears and sniffled, but wiping my runny nose with my fingers in front of him seemed too gross, so I lifted the hem of my blouse and used that instead. "Sorry," I mumbled. "This is *really* attractive, I know."

Atum chuckled and folded up the sheet of paper, offering it to me pinched between his index and middle fingers.

I took a deep, steadying breath, taking back the folded list. "Do you think about anything else when you do it? The ritual, I mean." I tucked the paper back into my pocket for safekeeping. "When you speak their names and—" My voice caught, and I struggled to finish the question. I took another deep breath. "And when you make each cut?"

Atum didn't answer right away, and I feared I had finally overstepped. "I apologize to each person," he said quietly, placing his hands on his knees. "Because since the moment I took each life, I have thought of dozens of things I could have done differently that may have led to a different outcome." He inhaled deeply, letting the breath out with a sigh. "But once I visit an era, that window crystallizes and becomes a fixed point in the timeline, forever closed to me. I cannot change what I have already touched."

My eyebrows rose. "That's why you're always watching the time tapestry," I said. "Checking and rechecking. You only have one shot at correcting each dissonance." I stared at the side of Atum's face, studying his stoic expression, my heart breaking for the dreadful responsibility Nuin had dumped on his shoulders.

"Please, don't." He bowed his head. "I don't deserve your sympathy," he said, repeating words he had spoken to me what felt like a lifetime ago. "After everything I've done . . ."

I reached out, covering his hand with one of mine and curling my fingers around the edge of his palm. "You *do* deserve it," I told him, squeezing his hand. "*Because* of everything you've done."

Atum's jaw pulsed. Tears welled in his eyes and streaked down his cheeks. "Not every victim was necessary to protect the timeline," he said, a hollow sound to his voice. "My brother, Osiris—" Atum bowed his head again. "I may not have ended his life, but what I did to him is truly unforgivable."

I didn't know what he had done to Osiris, my grandfather and his brother—only in the sense that Nuin had created them both—but I refused to believe it was as bad as Atum believed.

"You are *not* a monster," I whispered as I held the hand of the strongest, most selfless man I had ever known and watched him fall to pieces beside me.

I FOLLOWED ATUM AROUND for the remainder of the morning, not because he required me to stick to his side like before—he seemed satisfied with my will to live—but because I didn't want to be alone. He was a beacon of hope. He had survived this long with his humanity, so to speak, still intact. If he could do it, maybe I could, too.

"We should reach Rostau tomorrow afternoon," Atum told me as he escorted me back to our cabin carrying a tray laden with our lunch, whipped together from the last dregs of the larder—peanut butter and jelly sandwiches, wedges of hard aged cheese, and some dried fruit. There was also a chewable vitamin C tablet for each of us to prevent scurvy.

I offered to help carry the food, but I didn't push the matter when Atum refused. My sea legs were laughable. It was all I could do to keep myself upright as the ship rode the swells. Any food on a tray in my hands likely would have ended up splattered on the deck and swept overboard, and now that I had seen just how little food was left on the ship, I wasn't willing to risk wasting any of it.

"We arrive tomorrow? Really?" I asked, my interest piqued. I pushed open the door to the corridor that led to our private quarters and held it propped open with my shoulder while I waited for Atum. I stopped myself from adding an *already*, fully aware that I had a warped perception of the journey's length because of my weeks of deep depression followed by rounds of regenerative sleep.

I had surmised from the nautical charts on Atum's desk in our cabin that Rostau was an island somewhere in the Mediterranean Sea, but since none of the surrounding landmarks were labeled in a language I could read, I hadn't been able to pinpoint the island's location beyond that. And honestly, geography had never been my strong suit. The only reason I could tell the difference between Italy and Greece on a map was because even *I* knew Italy was shaped like a high-heeled boot.

"Really," Atum said, passing through the doorway to join me in the passageway.

I closed the door against the crisp sea air, then hurried ahead to the door of our cabin and pushed that open for him as well.

"There is something of a gauntlet surrounding the island," Atum explained, setting the tray on the small *At* dining table that formed in the middle of the cabin out of a cloud of otherworldly mist right before my eyes. A pair of chairs appeared next, and Atum set down his trays, then rounded the brand-new table to pull out one chair and stood there behind it, clearly waiting for me to come and sit.

Smiling to myself, I shut the door. "You don't have to do that." I crossed to the proffered chair. "I'm perfectly capable of pushing in my own chair," I said as he did that exact thing for me.

"You seem to be under the impression that everything I do is done out of a sense of obligation," he said, taking his own seat across from me. "And while that may be the case in nearly every other aspect of my life, please rest assured, Tarset, that when it comes to you, my every action stems from desire." His dark eyes locked with mine. "I *desire* to sit with you on the deck, and I *desire* to show you gentlemanly courtesy, and I *desire* to see your every need satisfied, because I *desire* to bring as much joy and pleasure to your life as I can while I am still in it."

I blew out a breath I hadn't realized I was holding until he finished. "How am I supposed to respond to that?"

Atum's lips twitched, but the hint of a sly smirk shone through. "I have a few suggestions." His midnight eyes danced with starlight and promise. "Would you like to hear them? Or better yet, perhaps I could show you."

I guffawed, grabbing one of the folded cloth napkins off the tray and tossing it across the table at him. "You're so method," I accused, teasing. "You dress up like a rakish pirate, and suddenly you have the personality of one, too." I gestured at him, thinking of *Pride and Prejudice* despite the fact that Fitzwilliam Darcy was no rake. However, the stoic, brooding charm was the same. "If Mr. Darcy became a pirate, he'd be you. You're pirate Darcy." I skewered Atum with a pointed finger. "This is not fair. No woman can resist pirate Darcy."

His smirk intensified. "I believe that is the point, dearest, loveliest Tarset."

I splayed my hands palm-down on the table and took a deep breath. My resistance was one hand-flex away from crumbling. I wondered if he could tell. If he knew how badly I wanted to stay with him. How deeply I loved this lonely, scarred, and incredibly charming and thoughtful man sitting across from me. I just wasn't sure if I loved him too much to stay or too much to leave.

"You are—" I laughed breathily and shook my head. "Thank you for making me laugh. I can't remember the last time I did."

Atum's dark eyes shone with warmth born of deep emotion. "Any time." He reached for a sandwich. "I apologize for the meager fare—"

I waved away his attempted apology and grabbed a sandwich of my own. "PB and J is a staple of my diet—or at least it used to be." I took a bite and smiled while I chewed. "Delicious," I said from behind my hand, despite being tired of the combo. I really did love peanut butter and jelly sandwiches, but not with every meal. "I'm sure this is much better than the alternative for sea voyages in this time period," I commented before taking another bite. I wasn't even sure if sea voyages were a thing yet.

Atum bowed his head in assent. "You would be correct."

"So, about this gauntlet," I prompted him, knowing he had meant to say more before I distracted him with all the pirate Darcy stuff.

"Ah, yes." Atum set down his sandwich and poured steaming tea from a pitcher into my cup first, then his. "I'll be helping the crew with preparations, so I won't be in the cabin much tonight."

I could already feel my inner demons creeping closer at the mention of Atum leaving me alone. "Can I help?" I asked, sounding a little too eager.

Atum watched me warily. "Will you be offended if I tell you *no*?"

I laughed under my breath and shook my head, despite feeling a pang of rejection.

"If you're worried about your dreams, I can force your mind into a deep, dreamless sleep before I step out for the night," he offered.

"Like you did with Kiya?" I asked, recalling the way she had passed out after he touched his thumb to her forehead.

He nodded sedately. "It's not a permanent solution, but it will at least let you pass the night untroubled."

Feeling like a wimp, I averted my gaze to the table. "That's probably a good idea," I admitted.

"Feeling so deeply is not a weakness," Atum said.

I nodded but didn't trust my voice, so I remained silent, staring at my half-eaten sandwich. Tomorrow, we would arrive, and I would face the decision I dreaded: stay with Atum or go home. I pushed the troubling thoughts away, not wanting to aggravate my soul.

"And in the morning, you will speak the names of your dead to the wind and mark your body with the scars on your soul," he said. "And perhaps then you may allow your heart to heal."

23

"I DON'T THINK I can do it," I said, my voice laced with fearful anticipation.

My knife hand trembled as I held the small At dagger over the heel of my thumb. I wanted my markings somewhere I could always see them, always feel them. I had taken six people's lives, cut their lifethreads short, but I could preserve their names. It was the least I could do.

Atum reclaimed the blade from my shaking hand, his own trembling slightly. "You don't have to do this," he said from beside me. "It was merely a suggestion, not a requirement."

We knelt along the starboard side of the upper stern deck, facing the rising sun. Atum was already well into his ritual, having paused only when I broke the silence with my statement of defeat. The slight tremor in his hands was his only outward sign of fatigue after his night of preparations for entering Rostau, but I thought I sensed a deeper weariness that resided in his soul. Whatever he had done must have required him to use his *sheut* extensively.

While I appreciated his words, I *did* need to do this. From the moment he first suggested I join him during his sunrise ritual, it had been ever present in my mind. I killed six people. I could withstand a moment of pain for each death. Inyotef had tortured me to the point of regeneration over and over again. A minor cut was nothing in comparison. This hesitation was ridiculous, but I couldn't seem to push myself past my own inner resistance.

Taking a deep breath, I held my left hand out toward Atum. "Will you help me? Just this once?"

Atum became very still, not even breathing as he stared at my hand. He had an extreme aversion to inflicting unnecessary pain on another living creature, and here I had selfishly gone and asked to do that exact thing *to me*. Sometimes I could be such an ass.

"It's fine," I said, retracting my hand. "I'll manage to—"

Atum caught my wrist and pulled it closer to him. "What did you have in mind?" he asked, his voice slightly strained as he ran the pad of his thumb over the heel of mine.

"Six dots," I said breathily. "In a line along here." I pointed to the outer edge of my thumb.

Holding my hand in a firm grip, Atum retrieved my discarded dagger and poised it over the area I had indicated. "The wounds will close quickly. You must be ready to rub gold dust in them as soon as I finish."

"I understand," I whispered.

His eyes met mine. "Are you ready?"

I nodded, my heart suddenly racing.

"I apologize for the pain I am about to cause you," Atum murmured, the words having the sound of a prayer. And then he pressed the tip of the dagger into my flesh.

I sucked in a hiss at the sharp bite of pain, then exhaled the name of my first victim on a sigh. Tears sprang to my eyes, born of relief rather than pain. Djau would be a part of me so long as I wore his mark on my skin. He would *always* be remembered.

Atum made another cut, and I whispered the next name. Guilt and self-loathing poured out of me, streaking down my cheeks in the form of hot tears, and I felt Atum's hesitation before making the third cut.

"Don't stop," I said, sobbing softly. "Please don't stop." It was as though every emotion I had been bottling up, everything that had been dragging me down, was emerging, excised from my heart with each short, sharp cut.

Atum made another cut, and I spoke another name. Another, and another, and another, and then it was done. I cried quietly as he sprinkled gold dust onto the open wounds, and I groaned as he gently rubbed it in with the pad of his thumb.

I bowed my head, my shoulders slumping, and felt the raw wounds with the pad of my other thumb. The contact stung, but my lips curved into a tremulous smile. "Thank you," I whispered.

"Perhaps this was a mistake," Atum said.

"No!" My head snapped up, and I stared into his uncertain gaze as I continued to rub the marks on the heel of my thumb. "No, it wasn't. I—" I shook my head. "I needed this. I *need* this."

Atum's eyes searched mine, moving back and forth, like he was weighing the truth in my words.

"I don't know why or how this helps," I said, holding up my hand so we both could see the six golden wounds, already beginning to heal and scar over. "But it does." Again, I shook my head. "It's like they know. It's like *they* accept this." I laughed, the sound high pitched and slightly hysterical. "I don't know how to explain it, and I know this makes me sound crazy, but—" I touched the center of my chest with my fingertips. "Inside me, they're backing away. They're slipping into the shadows, giving me space. *They're* letting *me* go."

Atum recaptured my hand and brought it up to his mouth, grazing his lips over the still sensitive marks. "That doesn't sound crazy at all," he murmured against my skin. His eyes met mine over my hand. "If I kissed you right now, would you tell me to stop?"

"I don't know," I breathed.

"Do you want to find out?" he asked.

I swallowed roughly and inhaled to respond, absolutely uncertain of what I was going to say.

"Captain!" Ode shouted, bounding up the stairs. He was one of the few crew members I had seen this morning. So far as I could tell, everyone else was below deck. "We're approaching the boundary's event horizon. Do you want us to hold back?"

Atum exhaled a growl. "No." He kissed my fresh scars one more time, then stood and pulled me up to my feet. "Let's go home."

MY HEART STILL HAMMERED as I followed Atum down the stairs from the upper stern deck and across the main stretch of the ship toward the bow. Would I have stopped him if he had kissed me? I honestly didn't know.

My own desires were clear enough—I wanted to be with Atum more than I had ever wanted anything in my life. But the decision to be with him was about more than just *my* wants. And for once, I was thinking of someone other than myself. I was thinking about the universe and the potentially dire ramifications should I stay with Atum, bind my soul to his, then accidentally blow him up.

And I was thinking about Atum, and what was best for him personally. I knew he wanted me, that his desire for me surpassed physical attraction and ran soul-deep. But that insipid voice whispered intrusive thoughts through my mind yet again: *He let them hurt you.* Did the man, Atum, truly love me, or was he merely falling prey to the lure of the potential bond?

Clenching my jaw, I scanned the horizon ahead of and on either side of the ship, searching for evidence of the "event horizon" Ode had mentioned. I imagined something dark and looming, similar to the inky void surrounding *Aaru*. And yet, I saw nothing but a clear blue sky and a glittering sea.

Ahead, Ode passed through the door tucked under the upper bow deck, which opened to the stairs leading to the underbelly of the ship containing the crew's quarters, the kitchen and mess hall, and a vast storage space. Two other members of the bare bones crew followed, leaving Atum and me alone on the deck.

"We must hurry," Atum said, placing a hand on my lower back as he quickened and lengthened his strides.

He stepped ahead of me and pushed the door to the stairs open, holding it with an outstretched arm so I could pass through ahead of him. I crossed the threshold and started down the stairs, Atum's heavy footfalls close behind me.

I sucked in a breath to ask him where to go next, but there was no need. Beyond the foot of the stairs, near the front of the low-ceilinged, wide-open berthing quarters filled with row after row of gently swaying hammocks, I spotted Ode and his two colleagues each climbing into a hammock of their own.

Their behavior was intriguing, but it was the occupants of the other hammocks who captured my attention. They lay completely immobile within their swaying, hanging beds. No snoring. No coughing. No sound save for the grunts of Ode and the other two climbing into their own hammocks.

I crossed to the nearest hammock, my eyes widening as I realized the reason for the sleeper's silent stillness. The man lying within appeared to be made of solid, shimmering moonstone. But I knew better, because for four thousand years, I had looked exactly the same. He had been transformed into *At*.

I looked up, peering past him to the woman lying in the next hammock over. She, too, appeared to be an *At* statue, as did the crew member beyond her. I scanned the rows of hammocks, discovering that every person looked the same.

A tingle of otherworldly energy caressed my skin, and I spun around to see Atum leaning over a hammock three rows over, one hand pressed to Ode's forehead, the other to his belly. Atum's eyes were closed, and he held his breath, his features locked in an expression of intense concentration. Finally, he released his held breath, and his expression relaxed. And Ode, who had been so lively a moment earlier, now appeared to be made entirely of shimmering, opalescent stone.

I slowly approached Ode as Atum moved on to the next hammock over, turning his back to me. Ode's eyes were closed, his expression peaceful. If I hadn't seen him walking around a minute ago, I would have thought Atum had come upon the man while he slumbered and transformed him before he woke. Ode had expected this. He was used to it.

I stayed put while Atum finished transforming the other two, and I watched him as he stood with his head bowed over the third, catching his breath and regathering his strength. Again, I scanned the rows of hammocks. Had he transformed *all* of these people into *At* last night? Were those the preparations he had claimed I couldn't help him with? If so, he was right. I wouldn't have been anything but a distraction.

Finally, Atum straightened and squared his shoulders, the top of his head nearly skimming the low ceiling. He inhaled deeply, let the breath out, and focused on me.

I approached, studying the woman in the hammock before him, then peered out at all the other frozen-in-time crew members. "They can't pass through the barrier surrounding Rostau?" I surmised.

Atum scanned his people as well. "It would tear their souls apart," he said.

My brows rose, and I glanced at Ode. "Even the Nejerets?"

"Even the Nejerets," Atum confirmed. "Only a *sheut* can shield someone from being consumed by the interdimensional fires." He stepped to the end of the hammock and gestured toward the stairs.

I looked at Atum as I moved away from the hammock. "Back to our cabin so you can transform me?"

Atum fell in step beside me, his hand settling on the small of my back once more. "That won't be necessary," he said as we started up the stairs, him a few steps behind me.

"It won't?" I asked and glanced back at him over my shoulder.

"You have a *sheut*," he said, like it was the most obvious thing in the world.

Except it wasn't, because I *didn't* have a *sheut*. Only the rare Nejeret born of a union between two Nejeret parents developed the additional part of the soul that afforded them extraordinary powers beyond the healing gifts and enhanced senses standard among our kind. And the only ways a female Nejeret could carry a baby to term without her regenerative abilities rejecting it were to become pregnant before her Nejeret power manifested when she reached full maturity, or to share a soul bond with another Nejeret. The bonding pheromone that linked the physical bodies of the bond-mates could suppress the female Nejeret's regenerative abilities, giving her the fragility of a human and allowing her body to sustain new life rather than rejecting it. And that new life would include not only a *ba* but also a *sheut*.

Of course, there was another way to gain a *sheut*. An extremely powerful Netjer—or a *really* powerful Nejeret like Kat, I supposed—could gift one to a Nejeret, but that hadn't happened to me.

I stopped on the landing between the narrow flights of stairs and turned to face Atum. "I *don't* have a *sheut*," I told him.

He remained a few steps down, and for once, I didn't have to look up at him. "I was not the one who teleported you out of our cabin to hover above the sea," he said. "That was entirely your doing. Only a being with a *sheut* could do that." He studied my face.

My brow furrowed, and I shook my head. "How is that possible?"

"I don't know," Atum admitted. "I believe it may have something to do with your death—the first one that resulted in your trip backward in time." He searched my eyes, like he might find the answers there.

"Really?" I asked, my brows rising.

He shrugged one shoulder. "When my father created the Nejeret species," Atum said, "he didn't understand all the nuances of their existence. Your people are the first of their kind, physical beings with the potential to exist as entities of pure energy. Perhaps a *sheut* exists within every Nejeret, sealed away somewhere even my father could not sense, only to be released when a Nejeret's body perishes and the *ba* emerges from its physical shell. Perhaps, if Nejerets weren't immediately sucked into *Aaru* upon the moment of death, we would know."

He raised a hand to my face, skimming his fingertips down my cheek. "Perhaps you are the first to ever escape that eternal fate." The pad of his thumb glided across my lips, and my breath hitched. Desire darkened Atum's eyes, and he pulled his hand away. "Regardless," he said, clearing his throat. "You now have a *sheut*, which means you are one of the few people able to witness the breathtaking glory of a journey across dimensional boundaries."

His hands settled on my hips, electrifying my nerve endings. I was suddenly hyperaware of where his body was in relation to mine. But he didn't pull me closer. Rather, he turned me away from him, angling me toward the second flight of stairs that would carry us up to the main deck.

"Let us not delay," he said, gently pushing me forward so I would start the climb up the stairs. "I have been away from the time tapestry for too long already, and I'm sure you're eager to see your mother."

His words were an unexpected gut punch, stealing my breath and bringing tears to my eyes. I was suddenly desperate to reach Rostau, to fall into my mom's arms and to confess my sins to her. Nejerets may have been capable of extraordinary healing, but there was no greater medicine for a guilt-ridden heart than that of maternal absolution.

I hurried up the stairs and out onto the ship's main deck, quickly moving out of the doorway so Atum could follow. He took the lead, making a beeline for the stairs up to the quarterdeck at the stern, and I followed close behind him. Atum toed off his boots and tucked them close to the railing, leaving him standing in only his trousers, the morning sun gleaming off his dark skin and golden scars. He planted both hands on the railing, and *At* quickly spread out from those two points of contact, consuming the railing and his boots, the deck beneath our feet, the wheel. Faster than I would have believed possible, Atum transformed everything on the ship into *At*.

Breathing hard, he faced me, his gaze skimming over my body. "Your clothing will be destroyed during the crossing," he said. "If you wish to preserve anything, remove it now."

I peered down at myself, quickly toeing off my boots. I wasn't in love with the jeans or T-shirt I had worn for the morning ritual, so I left them on. Besides, I doubted Atum needed the distraction of me stripping right now.

After placing my boots next to his and transforming them into *At*, Atum settled at the helm, his hands gripping the wheel. I stood beside him, my heart pounding.

"Don't take your eyes off the horizon," he murmured, glancing at me sidelong.

I stared hard at the place where the blue sky met the glittering sea. At first, I thought it was a trick of the eye. The air ahead shimmered, like the heat distortion birthing a desert mirage. And just like with a mirage, a shape gradually took form through the wavy air. A distant island, lush and green and surrounded by golden beaches, with a jagged, rocky mountain peak at its center, bleeding towering waterfalls. The sky beyond was a dark canvas thick with glittering stars.

"Oh my gods," I breathed, my blood humming with a thrilling combination of fear and wonder. "That's incredible."

As the bow of the ship pierced the distorted air, it disappeared into a wall of iridescent flames. More and more of the ship vanished with each heartbeat, and a roaring filled my ears, punctuated by the snap and crackle of a raging fire.

I gasped and gripped Atum's arm. "Is that supposed to happen?"

Atum angled his face toward mine, his lips curving into a mysterious grin. "Just wait," he said, raising his voice to be heard over the incendiary roar. "The best is yet to come."

The consuming distortion hurtled toward us, faster and faster, and I clung to Atum's arm. What if he was wrong? What if I didn't really have a *sheut*? I would be ripped apart in mere seconds.

A moment before that otherworldly fire swallowed us whole, Atum turned toward me, gripped my head in his hands, and crushed his lips against mine. The shock of the unexpected kiss was closely followed by a rush of pure, searing pain.

My flesh sloughed away as the interdimensional flames surrounding Rostau devoured me. Even with all the torture I had suffered through, I had never felt anything like this. But the agony quickly transformed into blissful ecstasy as Atum's exposed *ba* pressed into mine, and in that moment between realities, I was completely undone.

As we emerged from the interdimensional fire and recorporealized on the other side—not just in another place and time, but in another dimension entirely—I clung to Atum, panting, my eyelids squeezed shut and my cheek squished into the hollow of his shoulder. And I could tell, easily, that he hadn't been kidding about the crossing destroying our clothing. His trousers were *long* gone, as was every other stitch of clothing I had been wearing before the trip across dimensions.

Trust me. I could tell. Holy fucking hell, this man would be my destruction.

I understood now why Atum had removed his beloved boots and turned them into *At*, along with everyone and everything else he wanted to save. The otherworldly material seemed to be the only thing that could survive the trip.

Besides us.

Except, I didn't think we had emerged unscathed. Atum's skin felt different under my splayed fingers. The raised bumps and ridges of his scars were gone, leaving only smooth, soft skin stretched over hard muscle. My fingers trailed over his chest and down his sides, savoring the feel of him bared to me. Pressed *against* me.

Atum sucked in a sharp breath, his entire body tensing.

I opened my eyes and tilted my head back so I could see the rapturous expression on his face. Stars gleamed in a clear night sky beyond him. Despite apparently being the middle of the night here, the temperature was perfectly comfortable.

Atum lightly grazed his large hands down my bare back, and I gasped in pleasure, understanding his reaction. My nerve endings felt electrified, every point of contact between us far more sensitive than usual, and that benign touch sent aftershocks of ecstasy jolting through my body, making my spine arch and my legs tremble.

Atum wrapped his arms around me, pressing our bodies more firmly together, and for an indeterminate time, the feel of him overwhelmed my brain, blocking out all other sensory input and rendering me momentarily mute.

Slowly, my awareness of where I was returned, and I regained my ability to think coherently, and eventually, even to speak. "What—" My voice was barely audible, so I cleared my throat and tried again. "What *was* that?"

Atum chuckled, and goosebumps rose all over my skin. "That was just a taste of the bliss we could share if our souls were bound together."

I scoffed and tilted my head back so I could see his face. "Just a taste?" I laughed, disbelieving. "There's *more*?"

Atum pressed his lips to my forehead and inhaled, breathing me in. "Matter from the physical realm cannot cross dimensions, so you are reduced to your spiritual essence during the journey. For a brief moment, our exposed souls were able to interact without any barriers. And the resonance between us ensured the meeting was *charged*."

"Charged?" I barked a laugh. "That's one word for it," I said, thinking *climactic* was a little more appropriate.

The sails snapped overhead, and I looked up as they filled with a strong wind, propelling us toward the moonlit island.

Considering what else Atum had just said, I stuck out my elbow and peered down at my arm, then grazed my fingertips over his unmarked skin, tracing imaginary scars. My hand slowly traveled down his torso, moving over hard ridges of muscle. "What happened to our bodies?"

Atum caught my wrist, and only then did I realize how close I had come to caressing his erection. "As I understand it, they are instantly vaporized by the interdimensional fire, more or less. When we reemerge in Rostau, our *sheuts* pull matter from the atmosphere and recreate our physical forms."

My brows bunched together, unexpected hope swelling in my chest. "Does that mean you can't die? Like, if your physical body failed, could your *sheut* simply recreate another one?" If so, I posed no threat to Atum, and the only thing holding me back from jumping into a soul bond with him would be my uncertainty of the depth of his feelings for me.

Atum exhaled a sigh. "I don't know," he admitted, sounding reluctant. "I've never died."

"Except for every time you pass through the interdimensional fire," I countered, raising my eyebrows.

Atum frowned. "I'm not sure that counts," he said, his eyes searching mine. "I'm sorry. I know that's not the answer you were looking for." He chuckled darkly. "If I were a more devious man, I would lie and tell you I could not be killed. I would assure you that you could not harm me permanently, but I will not deceive you again. I would have there be honesty between us in all things."

I raised a hand to cup the side of his face. "You're too noble for your own good."

That dark chuckle rumbled through Atum's chest once more, and one of his hands slid up the column of my throat and gently but firmly gripped my jaw, turning my face away as he leaned in. "Do not mistake my desire for honesty between us for nobility," he murmured, his lips brushing the shell of my ear. "I wish to defile you in every deliciously wicked way you can imagine, body and soul."

My next breath was noticeably shaky as, once again, I thought back to the carnal scene I had witnessed in the Waset palace before everything fell apart. The way he had taken Nitocris on the floor of his room—he had been wild and unrestrained, more a savage creature than a tamed man. My heart beat faster as I considered being the focal point of all that animalistic power, not just for the rest of my life, but for all eternity.

Atum released my jaw and his arm relaxed around me, slipping away as he stepped back. His gaze seared over my nude form, and suddenly he was the one taking a shuddering breath.

"We should dress and rouse the others," he said, his voice rougher than before. "Those on land will have spotted our sails from the harbor and by now are preparing for our arrival." He reclaimed my boots, and they reverted to leather the instant his fingers touched them. He handed them to me, then retrieved his own footwear.

"Penelope will have my hide if I delay her reunion with Ode for too long," he added. "Let's hurry to our cabin to dress. If I don't cover you up soon, I can't guarantee we'll ever reach the harbor."

"Oh." Heat suffused my chest and crept up my neck and cheeks. "I see." I forced myself to turn away from the naked, godlike man standing before me and to walk toward the stairs. I could sense him close behind me.

Don't look back, I told myself, repeating the words silently.

By some miracle, my will held out, and I made it to the cabin below without turning on my heel and jumping Atum. We stood with our backs to one another as we dressed, seeming to silently agree that if one of us caved, the other wouldn't resist. And however he taunted me, Atum was still committed to ensuring I had a cognizant choice in whether we bonded. In whether I would give up my life and family in the distant future for an eternity in his vast present. In whether I was willing to risk his life—and the entire universe—every day for the chance to experience the truest form of happiness with him.

I dressed in the only garment that had been in my dresser but wasn't from the distant future, thinking it must have represented the current fashion on Rostau—whatever *current* meant here in this place that apparently existed in its own bubble of time and space. The flowy, off-white muslin dress had a vaguely ancient Mediterranean appearance, with short, cinched split sleeves, high slits cut up each side of the skirt, and a deep V in the front and the back. I assumed the long, matching strip of fabric I had found wound around the dress was a belt, and I wrapped it around my waist several times. The bottom hem of my skirt brushed the floor, but even with the length, the dress was more of a casual maxi than a formal gown.

I found a pair of silky underwear beneath the dress with a pair of sandals, and stepped into them, sliding them up my legs. Tucking my feet into the simple, leather thong-style sandals, I turned to face Atum, surprised to find his pirate-y attire remained, only he had left his coat thrown across the foot of his bed. He wore dark gray breeches, cuffed leather boots, and a loose off-white linen shirt, tucked into his waistband to show off the gilded winged scarab on the silver buckle of his belt. As had been standard for him while we were at sea, he wore no visible weapons, though I knew he could create a knife from *At* in the blink of an eye. Even so, it was nice to see him let down his guard. This was his place. His home.

"You look divine," Atum said, scanning me slowly. "Like you belong here, a goddess ruling over her enchanted isle."

"Thanks," I said, blushing at the compliment. I averted my gaze to my toes and smoothed down the front of my skirt unnecessarily, a seed of doubt taking root in my belly now that the moment of my big decision was closing in. I *wanted* to belong here, with him, desperately. But was that enough? Was I enough for him, long term? He craved me now, but would he feel the same in a year? In ten? In a hundred?

He let them hurt you, whispered through my mind yet again. I hadn't been enough for him then—not enough to convince him *not* to let Inyotef hurt me. That was before our potential to bond was so obvious. What did that mean about Atum's true feelings for me? Did he love me? Did he even like me? I knew he wanted me, physically, but were there any emotions there to back it up? Or was his attachment to me all the lure of the bond? When the novelty of my body and our new bond wore off, would he revert to a state of emotional ambivalence concerning me?

My gut told me my doubts were unfounded, but I didn't want to rely on a hunch for such a monumental decision. This was forever, after all.

Atum strode to the door and opened it, holding it for me to pass through the doorway ahead of him. He grabbed my hand as I passed him, giving my fingers a gentle squeeze before I crossed the threshold and he let go.

We walked arm in arm to the berthing quarters, and I watched from the bottom step as Atum awakened his crew with a single, sweeping rush of power that left me breathless and tingling all over. My anxious nerves drove away the dread as we made our way back up to the helm and watched the crew spill onto the main deck, Ode shouting orders to the men and women hustling about.

As the ship neared the harbor of a charming town that would have looked right at home on the Amalfi Coast, golden light glowing in the many windows like gemstones, I stepped forward from my position at Atum's side and gripped the smooth *At* railing. My mom was there, on that island, possibly in that town, maybe even on the docks, waiting for us. Waiting for me.

In a few minutes, I would get the reunion I had waited so long for. More than a fleeting exchange in the middle of the night, but a chance to truly reconnect. To let her know me, the woman I had become not only away from her, but because of her. Because she had begged Lex to help me when I was a dying little girl. Because she had cared more about me growing up than about keeping me close. Because her greatest act of love had been letting me go.

I wondered what she would say about my situation with Atum. I turned my head just enough that I could watch Atum out of the corner of my eye. Would she agree with Tefnut and tell me to let him go? Would she suspect the affection between us wasn't lasting and advise me to leave? More importantly, would I listen?

I gripped the railing tighter as power swelled in my chest, raging against the prospect of leaving Atum. My head bowed, my shoulders hunching. I squeezed my eyes shut, reminding myself that I hadn't yet made my decision. There was a good chance I would leave—I knew I *should* leave—but I remained undecided. I held that final thought at the forefront of my mind, and the power swelling within me slowly receded.

"Tarset?" Atum asked, his voice a gentle rumble from the helm behind me.

"I'm fine," I assured him, raising my head and taking a deep breath before glancing at him over my shoulder and forcing a smile. "I'm fine, I swear." And so long as I didn't succumb to my fatalistic thoughts, I would remain that way.

Atum studied my face for a long moment before returning his focus to the fast-approaching harbor. "Look," he said, pointing to the way ahead with his chin.

I peered beyond the bow to the gleaming quartet of narrow piers—apparently constructed of *At* like much of the town beyond—and to the pair of women standing close together on the leftmost pier. My mom wore a long, flowy dress very similar to my own, only hers was dyed a brilliant cerulean, and she wore her wavy, gray-streaked black hair loose around her shoulders. The diminutive woman beside her wore tan breeches, a loose, white shirt, tucked in, and cuffed boots much like Atum's, her pixie cut showing off her bold features.

"Kiya," I whispered, my lips spreading into an unsteady smile. And this time, I felt certain that I was seeing the real Kiya.

She looked well—healthy and proud, far better than I had expected to find her. We had been through so much together. We had *survived* so much. She had seen me at my absolute worst and had kept me alive when I had wished for death, and I could have kissed her for that, because whatever my future would hold, I wanted to live to see it.

I rushed to the steps and raced down, hurrying to the side railing. The ship slowed as we neared the leftmost pier, and I barely waited until the *At* gangplank had solidified out of the otherworldly mist to run down to the dock.

My steps slowed as I approached my mom and Kiya, tears already streaming down my cheeks. I threw my arms around my mom, my chest convulsing with quiet sobs as she embraced me back. I felt like I could have hugged her forever, but she relaxed her hold and stepped backward, making room for Kiya.

The smaller woman held her hands out to me, and I placed my palms against hers, gripping her tight. "Hello again, my friend," Kiya said.

My cheeks were soaked, and my nose was running, and I was definitely still crying, but suddenly I was laughing, too. Because she could talk. Because she had a tongue. "How?" I laugh-cried.

Kiya stuck out her tongue at me. It wasn't pink but colorless and semiopaque, like gleaming moonstone.

My mouth fell open. Kiya had an *At* tongue.

"It's Tefnut's doing," she said. "Don't ask me to explain how it works, because I don't understand either."

Still laughing, with tears streaming down my cheeks, I grabbed Kiya's shoulders and pulled her in for a hug. "I am *so* happy to see you," I cried.

Kiya snorted. "Could have fooled me," she said dryly, but she held me just as tightly as I clung to her.

Whatever harsh feelings I had toward Atum's prickly daughter and the role she had played in my unraveling, at the moment, I loved Tefnut because she had done this for Kiya. She had healed my dearest friend, body and mind. And for that, I would be forever grateful.

26

"A PLEASURE TO SEE you again, Sesha," Atum said, reverting to Old Egyptian as he bowed his head to my mom.

"You as well," my mom drawled, a merry light dancing in her rich brown eyes.

Atum's focus shifted to Kiya. "And I am pleased to see you're looking well, Kiya," he said with another incline of his head. He turned to me and captured my hand. "I must go to the observatory and check on the time tapestry." He raised my hand to his mouth, and I felt the barely perceptible tremor in his touch. He was exhausted from the power he had expended during the interdimensional crossing, though he hid it well.

"Must you?" I asked, thinking he could spare a few hours to rest. After the weeks he had been aboard the *Bennu* without access to the time tapestry, what was a few more hours?

Atum's eyes remained locked with mine as lips brushed across my knuckles, making my cheeks heat and my belly flutter. "I must," he said, lowering my hand and looking inland. "Stretch your legs." He gave my hand a squeeze, a silent reassurance that he would be all right. "Explore the island. I'll come find you when I'm finished."

With that, he released my hand and strode up the dock, leaving Kiya and my mom to show me around Rostau. I watched him go, his strides deceptively sure despite the bone-deep weariness I knew he felt, then turned toward my companions. My mom wore a small, secretive smile, but Kiya grinned wolfishly.

"Don't start," I told them. "It's complicated, and I don't know what we are." Either everything or nothing. There was no in between.

My mom's face filled with warmth and understanding, and she released a sigh. "I know all too well the difficulties of loving a powerful man." She curved an arm around my waist and guided me up the pier, toward shore. "Come, daughter. I'm sure you're hungry for something that isn't dried, salted, or otherwise preserved." Kiya fell in step on my other side, and I reached for her hand. "The gods know I was dying for some fresh fruit after my journey to the island."

At the mention of fresh fruit, my mouth started watering. "Yes, please!"

N OW THAT I WAS exploring it on foot, the town reminded me even more of those I had visited on the Amalfi Coast a few years back, before the world was turned into a hellscape by the invading Net-jers. The buildings of Rostau were built upon a steeply inclining hillside, with sheer cliffs of warm golden-brown stone rising high behind the town and zigzagging streets winding up and down the slope, connecting the levels of gleaming opalescent white buildings.

My mom and Kiya led me up a steep flight of stairs to a triangular town square surrounded by quaint shops and restaurants, many of which appeared to be open despite it being the middle of the night. A smattering of people went about their night: shopping, eating, chatting, cleaning. It was not at all what I had expected from a mystical island located in a dimension completely separate from reality.

We ended up in a cafeteria of sorts, the tables arranged in the center of the large, open-air room overflowing with fresh fruits and vegetables, cheeses, bread, and pastries. I didn't see any sign of meat, and a small smile touched my lips. It looked like Atum's personal ban on consuming animals applied to his island as well.

I gorged myself on the fresh food, sitting back and sighing when I was sated. "I feel like I could sleep for a week," I groaned. Not regenerative sleep, but normal sleep for sleep's sake alone.

"I can walk you to the observatory," Kiya said, looking from me to my mom. "I know the hill bothers your knee, Sesha."

My heart twinged with sorrow that Kiya knew something so intimate about my mom, while I was clueless as to the cause of her aches and pains. Did she injure her knee? Or was it simply aging joints?

At my mom's torn expression, I held in my hurt and offered her a cheerful smile. "It's fine," I told her. We had reunited briefly barely a month ago, after Atum rescued both my mom and me from separate deaths at Inyotef's hands, but this longer reunion only left me wanting more time with her. "I'm just going to pass out for a few days, then we can catch up on *everything*," I promised both my mom and myself.

"Can you walk, or do I need to roll you up the hill?" Kiya asked, chortling.

I scoffed, feigning affront. "I didn't eat that much!"

Kiya snorted and grabbed my wrist, pulling me out of my chair—which was no small feat considering how lethargic I felt after that feast. "Come on," she said. "Let's get you tucked into bed before you fall asleep right here."

I paused to hug my mom, then let Kiya lead me away from our table and back out into the square. "What's wrong with her knee?" I asked when we were out of human earshot.

"An old injury aggravated by age," Kiya told me. "The healers recommend surgery, but she's resisting." Kiya eyed me sideways. "Perhaps you can convince her."

I nodded absently. "You know, you don't need to take care of me," I said. "I appreciate your company, of course, but I'm not your charge anymore."

"I owe you my life," she said simply.

I guffawed. "You nearly *lost* your life because of me."

"A life that was not mine," she countered. "Inyotef owned me. Until you came along, I was his blade, his tool, his possession. Only now do I know true freedom."

I considered her words as we left the town square behind and started up a narrow, winding street between connected buildings.

"What happened to your family?" I asked. "Did Inyotef hurt them?"

Kiya shook her head, smiling. "He didn't have a chance. Atum arranged for them to be hidden away until after . . ." Her smile faltered, her thoughts almost certainly returning to her time as Inyotef's captive. "Tefnut showed them to me on the time tapestry. They are alive and well."

I sniffed dismissively at Tefnut's name.

"You don't like her, do you?"

My eyebrows rose, and I looked at Kiya. "What?"

"Tefnut," Kiya clarified. "You make a face—" Kiya scrunched her nose like she smelled something foul. "—every time I mention her. I know she can be difficult, but her heart is true."

I held my tongue, having been taught that if I didn't have anything nice to say, I shouldn't say anything at all.

"Something happened between the two of you," Kiya guessed. "What was it?"

Tefnut's remembered words whispered through my mind. *Leave, now—before you destroy him. Before you destroy us all.* Power thrummed in my chest, roused by the recollection of why I should leave Atum and return to the future I had once been so desperate to get back to.

Stumbling over my next step, I gasped and clutched my chest. Kiya gripped my elbow, but I jerked away from her and backpedaled until I hit a wall. I doubled over and squeezed my eyes shut. "I'm not leaving him," I muttered under my breath. "I haven't decided yet. I'm *not* leaving."

"Tarset?" Kiya said, her hushed voice coming from only a few feet away. "What is it?"

I held out a hand to keep her at a distance while I continued my muttered mantra, attempting to convince my soul not to lose its shit. The power's chokehold receded, and I worked to catch my breath. Slowly, I straightened, my entire body trembling.

"You were glowing," Kiya noted. "But I'm guessing you already knew that." She tilted her head to the side. "Tefnut mentioned that her father was nearly killed in an explosion. It was you, wasn't it?"

I nodded, not trusting my voice yet.

"Did it happen again?" she asked, drawing on the incredibly quick wit that had qualified her for a position high up in the ranks of Inyotef's guards.

Again, I nodded, my chin trembling.

Her eyes narrowed. "And someone was hurt," she deduced, her no nonsense expression holding fast.

"Six people," I rasped, my shoulder leaning against the wall. "I—" My voice hitched, and I cleared my throat. "I killed them." I rubbed the side of my thumb, where the scars should have been, but the trip across dimensions had erased them.

"Tefnut told me to leave," I confessed, my voice sounding remote as I attempted to distance myself from the words' meaning to prevent them from riling up my soul again. "She told me to take a portal back to my home." I inhaled shakily. "She told me I'm the greatest threat Atum has ever faced, and that if I don't leave him, I'll destroy him, and—"

The power pulsed, threatening me. Letting me know it was still there. Always there. Ready to blow.

I drew in a deep breath, reminding myself I was still *here*, with Atum, which meant there was still a way to make this work. "Every time I start to believe she might be right, something snaps inside me, and I lose control."

Kiya studied me for a long moment. "Let me get this straight," she finally said. "You think you should leave him because you might hurt him—"

"I *will* hurt him," I blurted. "I *have* hurt him."

Kiya rolled her eyes. "He seems fine to me."

"You don't understand," I said, throwing my hands up.

Crossing her arms over her chest, Kiya pursed her lips and raised her eyebrows.

"If I kill him, everyone dies," I explained. "Every single spark of life will be snuffed out. I will be the greatest mass murderer in history, except there won't be any history, because without Atum around to tend to the time tapestry, the timeline will unravel and the entire universe will collapse in on itself."

Kiya scoffed. "You speak as if you have seen this doomed future. Have you? Have you witnessed his murder at your own hands in the time tapestry? Or perhaps in an echo?"

"Well, no, but—"

Again, Kiya raised her brows, silencing me with a look. "There are many ways to die," she said curtly. "Sometimes it is violent and sudden, and sometimes it is slow, almost imperceptibly so, as a person loses their will to live and simply fades away. You seem so certain that staying with Atum will lead to his death, but how do you know that you leaving him won't have the same outcome?"

I hugged my middle and slumped back against the wall. "I don't know what to do."

Kiya let out a heavy sigh. "I don't know either, and I certainly don't envy the position you're in."

A humorless laugh shook my chest. "Thanks."

"But," Kiya mused, "I do find *this* interesting: when you think about leaving, you explode. You're thinking about leaving *because* you explode. Perhaps if you were to remove *leaving* as an option, your volatility would no longer be an issue, and you would no longer be a threat to him *and the entire universe.*"

I frowned, not yet having considered the situation from that angle.

"Something to think about," she suggested, turning and meandering up the street.

A stranger to this place, I had little choice but to follow.

THE OBSERVATORY WASN'T A building at all, but a structure cut into the cliff jutting up above the town. Kiya led me through the tall arched entrance and down a long corridor lined in gleaming *At*. We passed a handful of arched doorways, then climbed a short staircase topped by yet another archway. Atum came into view as I neared the top step.

He stood at the end of a walkway that extended into a deep cavern. The smooth *At* walls glowed with a gentle iridescence created by millions upon millions of entangled lifethreads, with tiny spots ranging from subtle rose to angry crimson drawing the eye throughout the pattern.

Kiya stopped on the second to last step, leaving me to enter the strange cavern alone. My lips parted as I followed the line of the walls up and over my head, then back down on the other side. A peek over the edge of the walkway told me the glowing surface continued unbroken below. This was the time tapestry in its entirety. The patches I had seen before were impressive enough, but this was absolutely breathtaking.

Atum's footsteps on the walkway alerted me to his approach, but I couldn't tear my eyes from the walls. "This is incredible," I whispered.

He stopped in front of me and touched my chin, turning my face toward him.

My focus snapped to his face, and I registered his troubled expression. "What's wrong?"

"The Waset dissonance has infected the rest of Kemet," he said, his voice hushed. "Nitocris is mobilizing her forces against Waset. I must return to assist in the correction."

Clearly Nitocris, the queen of the northern half of Egypt, hadn't responded well to Atum's forged note breaking her engagement with Inyotef. She had proved herself to be both paranoid and formidable during our brief acquaintance, so I couldn't say I wasn't surprised she had taken this course of action. Apparently, if she couldn't unify the land via marriage, she would attempt to do so by force.

Even so, I didn't see why Atum had to rush back. This island existed outside of the timeline. What harm was there in waiting a few days when Atum could easily hop back into the era we had just left?

"But we just got here," I said, not understanding the rush.

"I know." Atum brushed the pad of his thumb over my lips, then withdrew his hand. "I will leave after sunrise."

"I thought I'd have more time with my mom before—"

"You're not coming," he said definitively.

I stared at him for several heartbeats, my mouth hanging open, not quite believing what I was hearing. I snapped my mouth shut.

"I can't afford the distraction of constantly wondering if you'll leave," he explained. "Until you make your decision, I must carry on my duty without you." His eyes searched mine, and a crease formed between his brows. "This is not a punishment for your indecision, Tarset; it is merely a consequence of it. I hope you can see that."

I nodded, knowing that if I spoke, my unsteady voice would give away my absolute heartbreak.

"Come," Atum said, wrapping an arm around my shoulders and turning me back toward the archway. "I'll show you to my private chambers. Take a long bath if you like. I must go to the harbor to alert Ode to make preparations for the voyage, but I'll return shortly. There is something I wish to show you before sunrise."

I spotted the hope shining like starlight in his midnight eyes. There was still time. If I made my decision now, before he left, maybe he would postpone for a while–or, at least, I could go with him.

But only *if* we completed the soul bond.

T HE BATH—MORE LIKE A swimming pool—was luxurious, but far from relaxing. I found myself locked in a never-ending cycle of thinking about bonding with Atum, then thinking about leaving him and fighting off the resulting swell of explosive power within me. I washed, donned a turquoise dress nearly identical to the other, and paced back and forth across Atum's sleeping quarters, my bare feet quiet on the smooth *At* floor.

My things from the ship had been transported to a dresser in his room, added to a fresh collection of Rostau-appropriate clothing, but none of the books or anything else appealed to me in my present distracted mood.

I didn't even have the urge to snoop through the other dresser or the cabinets and chests, which was really saying something.

The only upside I could see to Atum being away for a while was that the distance would enable me to consider the situation without the raging desire I felt around him clouding my mind. I tried to hold on to that, to remind myself that just because he was leaving in a few hours didn't mean I had to decide *right now*.

"Tarset," Atum said, his voice a gentle rumble.

I spun around, my heart suddenly hammering.

He stood in the peaked archway to the sleeping chamber, appearing to be a shadow surrounded by the subtly glowing *At* walls. He extended a hand toward me, his full, sensual lips curving into a slight smile, though only sadness shone in his dark eyes. "Come," he said. "I have something to show you."

A herd of horses galloped in my chest as I approached him. I scanned his face as I placed my hand in his, searching for some clue to where he was taking me. Perhaps he wished to show me some new amenities in town, something to sway me into deciding once and for all to bond with him. To stay.

Atum's grip was firm, but a slight tremor still shook his hand. He led me out of the sleeping chamber and up the hallway toward the observatory's main corridor. We crossed to another archway leading to a descending staircase and another hallway stretching out beyond the foot of the stairs.

As we neared the bottom, more arched doorways came into view, except they seemed to be doorways to nowhere. Each led to a shallow alcove, barely six inches deep, reminding me of the false doors in Egyptian tombs. We passed dozens of such doorways, each with only a few feet separating them, and headed for the end of the corridor.

Yet another archway was carved into the far wall at the end, but this one was different. A filmy white iridescent haze filled the doorway, ever moving like a liquid. Through it, I could see vague shadows, tall and narrow, slowly shifting about. The closer we drew, the clearer the shadowed shapes became, until they were recognizable as people. Until they were *identifiable* as my family—not my ancient family, here with me on Rostau, but the one I had left behind in the distant future.

My steps slowed, and Atum didn't press me to move faster. He released my hand, letting me approach the archway alone. I stopped inches from the undulating mist, my eyes constantly moving as I scanned the scene beyond.

Through the cloudy barrier, I could see my dad. He sat with his back to me beside a bed—a hospital bed if I wasn't mistaken. Lex was in the bed, unconscious, a ventilator helping her breath. Shoulders slumped and head bowed, my dad gripped her limp hand in both of his. Aset stood on the other side of the bed, her expression somber as she watched them both.

"What is this?" I asked, my voice weak and thready. My eyes stung with a sudden welling of tears. Whatever was going on in that room beyond the barrier was serious, and my dad was in emotional distress. I wanted to go to him. To comfort him. To let him know that whatever else was going on in his life, he didn't need to worry about me.

Atum placed his hands on my shoulders, letting me know he was directly behind me. "This is the portal I promised you." He settled something cool around my neck, then removed his hands.

I glanced down to see I now wore a necklace, both the chain and pendant made of *At*.

"This pendant will allow you to pass through, if you so choose," he explained. "Without it, the portal is merely a window, rather than a door."

"This is the future," I said numbly. "*My* future?"

"It is the time beyond," Atum explained. "My temporal control outside of my timeline is imprecise, so I don't know exactly when this is, but it should be *some time* in the year following your initial death."

I turned around to face Atum. "Why are you showing me this? Why *now*?"

Atum inhaled and exhaled slowly, his eyes searching mine. "I promised you a portal home," he finally said. "It would have been unfair of me to leave you stranded here without fulfilling that promise."

My chin trembled. This was not at all what I had been expecting him to show me. I had been expecting some new form of persuasion. Not that he would throw in the towel. The tears that had been threatening since I first saw my dad breeched the brim of my eyelids and spilled down my cheeks.

I touched my fingertips to the pendant. "Can I use this to come back here?"

"No," Atum said resolutely. "Portals outside of my timeline only work one way."

"Why?" I asked, a whine in my voice.

Atum shook his head. "I'm not sure exactly," he admitted. "I believe it is because the dimensional bubble containing Rostau is linked to me, and *I* am bound by the boundaries of the time tapestry. I cannot personally access that era, therefore, Rostau is closed off from it as well. I can build you a bridge, but I cannot cross it without risking the destruction of Rostau and everyone living here."

At a complete loss for words, I slowly shook my head.

Atum glanced down at the necklace. "I keyed the pendant to close the portal, automatically untethering Rostau from this era as soon as it passes through. Only then will the *Bennu* be able to depart." His expression turned pained, and he took a backward step. "If you decide you need more time and would prefer to wait until I return from this correction, come find me. I'll be on the bluff above the observatory during sunrise. The last door on the right before the stairs to the time tapestry opens to a lift that will bring you up there. If I sense the portal is still open when I finish, but you have not yet joined me on the bluff, I'll come down to close it and bid you farewell before I depart."

I sucked in a breath to speak, but when my lips parted, no words came out. He had stolen them with this selfless gesture.

"If you're not still here . . . if you decide to leave—" He closed his eyes, setting free a string of tears to glide down his dark cheeks. "Please know that I love you, Tarset." He raised his lids, his red-rimmed midnight eyes alight with vehement devotion. "Whatever you choose, I will continue to love you until the end of time." He stepped forward, his hands gripping either side of my face, and pressed his lips to mine.

I clutched the front of his shirt, tugging him closer, holding onto him.

But he pulled free from my grip, stepping back and turning around to stride away.

My shoulders shook with silent sobs as I watched Atum go, unsure if I would ever see him again.

N UMB WITH SHOCK, I turned back to the portal. My dad and
Aset were gone, leaving Lex alone in the hospital bed. Remotely,
I recognized the room as one in Nuin's palace in the Netjer-At Oasis.

I took a small step closer to see more of the room. Power pulsed in my
chest, and I immediately backed up a few steps, almost as though repelled
by the portal. I couldn't step through. Not right now. The thought of
doing so was utterly abhorrent.

As my resolve to stay settled within me, the swelling power receded.
The thought of leaving Atum was what had always triggered my soul to
explode, and accepting that I would stay made me feel more in control,
banishing the fear that I would one day destroy him. That fear no longer
held me in its grip, but I still hesitated to commit to him.

Why had Atum done this? Why create the portal *now*? Why not pull
me closer, hold me tighter? Why was he so willing to let me go?

Because he loved me? Was he willing to let me go because he believed it was what was best for me? Because he thought this was what I needed to heal?

It wasn't, and I dismissed that as a reason to leave. Only one hangup remained.

He had said he loved me, and so far as I could tell, he had meant it. But was it really love, or was it the lure of the potential bond? Before we knew about our potential to bond, he had let me be imprisoned and tortured. For twenty-six days, he stood by and did nothing.

I gripped the pendant so tightly that my nails cut into my palm. The bite of pain reminded me of my vanished scars. An image of Atum's trademark gold markings flashed through my mind's eye. Of his newer, longer scars. Thirteen running the length of either forearm. Thirteen on each arm, twenty-six total. They hadn't been there before my imprisonment, but they had been there after.

I backed up another step, putting more distance between myself and the portal.

Unbidden, Atum's voice whispered through my mind. Words he had spoken while I wallowed in the pit of despair on his ship.

Even in your darkest moments, you have never been alone . . . I have always been with you.

At the time he spoke those words, I had understood him to mean I hadn't been alone after the explosion in Waset, when I had inadvertently killed six innocent people. But now, I wasn't so sure. Could it be—was he talking about earlier, as well? Was he referring to my time in the dungeon? Had he *been* there with me the whole time?

I closed my eyes, attempting to recall his visit to heal my ravaged back. I had been delirious with pain, but I could remember thinking it was strange that I hadn't heard the door to my cell open. It was like he had appeared out of thin air. While I now knew that was a definite possibility, considering he could teleport, I realized there was another option. He could have already been in there.

Another moment from the cell replayed in my mind, when Inyotef visited me mere minutes before Atum freed me. I recalled the way Atum had stepped out of the shadows in the corner, his form seeming to coalesce from the darkness itself. He could disguise his appearance, even going so far as to make himself melt into the shadows until he was effectively invisible.

But what if Atum hadn't only hid in the corner during Inyotef's last visit? What if he had been there the whole time?

I backed away another step. Another.

I recalled Kiya's words from earlier.

There are many ways to die. Sometimes it is violent and sudden, and sometimes it is slow, almost imperceptibly so, as a person loses their will to live and simply fades away. You seem so certain that staying with Atum will lead to his death, but how do you know that you leaving him won't have the same outcome?

I didn't know that–couldn't predict it. If I left, would Atum lose his will to live? Would he simply give up, leaving the timeline in his children's care? The possibility horrified me.

One more backward step, and I spun on my heel, my stumbling strides becoming more sure until I was running toward the stairs. On swift feet, I retraced the route to Atum's private quarters. I yanked the dresser drawers open until I found the one holding my used notebooks, grabbed one at random, as well as a pen, and tore out a page. There was already writing on the front, but I didn't care. I flipped the page over to the blank backside and started to write.

Dad,

I miss you. So, so much. I wish I could see you again, and I <u>will</u> try to find a way. But if I don't, I want you to know that I'm OK. I'm not lost or scared or alone. I think I finally found where I belong.

I love you!!!

- T

Gripping the note tight, I raced back to the portal corridor, tugging the necklace off over my head. I wrapped the hastily scrawled note around it, compressing the paper into a tight ball, and skidded to a stop before the portal. My heart hammered as I stared through the filmy barrier.

Lex lay in the bed, the ventilator helping her breathe moving silently. As I stood there, panting, I wondered what had happened. Kat had mentioned that my dad's soul had exploded. Had Lex been caught up in the blast?

It didn't matter. Much as I wanted to comfort my dad and to make sure Lex was going to be all right, my presence wouldn't change what had happened. *They* didn't need me.

I swung my arm backward, then threw the paper-wrapped pendant into the portal, aiming for Lex's bed. Iridescent lightning crackled over the portal's surface the instant the bundle crossed the threshold, consuming the mist like corrosive acid. In a blink, the portal closed, leaving me staring at an arched doorway to nowhere.

Electrified with purpose, I turned and marched back up the corridor, my fast walk quickly turning into a run. I raced up the stairs and found the elevator door right where Atum had said it would be, the last on the right before the stairway to the time tapestry chamber.

I rushed into the lift and spun around to face the open door. A column of buttons lined the wall to the right of the door, each labeled with a hieroglyph. I didn't even bother to read them. I punched the topmost button once, then punched it again and again and again.

Silently, the door glided shut, and the lift propelled into motion. I stood in the center of the lift car and bounced on the balls of my feet. Now that I had made my decision, I felt light enough to float up to the top of the cliff all by myself.

The lift slowed gradually, then stopped, and the doors slid open without even a whisper of sound. I stepped out into a narrow alcove at the foot of yet another gleaming *At* staircase, this one open to the rosy sunrise sky.

Heart thudding in my chest, I started up the stairs. My entire body hummed, my blood thrumming through my veins. I felt remote and hyperaware at the same time, both out of body and like I had never been more present, more *here*.

As I closed in on the top of the stairs, Atum came into view near the edge of the grassy bluff. He sat on his knees facing the rising sun, as he did every morning for his sunrise ritual. Except, he wasn't moving, despite the pattern of scars on his body only being partially completed. His head was bowed, and his black dagger rested on the ground beside him, his fingers still curled around the hilt. His other hand sat limply on the ground on his other side, gold dust spilling out from between his fingers and onto the earth.

A twig crunched under my bare foot as I stepped onto the grass.

Atum's head snapped up and around, his cheeks wet with tears, his eyes locked on me. His expression was torn between disbelief and that of someone seeing a ghost. "I thought you left," he breathed, his words barely audible, even to my sensitive ears. "I felt the portal close, and I thought—" His voice broke.

I shook my head as I approached him, a small smile curving my lips. "When did you first know you loved me?"

"Before I met you," he said, not a second of hesitation. "You were on the cliffs above the Waset necropolis. You fell asleep, and I stood there, watching you, knowing I should take your life, but finding I couldn't bear the idea of a world without your light."

My eyes widened. I had known he had disguised himself as the boat-man who ferried me to the necropolis, but I hadn't realized he followed me up to the cliffs as well. His answer only solidified my decision.

"You were there," I said, my steps slowing. "In the dungeon. You were there the whole time, weren't you? You never left me alone. You witnessed my every agony."

He nodded, his throat bobbing. "I *felt* every agony," he said, a rough, raw edge to his voice. "Every injury you suffered, I inflicted upon myself. It was the only way I could justify letting it continue. But I had to know. If I was going to allow myself the indulgence of letting you live, I had to be certain you would do anything to protect the timeline."

I stopped in front of him, blocking the sunlight and basking in the way his gaze drank me in. "And those?" I asked, my gaze flicking down to the fresh, longer scars on his forearms. Thirteen on each arm.

"One for each day you were in that dungeon," he confessed, confirming my suspicions.

I nodded to myself and gathered up the long skirt of my dress so I could push down my underwear, letting the silky fabric fall to the ground along with my skirt. Then I eased down to my knees before Atum. I reached for the dagger held loosely in his grip and claimed it, curling my fingers around the hilt. He didn't move as I angled it toward his abdomen, didn't flinch as I jerked it over the ties holding his breeches shut. His eyes remained locked on my face, his chest rising and falling faster with each breath. His heart beat so hard that I could hear it, the rhythm seductive and intoxicating.

I tossed the dagger away on the ground and raised my hands to Atum's face, sweeping my thumbs over his wet cheeks. "And these tears? What are they for?"

"For you," he rasped.

I stood up on my knees and gathered the sides of my skirt as I scooted forward to straddle his lap. With minimal effort, I pushed the front of his pants down enough that his erection sprang free. His hands settled on my hips, but he didn't try to guide me. I reached down between our bodies and took him in hand.

Atum hissed in a breath.

I leaned in until my lips were a hair's breadth from his and shifted my pelvis closer. The head of his arousal grazed over my slit, and I released a shuddering groan when it rubbed against my most sensitive of places.

"Are you sure this is what you want?" I asked. "You're not afraid of me? And you're not worried about the timeline?"

"I have never been more sure of anything." Atum gripped my hips more firmly, his arms shaking with restraint. "Are *you* sure?"

"With all my heart," I said, kissing him softly.

His arms flexed, his hold on me tightening further, and he shifted me forward as he thrust his own hips upward, plunging into me as far as my hand, which still gripped him, would allow.

I gasped and closed my eyes, resting my forehead against his as I savored the sensations of finally being joined with him. I released him and moved my hands to his shoulders, using them for leverage as I worked him deeper into me. He helped me, guiding my hips up and down, but he let me set the pace. My breaths came in ragged pants as the pressure of him filling me fueled an intense pleasure, winding ever tighter within me.

Once he was fully sheathed inside me, I stilled, needing a moment to regather myself. My inner thighs quaked, and my heart beat erratically. I searched his face, his eyes, memorizing the rapture transforming his features.

"I love you, Atum," I whispered. "I *choose* you."

Atum's hands were suddenly on my face, and he kissed me, claiming my mouth as I moved atop him, claiming his body. I rocked my hips, settling into a slow, deep grind that set my every nerve ending on fire.

Inside me, my *ba* roused, pulsing in time with our movements. It swelled, seeking, reaching. Tingles danced over my skin, and I recognized it as Atum's power, his soul, swelling in response to mine.

The first brush of his *ba* against mine made my back arch and sent bolts of orgasmic pleasure streaking out from my core, but instead of waning, the pleasure only built, climbing higher, winding tighter.

My movements against him grew more demanding. His hands returned to my hips, helping me take him more forcefully. Gasps and moans gave way to groans and growls. Tendrils of my *ba* plunged into him as his *ba* entered me, twining, weaving together, fusing us into one being. One soul. I no longer knew where he ended and I began. We were bound together.

I sucked in a breath, the pleasure narrowing to a pinprick, threatening to implode. It snapped on my next heartbeat, bursting out from my core, and my mouth opened in a silent scream. Atum grunted, dragging my hips down until he was buried as deep as he could get inside me, body and soul.

And as I floated along in the moment of bliss, I couldn't help but feel that this was what was always supposed to happen. Fate had driven us to this point. *We* were inevitable.

Because nothing had ever felt more right.

PRESENT DAY

29

NIK

I LEANED BACK AGAINST the edge of the counter running along one
side of the lab and watched my mom work on Kat. In a little over a
week, my mom had gained impressive control over her ability to touch
another's soul. She could now pull only part of a Nejeret's *ba* out of their
body, like she did at this very moment, with Kat. My mom held Kat's
golden, ethereal hand, extending the arm of Kat's soul out from her body
while Kat's physical arm rested on the worktable.

It was fucking weird.

Kat's *ba* looked different from mine or any of the others I had seen
my mom pull from their bodies. For the most part, she glowed golden,
just like everyone else, but veins of moonstone *At* and obsidian *anti-At*
cut through her golden light, and the scars from her battle to save the
universe darkened patches of her soul. I couldn't see it when I looked
directly at her, but when I watched her out of the corner of my eye, I
saw the hint of a rainbow luminescence coating the dark scars, like the
soul-energy was a bandage over her wounded *ba*.

Feeling useless just standing there watching, I strode forward. "I'm going to head upstairs," I said and placed my hands on Kat's shoulders. "See how it's going with Lex and Heru." Today was their first day of training their souls with Anapa. They were upstairs, their bodies hooked up to life support while their *bas* were off playing.

I bent down to plant a kiss on Kat's head, but my mom stopped me with a sharp hand gesture.

"Wait," my mom said. "Remove your hands from Kat."

"Uh, sure," I said, watching Kat's soul arm as I straightened and pulled my hands away.

My mom's eyebrows climbed higher, and she tilted her head to the side, studying Kat's *ba*. "Now, return your hands to her shoulders."

Brow furrowing, I settled my hands on Kat's shoulders once more.

"How fascinating," my mom murmured, but whatever she was seeing wasn't visible to me. "That's enough," she said, her gaze flicking to mine. "You can let go again."

"Do you need me to stay?" I asked, removing my hands again.

"No," my mom said with a shake of her head. She leaned over Kat's disembodied arm, and just like that, I was forgotten.

Kat angled her head to the side, offering me her cheek.

"I won't be long," I said and pressed my lips to her smooth skin, then straightened and strode from the lab.

I hurried upstairs, passing rooms occupied by Nejerets recovering from injuries suffered during soul explosions, and made my way into the room Lex had recovered in after Heru's first disastrous detonation months ago. Now, both she and Heru occupied the room, lying on twin hospital beds, their bodies hooked up to life support machines to keep them alive while their souls were away.

I scanned the room, but unless they were experimenting with appearing invisible, neither Anapa nor Lex and Heru were here in *ba* form. Disappointed, I crossed the room to the window overlooking part of the oasis, wondering if they were out there somewhere. I leaned one shoulder against the windowsill and watched the Nejerets tending the orchards and gardens below. At any second, one of them could blow, seriously injuring everyone around them. In my gut, I felt like we had the solution—discard our physical bodies and ascend to a higher existence as energy beings.

Finding that there was nothing for me up here, I turned away from the window and headed back toward the doorway. I glanced at Lex and Heru's bodies as I passed their beds. And froze.

A crumpled wad of paper sitting at the edge of the shadows under Lex's bed caught my eye. I cocked my head to the side, my eyes narrowing. A delicate *At* chain trailed behind the paper.

"What's this?" I said to nobody as I stepped into the space between the two beds. I crouched and reached under Lex's bed, sliding the ball of paper closer. The *At* chain followed, like part of it was wrapped up inside the paper.

I unfolded the paper, revealing a pendant identical to my mom's—a small *At* disk engraved with a winged scarab. Except the pendant Atum had given my mom as a thank you for saving his life hung from a delicate gold chain. This wasn't hers.

The words written on the wrinkled paper drew my eye, and I wrapped my fingers around the pendant as I read.

Dad,

I miss you. So, so much. I wish I could see you again, and I __will__ try to find a way. But if I don't, I want you to know that I'm OK. I'm not lost or scared or alone. I think I finally found where I belong.

I love you!!!

- T

"Holy shit," I said, staring at the note. Slowly I stood, but I couldn't tear my eyes from Tarset's words. How—not to mention *when*—this note had come to be here, under Lex's bed, was beyond me.

I gripped the pendant tight in my fist and dazedly left the room.

30

ASET

"DOES IT HURT?" I asked Kat, gently pressing on one of the darker patches on her golden forearm. Multicolored energy danced just under the surface, reminding me of the dark iridescence of an oil slick.

Kat shook her head. "It actually feels less, if that makes any sense. Like that part of my arm is asleep."

"Hmmm . . ."

I didn't look up as Nik quietly entered the lab, but when he stopped beside me and gently placed a necklace on the worktable, curiosity drew my eye. As soon as I saw the winged scarab pendant, I released Kat's hand, letting that fragment of her *ba* sink back into her body.

"Where did you get that?" I asked Nik, my stare glued to the pendant on the table. I reached up, curling my fingers around my pendant to assure myself it was still there.

Nik set a wrinkled piece of paper on the table. "I found it with this," he said. "It was under Lex's bed."

I skimmed the note, then read it again more slowly. "I don't under-stand," I said, slowly shaking my head. "This was under Lex's bed?"

Nik shrugged one shoulder. "I can't explain it," he said. "It was just there. They shifted Lex's bed to the side to make room for Heru's once Anapa started their incorporeal training. It could've been there for months, hidden until the bed was moved."

"Months," I mused. I pressed the pad of my index finger to the pen-dant and slid it closer. Curious, I removed my pendant and placed it beside the one Nik had found, wanting to study them side by side. The only discernible difference was the chains.

"When Atum gave me this," I said, tapping my pendant, "he told me it would allow me safe passage through the fires surrounding the island of Rostau." I looked at Kat, and then Nik meaningfully. "*The island* of Rostau."

"Wait," Kat said, raising one hand. "Are you saying that the random island that appeared for, like, a couple of hours is *Rostau*?" she asked, her eyebrows climbing halfway up her forehead.

"I don't know," I admitted. "But an island that appears, then vanishes again is too strange to ignore."

"We could go check it out," Nik suggested. "I know people are already hunting the coordinates for it, but they don't have your pendant. If it really is Rostau, maybe we could break through where they can't."

"Maybe," I said, nodding slowly. "I wish my father was still around."

"Osiris?" Kat asked.

Nik let out an ugly, dismissive laugh. "I don't."

"Nekure," I admonished. "He was your grandfather."

Nik scoffed, crossing his arms over his chest. "And he was a cruel bastard who treated you like a servant and me like trash. We're better off without him."

I stiffened, hurt by the truth in Nik's words. Osiris had never been a kind or loving father to me, but he had been a good leader to our people. I took a deep breath, shoving the old wounds into a deep, dark corner. "Be that as it may," I started, "my father grew up with Atum. He knew the most about the lore surrounding his brother, and he likely would have been able to tell us if the vanishing island was, in fact, Rostau."

Kat raised her hand meekly, waiting for us both to look her way. "Not to dredge up the past, but shouldn't Osiris have been resurrected along with the rest of the Nejerets?"

Nik's eyes widened, his lips parting, and I imagined that my expression was much the same.

"It has been so long since he died, I never even gave him a second thought," I said. In fact, I seemed to have formed a mental block around the events surrounding his death, as they were muffled and hazy in my memory.

"Me either," Nik admitted.

"Are any other Nejerets missing?" Kat asked. "Besides Tarset, I mean?"

I shook my head. "I don't know." I felt horrible admitting it, but the thought of checking for missing Nejerets had never crossed my mind.

"Let's mention it to Heru when he's back," Nik suggested. "He can bring it up at the next gathering."

"If a bunch of Nejerets *are* missing," Kat said, "I can ask Isfet about it the next time I talk to her . . . whenever that might be." Her shoulders bunched up, then slumped, her frustration palpable. It wasn't safe for her to enter *Duat* to reach out to Isfet—not after the last time, when soul-energy stuck to her wounds like leeches, strengthening its hold over her—which meant she likely wouldn't be talking to Isfet until we figured out how to heal her *ba*.

"Ah!" I said, straightening. "You just reminded me—I want to try something." I looked from Kat to Nik. "I'll need you both outside of your bodies, so we'll have to head upstairs." That was where we kept all the rooms set up with life support equipment for the physical bodies of the Nejerets exploring their soul's capabilities.

Kat and Nik exchanged a look. Kat shrugged first, and Nik nodded, then looked at me. "All right." He stepped back, extending an arm toward the doorway. "Lead the way."

I STOOD AT THE foot of a pair of hospital beds, studying Nik and Kat's still forms. It had become standard procedure to sedate and intubate before extracting the souls after we nearly lost a subject in the moments between when I pulled their soul from their body and when Neffe got them hooked up to life support.

I stepped into the space between their beds and pressed my hand to Nik's chest. Closing my eyes, I focused on his heartbeat as I sought the tingle I associated with a Nejeret's *ba*. Once I had a lock on his soul, I pulled my hand away, knowing instinctively that his *ba* was following with his *sheut* in tow.

"Very smooth," Nik said from directly in front of me.

I opened my eyes and smiled at my golden, glowing son.

"You're getting better at this," he said, the golden glow fading as color bled into his appearance. Within a few seconds, he looked indistinguishable from his physical body, still lying on the bed. He squeezed past me to stand at the foot of Kat's bed.

"Practice makes perfect," I murmured and turned toward Kat. I pulled her *ba* free the same way, and her appearance normalized the instant she was fully untethered from her body. If I focused, I could look past the illusion masking their appearances and see their souls in their full, golden glory.

Kat shivered, staring down at her body lying on the bed. "This is never *not* weird."

Nik let out a single laugh in agreement. "So, what now, Mom?"

I stepped out of the alley between their beds and waved Kat forward to follow. "When you touched Kat's shoulder earlier," I said, looking at Nik, "the soul-energy adhered to the bruised parts of her *ba* wavered, like it was losing its grip on her." I moved to one side of the room, while Nik and Kat stood close together at the foot of Kat's bed. "Hold hands, please. I'd like to see what the contact does now that Kat's free of her body's protection."

Nik and Kat exchanged another look, their hands drifting closer together, but not quite touching.

"What are you waiting for?" I asked, gesturing to them with a flick of my fingers. "Hold hands."

Kat's cheeks reddened, and Nik cleared his throat. "Uh, yeah . . . about that," he said, rubbing the back of his neck. "When our souls touch, it can be kind of intense."

"Intense?" I asked, my brows drawing together.

Kat stared at the floor, her cheeks on fire.

Nik chuckled, looking embarrassed for the first time I could remember. "I don't think either of us feels comfortable doing that with you in the room."

Did he mean the sensation of their souls touching was a sexual feeling? "Oh," I said, my own cheeks heating. "I see." I clasped my hands together and looked around the room, anywhere but at my son and his bond-mate. "I'll just—" I started toward the door and stopped right after I passed Nik. "Since I won't be in the room to witness the effect your soul has on hers, please be thorough in the contact—to increase the likelihood that I'll be able to see a difference on her *ba* after."

Nik's attention was locked on Kat, who appeared completely mortified. His lips curved into a sly grin. "I think we can manage that."

I WAS MAKING A list of every Nejeret I had yet to hear mention of since the resurrection, intending to follow up with their nearest and dearest to see if they were missing as well, when I heard footsteps out in the hallway. I set down my pen and stood just as Nik and Kat entered the lab. Nik strode in like he owned the place, but Kat hesitated just inside the doorway.

"Come here," I said, waving her forward. "Let me get a look at you."

Her cheeks reddened.

I glanced at Nik, who grinned wolfishly. "Don't be silly," I told Kat, hurrying toward her. "I don't care what the two of you do when you're alone, so long as it makes you both happy."

I linked my arm in hers and pulled her into the lab. The best light was near the worktable where I had been sitting a moment ago. I situated her there and stepped back, squinting as I focused on seeing her true appearance through the illusion.

The dark patches were still there, but they seemed less intense than before. I moved closer, leaning in to study the dark patch on her forearm.

My lips slowly spread into a grin, and I straightened, looking from Kat to Nik and back. "There's no hint of soul-energy," I told them. "When your souls touch directly, because the connection you share is stronger than Kat's connection to the soul-energy, I think your *ba* dislodges the soul-energy."

I tilted my head to the side, studying Kat's arm again. There was an extra shimmer over the dark patch. I placed my hand over the dark patch on her forearm and closed my eyes. My gut told me I was touching Nik, not Kat. My lips parted, and my eyes opened wide with wonder. "Your *ba*—" I looked at Nik. "Pieces of it remain on her, as though it's coating her weak points like a bandage."

Nik leaned back against a nearby worktable, gripping the edge with his fingers. "So, what does that mean?" he asked, his eyes narrowing.

"I believe it means she will finally have a chance to heal."

Kat blew out a breath that transformed into a laugh, and she turned hope-filled eyes on me. "Really?"

"Really," I said with a nod. I glanced at Nik. "When your raw souls touch, it's like therapy for her *ba*."

"Therapy, huh?" Nik smirked and locked eyes with Kat. "I have an opening in my schedule, if you feel like you need another session."

Kat's cheeks flamed tomato-red.

"Not yet," I told them. "Take it slow. For now, I'd like you to return to your bodies." I looked at Kat. "If the improvements hold until tomorrow, let's try it again. We don't know what we're dealing with here, and too much too soon could do more harm than good."

ANCIENT TIMES

TARSET

A TUM SAW REASON AND delayed our departure from Rostau for
a few days. It didn't really matter how long we waited—the dissonance wasn't going anywhere, as we were currently outside of the
timeline. However long we spent in Rostau, we would be returning to
the same moment in time.

After sending his message about the postponement to Ode via a
charmed *At* pigeon, Atum led me back into the lift. We retreated into
his bedchamber, and didn't emerge for a very, *very* long time.

"Another?" Atum asked as I lay boneless atop him in the bath, my
back to his chest. He cradled my body with his own, the back of my head
resting on his shoulder and my legs splayed over his. My hands rested
atop his as his fingers grazed lightly over my abdomen and thigh.

I shook my head, my body still thrumming with little aftershocks of
pleasure from the latest climax. I had lost track of how many he had
given me in the bath, and I had given up on trying to return the favor.
He refuted my every attempt, saying this was recompense for the pain he

had allowed me to suffer. Who was I to turn down freely offered orgasms with no strings attached?

"Just one more, I think," Atum said, dragging a fingertip along my slit. "An even dozen."

He dipped that lone finger inside me, and I shuddered at the overwhelming sensation from even such a gentle touch. Every part of my body felt overstimulated and hypersensitive. He pressed his palm to the apex of my sex and I whimpered, the electric contact making me squirm. Atum wrapped his other arm around my middle, holding me tight against him and keeping me from wiggling away.

"Atum, please," I begged, though I wasn't even sure whether I was asking him for more or to stop.

A tendril of his *ba* slipped inside me and teased along the edges of mine.

I gasped, arching my back. No words could describe the blissful sensation, just shy of too much. It felt so good I thought it might kill me, and I never wanted it to stop.

"Please, what?" Atum asked, grinding the heel of his hand against me in a slow circle.

My hips rocked, seeking more direct contact.

His grip around me tightened, and he stilled his hand. "Please, *what*, Tarset?"

"More," I whined. "Please, *more*."

His low, satisfied chuckle vibrated against my back, and he withdrew his finger from within me and slid it higher to slowly, deliberately circle my most sensitive place. "Like this?"

"Mmm," I moaned. "Yes . . ." I raised my head to watch his hand work between my legs under the water, the sight almost as arousing as his touch.

Another rough chuckle rumbled through him. He shifted me higher on his body until the head of his erection nudged my entrance. "How about this?" he asked as he pushed the tip inside me. "Do you want more of this?"

"Yes," I groaned, straining to watch him enter me.

"As my fallen star wishes." He raised his hips, thrusting deep inside me.

I gasped, letting my head fall back against his shoulder as the sinful sensations swept me away.

It went on like that for days of pure bliss. We only emerged from his private quarters to eat on a terrace in the cliff that overlooked the town and harbor or to greet the rising sun on the bluff. We saw no one, but that was probably for the best, because we couldn't keep our hands off one another.

And I didn't mind one bit.

I FELT DISORIENTED AS I walked down the pier toward the *Bennu*. The ship had been a place of darkness and despair for me during the trip *to* Rostau, when I had believed my situation in this era—in any era, really—to be utterly hopeless. But now, arm in arm with my mom, I felt a slow rising of excitement.

Gone was the insidious dread that this day might be my last with Atum, as was the constant fear that I might inadvertently kill him—or anyone else. For three days, my soul hadn't stirred for anything but to mingle with Atum's in pure ecstasy, and I dared to hope that finally accepting the bond with Atum would quiet it permanently. After all, the thought that we could never be together was what had always set me off in the first place. Even the first few times I detonated, when I believed he had deceived me and then later, when I thought he had killed my family, I could see now that it was my belief that he wasn't a man I *could be with* that had set me off.

Atum was already on the ship when I arrived, having spent the morning hours after our sunrise ritual preparing for our departure while giving me that time to spend with my mom. Being with her, swapping stories of things that had transpired during the two decades we were separated, both wrenched and warmed my heart. Between the soul bond with Atum and my second chance at having a relationship with my mom, I felt settled in a way I had never experienced before. I felt *at peace*, and it was intoxicating.

Kiya stood at the bottom of the gangplank in a slightly more feminine version of Atum's pirate-esque attire, one hand resting on the butt of her khopesh sword's hilt. The blade of the curved sword she favored had been upgraded from bronze to gleaming *At*. She watched my mom and me approach with glittering eyes and a curious smirk, and once again, I was overcome with gratitude toward Tefnut for rekindling Kiya's vibrant light.

I had been pleased to discover similar clothing laid out for me on the bed when I emerged from my bath this morning. As comfortable as the sweats I had lived in during the voyage to Rostau had been, I was definitely looking to up my seafaring fashion game, and the beautiful long, flowy dresses and sandals I had adored while on the island weren't going to cut it at sea.

"You didn't have to come all the way down here to see me off," I told Kiya as my mom and I stopped at the nearer edge of the ramp up to the ship.

Kiya's lips twitched, her eyebrows rising. "I'm not seeing you off," she said. "I'm coming with you."

My mouth opened, but no words came out. I shook my head, too stunned to speak.

"I offer you my sword. It is my first act as a free woman," Kiya said, bowing. She looked at me, though her face was still angled toward the dock. "Unless you would prefer someone else guarding your back . . ."

I rolled my eyes. "Don't be so dramatic," I said, laughing. "So far as I'm concerned, there *is* no one else."

Grinning, Kiya straightened. "Excellent." She nodded toward my mom and murmured, "Until we meet again, Sesha," then strode up the ramp. She had more swagger in her step than literally anyone I had ever met, and with all the time I had spent in Hollywood *and* among Nejerets, that was really saying something.

My mom and I watched Kiya until she reached the ship's main deck. "Watching her transformation has been—" Seemingly at a loss for words, my mom shook her head. "I have never met anyone so resilient, save your aunt."

I nodded my agreement, assuming she was speaking of Aset and what she had suffered when she was abducted as a young woman, shortly before she manifested her Nejeret traits. Her harrowing experience had resulted in a child, Nekure—Nik, as he preferred in the future—but even I had heard the whispered stories of how she had struggled for years after being rescued.

"You're lucky to have such a loyal companion." My mom hugged my arm closer. "She would follow you to the ends of the earth."

I glanced at my mom, but my attention wandered back to Kiya, and I frowned. "She doesn't need to do that."

"Did your father teach you nothing?" my mom asked, releasing my arm as she stepped in front of me. She placed her hands on my upper arms and gave me a gentle shake. "Want and need are not the same. Need is a requirement. Want is a choice. Kiya *wants* to follow you, and that is a far more powerful brand of loyalty than anything forced or required." Her lips spread into a warm smile, and she pulled me in for a hug.

I wrapped my arms around my mom. She felt far more frail than I remembered as a little girl but still sturdier than she looked.

"I love you, my child," my mom murmured, her voice filled with motherly warmth and more than a hint of sorrow. "Be safe during your travels and come back to me." She kissed my temple, then released me and stepped back. "Now go," she said, a wobble to her words. She made a shooing motion with her hands and sniffled. "Board the *Bennu* before I fall to pieces."

But I didn't leave. I closed the distance between us and threw my arms around her, holding her tight. "I love you, too," I whispered. And then I released her, turned away from her as I stepped back, and boarded the ship. I almost couldn't believe I was voluntarily leaving her again after fate had miraculously brought us back together. But I *would* see her again.

"Ready?" Atum asked, striding toward me from the mast. Seeing that striking, swarthy man banished all doubts about leaving my mom.

Him. Atum. The bond-mate I hadn't expected and didn't remotely deserve, but who I planned to cherish for the rest of forever. *He* was the reason I was walking away from my mom. I smiled to myself as he drew near, taking my elbow gently in his large hand. I didn't feel the least bit ashamed to admit that, from now on, he was my reason for everything. Not because he was a man or anything stupidly misogynistic.

But because before him, my reasons had been hollow. Shallow. Paper thin. But Atum and everything he stood for, everything he had done to protect this universe—that was the definition of substantial. Through him, my life now had meaning.

And for that, *I* would follow *him* to the ends of the earth.

"ARE YOU READY?" ATUM asked, standing near the cabin door. He wore a robe loosely belted around his trim waist and nothing else, the gaping V revealing an enticing peek of his muscular torso and golden scars.

I stood with my back to him, my hands trembling as I tightened the robe's belt around my waist. Was I ready to make the interdimensional boundary crossing with him again? Hell yeah. And yet, I hesitated, inhaling a shaky breath as I recalled the intensity of the first crossing—the excruciating agony followed by obscene pleasure.

"Is it going to be the same as before?" I asked, facing Atum. I gulped. "Or will it be *more*?" If the euphoria was any more extreme, I honestly wasn't sure my mind would survive.

The corner of Atum's mouth tensed, hinting at a wicked smirk. "Are you worried I'll drive you mindless with pleasure?"

I gulped and nodded. "Pretty much, yeah."

The smirk finally appeared. "Do not fear," he said, his dark gaze smoldering. "I'll be inside you the whole time." He pulled the door open and gestured to the corridor, all nonchalance, like he hadn't just rocked my world with words alone. "After you."

For long seconds, all I could do was gape at him. He would be *inside me* the whole time? Not just *with* me, but *inside* me? I shut my mouth, swallowing roughly, and forced my feet to carry me toward the open door. He had promised to defile me, body and soul. Apparently, he was about to attempt both.

Atum followed me onto the quiet main deck, close enough behind me to steady me should I lose my balance. My sea legs were as hopeless as ever, and I appreciated his attentive care. I appreciated his sure hands finding their way to my body even more.

The barrier between dimensions shimmered ahead, my amateur estimation placing it a few minutes out. Atum had already transformed the crew into *At* for the crossing, along with pretty much everything else on board the ship, leaving the usually lively deck eerily quiet. The only sounds were our footsteps on the unyielding *At* boards, the sea spray as the *Bennu's* hull cut through the water, the groans of the rigging, and the gulls crying out overhead.

My heart hammered as I ascended the steps to the quarterdeck at the stern of the ship. My belly fluttered with anticipation—both excitement and fear. Last time I made the crossing with Atum, I hadn't known what to expect, and it had been a revelation. A preview of what it might be like to be together. To not merely be committed in our hearts, but to have our souls bound inextricably together.

When I reached the top of the stairs, I stepped off to the side, letting Atum pass. He approached the wheel, untying his robe and shrugging it off his broad shoulders to reveal the intricate pattern of golden scars standing out in stark contrast against his dark skin. He tossed the robe onto the railing, transforming it into *At* a moment after it landed.

My greedy gaze roamed over him, taking in every delicious inch of hard muscle and dark umber skin. He was too beautiful to be real, but here he was, all the same. And he was all mine.

"Come here, Tarset," Atum said, extending his hand toward me. His eyes glittered with approval. Apparently, he enjoyed my covetous stare.

I drew my bottom lip between my teeth and stepped closer to him, placing my hand in his.

Atum glanced toward the bow and the barrier beyond, then returned his attention to me. "Not much time now," he said, reaching down to tug the end of my knotted belt.

My robe fell open, and Atum's gaze skimmed over all that was visible of my naked body through the several-inch gap. By the time his focus returned to my face, his gaze burning with unbound desire, my breaths had quickened, and my skin felt flushed.

He released a murmured growl and slid his large hands into the opening at the front of my robe, palming my breasts. I used to be underwhelmed by men's obsession with my breasts, their attentions to that part of my anatomy predictable and completely uninspired. But with Atum, his focus remaining on my face to gauge my reactions to his every caress, noting the way my breath hitched when he skimmed his fingertips along the weighty underside of my breasts or flicked a thumbnail over my nipple, it was as though he had awakened a brand-new erogenous zone.

Atum's hands grazed up and over my shoulders, pushing the robe off and letting it fall to the deck. Movements slow and commanding, he caged my head in his hands and angled my face up toward his as he leaned in, claiming my mouth. My lips parted with a sigh, and I opened for him, savoring the contrast between his unyielding hold and the tenderness in his kiss.

My feet moved automatically as he turned me part way and guided me backward. My shoulder blades and butt pressed against the helm, and only then did Atum release his iron hold on my head. His hands slid over my shoulders and glided down my arms, each capturing one wrist. He raised my arms and pressed them back against the wheel.

"Hold on tight," he practically growled, curling the fingers of each of my hands around an upward projecting handle. He pulled back, again glancing toward the bow before his eyes locked with mine.

Heart hammering, I gripped the smooth handles for all I was worth, already anticipating where this was headed.

Atum's hands glided down my arms and over the curves of my body until he reached my thighs. His long fingers curved around the backs of my legs, and he hoisted me up, guiding my legs around his hips.

I flexed my arms, supporting some of my weight, and hooked my ankles together behind Atum, helping however I could. The head of his erection slid along my slit, and I tilted my pelvis slightly higher, affording him a better angle.

Atum's grip shifted to my hips, his fingertips digging into the swell of my backside, and he thrust forward, filling me completely in one smooth, hard motion.

I gasped, my head falling back against the rim of the wheel and my eyes drifting shut as I sank into the pleasure-pain of the sudden joining. Atum pulled out, then rammed back into me, taking me rougher than he ever had before, again and again and again. The friction fueled a deeper pleasure. This was the version of him I had seen with Nitocris that fateful night in the Waset palace, more beast than man. He was wild and unrestrained, and I *loved* it.

"More," I demanded, raising my head and staring into Atum's eyes. I dug my heels into his ass to encourage him. "Give me *more.*"

"As my lady wishes," he growled, then crushed his lips against mine as he thrust into me with even more force than before.

The friction-fueled pleasure wound tighter and tighter. Whispers of Atum's *ba* grazed against mine, and my soul responded, swelling and pulsing in an erotic rhythm with his thrusts. I climbed higher and higher, a tingling heat deep inside me hinting at the intensity of the coming release.

I gasped, the interdimensional fire licking at my skin. My pleasure crested an instant before I was engulfed completely. I came apart, destroyed by ecstasy and agony, my nerve endings singing with the height of my pleasure even as they disintegrated.

Suddenly free, my throbbing *ba* clung to Atum's, thrusting tendrils of itself into Atum's soul and escalating the blissful euphoria to new heights. I melted into him, the fibers of our souls fusing together until I could no longer tell where I ended and he began. I knew his every thought and feeling. His awareness was my own. His ecstasy *my own.* His thousands of years of existence played out for me like a movie, watched from beginning to end in an instant, like I had lived his life myself. I knew every piece of him, and I loved him all the more for it.

We reformed in an explosion of sensation. One moment, the strands of our souls were woven together, forming a single being; the next, I was gripping the handles of the ship's wheel, my legs wrapped around Atum's hips as he thrust into my newly formed body and buried himself to the hilt, sending me hurtling into another release.

I groaned as pleasure electrified my brand-new nerve endings. Atum went rigid, holding me as close as he could get, like he was attempting to meld our bodies together as closely as we had just fused our souls.

My legs trembled as my pleasure abated. I mourned as the details of Atum's life slipped away from my memory, leaving behind only a vague impression. Slowly, Atum relaxed his grip on my backside and let me lower my feet to the deck. My knees felt wobbly, and I gripped his shoulders for support, though he didn't feel much steadier than me.

Finally, Atum raised his head. I gasped when I saw his eyes—his dark-as-midnight irises now included a brilliant copper ring directly around his pupils. "Atum, your eyes! Are mine—"

"Changed," he finished for me. His throat bobbed, and he nodded. I assumed that meant there was now a ring of midnight encircling *my* pupils.

"What—" I shook my head, my brow furrowing. "What does that mean?"

His eyebrows drew together, forming a crease. "I don't know," he said. His lips curved into a quiet, closed-mouth smile. "But I like it."

34

"I'VE GOT YOU," I said as the colorful mist dissipated to reveal the landing outside Atum's hideaway high in the Waset cliffs.

As before, each additional jump through space sapped more and more of Atum's strength. We had reached our final destination, but we would still need to rest for the night so Atum could recharge his *sheut* enough to disguise himself before we crossed to the palace on the eastern side of the river.

Atum slumped against me, still supporting himself on his own two legs, but just barely. I dropped the basket of supplies from the ship that I had been carrying and pulled Atum's heavy arm over my shoulders. I tucked in close against his side, curving my arm around his back and gripping the side of his coat.

Kiya, Ode, and the others remained on the ship, sailing up the Nile toward Waset, but as soon as we saw the impacts of Nitocris's troops marching south with our own eyes, Atum had felt an urgency to reach Waset immediately. She had to be stopped as soon as possible.

Very aware of the steep ledge behind us, I shuffled Atum closer to the cliff wall. His breathing was ragged, and he bowed his head, seeming to focus all his effort on remaining upright. He was barely holding on to consciousness. I gripped his wrist and lifted his hand, pressing his palm flat against what appeared to be rough limestone, though I could feel the faint thrum of otherness that had become more and more apparent to me since crossing the interdimensional boundary a second time emanating from the *At*, like some of Atum's *sheut* had seeped into me, as well.

The tingle of Atum's rising power surrounded me, vibrating through my blood and electrifying my nerve endings. The pale color of the limestone faded to shimmering, opalescent *At*, and a moment later, the wall melted away.

Atum dropped his hand, and his head fell forward, his weight seeming to quadruple as his knees threatened to give out.

"Oh, no you don't," I murmured, dragging him forward and into the cavern.

Three steps in, Atum went boneless, and it was all I could do to keep him from dropping like a stone and cracking his head on the unyielding *At* floor. I wrapped both arms around his torso and eased his dead weight down to the cavern floor as gently as I could, settling him flat on his back.

On my knees beside Atum, I glanced at the mouth of the cave, wide open to the world beyond, and sighed. There was nothing I could do about that beyond watching over Atum while he was unconscious and exposed. Unless . . .

Could I draw on my latent *sheut* powers and pull *At* into the physical realm? My *sheut* existed, proven by my ability to cross the interdimensional boundary without being obliterated. I had yet to succeed in purposely drawing on that uniquely powerful aspect of my soul, but I couldn't help but wonder if, like my eyes, something within my *sheut* had changed during the crossing as well. After all, I *could* sense the solidified *At* now. That was definitely new. Maybe I had other yet-to-be-discovered new abilities.

I regained my feet and retraced my steps to the cave mouth, where I stood just inside the threshold and studied the roughly arched entrance. Atum always made manipulating *At* look so easy, like it took little more thought or effort than breathing. How hard could it be?

Raising my hands, I held them in the place where I wanted to create a barrier and closed my eyes. I pictured that rainbow mist appearing and filling the cave mouth. I imagined it solidifying and turning into the same unbreakable crystalline material that coated the cavern floor, walls, and ceiling. My brows bunched together as I squeezed my eyes shut tighter, and I gritted my teeth, concentrating hard enough to make my brain throb.

After a solid thirty seconds, I cracked one eyelid open and peeked at the mouth of the cave. It was still open, no hint of solidified *At* or even a shimmer of rainbow mist.

I blew out a breath and lowered my arms, my shoulders slumping. I stared out at the Nile Valley far below, studying the flooded farms lining the banks of the river and the walled town in the distance. There was no sign of Nitocris along the northern horizon, but then, we had just seen her encampment far to the north, near Khmun, a town about halfway between Men-nefer and Waset. It would take the queen and her troops another few weeks to reach this region.

Turning my back to the opening, I surveyed the cavern. Nothing had changed since we were last here, a little over a month ago.

I crossed to the back of the cavern, where we had draped our blankets and sleeping pads over the storage baskets filled with non-perishable supplies. I arranged the sleeping pads and blankets on the reed mats surrounding the dormant fire pit, quickly working up a sweat in my long coat that was far too heavy for Egypt's heat, even within the cooler cavern.

After shucking my coat and draping it over a basket in the back of the cavern, I returned to Atum, crouching at his side. I stared down at his slack face, stunned for about the thousandth time by his inhuman beauty. Even after the honeymoon of sorts we had spent locked away together on the island and the week on board the *Bennu* while we crossed the Mediterranean, it had yet to truly sink in that he was mine—and that *I* was *his*—forever. Not just while our bodies lived, but our souls were bound for all eternity.

I crouched beside Atum. "Let's make you a little more comfortable," I said, knowing full well that he couldn't hear me.

He was locked in a deep, regenerative sleep, his overuse of his *sheut* having taken a toll on his physical body, and I knew from experience that he would remain that way for at least five or six hours. Not as long as if he had sustained an actual physical injury, but long enough to put us in a temporary holding pattern. I hooked my elbows under his armpits and stood part way, grunting as I dragged him closer to the bedding. He was not light, but I managed.

I considered attempting to remove his coat, but it was leather and molded to his body so well that I would have had to roll him back and forth and back again. Boneless as he was at the moment, the task would have been nearly impossible, with a high likelihood of injuring him. The last thing I wanted was to prolong his regenerative sleep. So I left him in his long leather coat, hoping he wouldn't overheat. I did, at least, remove his cuffed boots and socks.

While Atum slept, I retrieved the basket I had abandoned on the ledge and carried it into the cave, setting it by the low *At* table beside the dormant fire pit, then rummaged through some of the supplies stashed in the baskets at the back of the cavern. I dragged the basket of waterskins closer to the table, then pulled out another basket filled with women's clothing, including an assortment of era-appropriate white linen shift dresses, desert robes, and leather sandals, as well as a small wooden box stocked with jewelry, all gold and most decorated with a solar scarab.

Quickly changing out of my seafaring attire and into a delightfully lightweight linen dress that reached mid-calf, I added a delicate gold belt made of interlocking solar scarabs with lapis lazuli bodies, but no other accessories. I puttered around, digging through a few more of the baskets until I found one containing folded up schentis, the white linen kilts favored by men in this time period, and a few leather weapons belts and pairs of larger sandals.

Knowing next to nothing about what made a good schenti, I picked a bundle of linen at random and set it on the reed mats near Atum's bedroll, along with a weapons belt. It was sweltering outside and not much cooler in the cavern. He would definitely want to change as soon as he woke. He would want to eat to replenish the energy his body had burned through to repair his cells as well, but it would be hours yet until he roused.

With nothing else to do but wait, I left the cavern with a notebook in hand and sat near the ledge to observe the valley below while I jotted down song lyrics, not a macabre note among them.

THE SUN WAS NEARING the western horizon when Atum finally
let out a muffled groan, the first hint that he was rousing. I set
down my notebook and glanced over my shoulder. He had rolled onto
his side while my back was to him, another sign that he had shifted from
regenerative sleep to a natural slumber and would wake soon.

I reached my arms high over my head and arched my back, stretching
first to one side, then the other. With a heavy exhale, I stood and brushed
off my backside, then bent down to retrieve my notebook.

I headed for the low table and knelt on a sitting cushion while I pulled
out various food items from the basket, including vitamin C tablets and
all the fixings for peanut butter and jelly sandwiches, both of which I
had come to understand were staple items for Atum's crew during their
frequent sea voyages. Though I was relatively sick of PB&J at this point,
I took my time making these sandwiches perfect, knowing they would
be the last I would have for some time, until we returned to Rostau.

Atum groaned again, louder this time, and rolled onto his back. "Tarset," he said, his voice rough with sleep, his hand searching the bedroll beside him.

"I'm here," I told him and stuck the knife back into the peanut butter jar. I stood and started around the fire pit toward him. "How do you feel?"

"Lonesome," he said, lifting his lids and locking onto me with his midnight stare. He raised a hand, extending his arm toward me. "Come here."

I placed my hand in his and started to kneel. Atum took advantage of me being momentarily off balance and tugged on my arm, pulling me down on top of him. I let out a squeak that transformed into an oomph as he rolled us both, trapping me beneath him.

"Atum!" I protested, but then his lips were on the side of my neck, and his hand was moving up my bare thigh, bunching up my skirt, and my protests died on my tongue.

He somehow managed to unfasten his belt and pants with one hand—or maybe he just transformed the fastenings into *At* and made them vanish—but suddenly, he was nudging my entrance. Need pulsed deep in my core, and I shifted my hips to a better angle. He thrust into me, and I gasped, letting my head fall back against the sleeping pad as Atum claimed my body anew with each pump of his hips. Pleasure coiled within me incredibly quickly, and it wasn't long until we were both shuddering, overcome by ecstasy.

Atum raised his head and pressed a gentle kiss to my lips. "Apologies," he murmured. "I don't know what overcame me."

I laughed, the sound sultry. "If there's one thing you never need to apologize for," I told him, "it's *that*."

Atum chuckled. "I'll keep that in mind," he said and rolled off me.

I sat up and adjusted my skirt to cover myself. "Do you need another round?"

Atum paused in the middle of removing his coat and met my eyes, a wicked glint in his dark stare. "Always."

I smacked the outside of his thigh with the back of my hand. "Another round of regenerative sleep," I said, laughing.

His lips curved into a seductive grin, and he removed his coat. "I prefer my interpretation."

Smiling, I shook my head. "I'm sure you do." I glanced past him to the schenti I had laid out earlier. "There's fresh clothes for you, and dinner's ready." I shifted to my knees, then stood and headed back to the table. "Are we crossing the river tonight, or are we sleeping here?"

"We cross tonight," Atum said, pulling off his shirt. I didn't bother hiding my ogling stare as he quickly shed the rest of his clothing. He wrapped the schenti around his hips, knotting it under his navel, but left the weapons belt and sandals where I had set them out. Worry lines had formed between his brow by the time he joined me at the table.

"No time to waste?" I asked, tearing off a corner of a peanut butter and jelly sandwich.

Atum shook his head and scooped a handful of roasted mixed nuts out of the bowl at the center of the table. "Not with this dissonance," he said. "It's among the worst I've seen."

"I'm sorry," I said, averting my gaze to the sandwich in my hands. None of this would have happened if not for me.

"Tarset," Atum said, my name a plea. A command.

I reluctantly met his stare from across the table.

"*I* did this, not you," he said. "*I* killed Inyotef."

"But—"

"I didn't have to kill him," Atum said. "Just as I didn't have to slaughter his warriors." He was quiet for a moment, but I didn't protest further. "I made a choice, and now I must deal with the consequences of that choice."

"*We* must deal with the consequences," I said, reaching across the table and capturing his hand. I threaded my fingers between his and pressed our palms together. "You're not alone in this. Not anymore."

"How do I look?" Atum asked, his divine luster dulled to make him appear perfectly human in the moonlight pouring in through the mouth of the cave.

"Like the man I fell in love with," I said, moving closer to him. I placed my hand on his upper arm and slowly walked around him, trailing my fingertips over the smooth skin on his back and the raised scars on his chest, now the same dark color as his skin instead of the striking gold I had grown used to.

"Did you truly love me as Temu?" Atum asked, his midnight eyes smoldering down at me.

I stopped with my palm pressed against his chest, directly over his heart, a small, sad smile curving my lips. "You broke my heart as Temu," I said and raised my gaze to meet his. The copper that remained in his irises from our souls merging so completely reminded me of shooting stars streaking through the night sky.

Atum clenched his jaw, his throat bobbing. "Tarset, I—"

"Don't," I said, cutting him off. "I wouldn't change anything that happened before this moment, because it all led to *this* moment." I raised my hand to cup his chiseled jaw. "I do think about it a lot," I murmured.

"What was done to you—"

"Not that," I said. "I think about what I saw the night of the party. I think about you . . . with *her*."

Atum inhaled like he was going to speak again but wisely remained silent.

"I think the memory of you fucking her is seared into my soul."

Atum made a low, rough sound and turned his face toward my hand, pressing his lips against my palm. "Well then, I guess I'll have to think of some way to burn that memory away," he mused, his eyes glittering with dark promise. "I'm sure we can create a new memory to banish the old."

My belly fluttered at the thought, and I let my hand glide back down to his chest. I traced scars that I knew from experience were more sensitive than his unmarred skin. "I look forward to it."

Atum chuckled. "As do I." He leaned in and wrapped his arms around me, claiming my lips with tender persistence. When he held me like this, I felt tiny and fragile and fearless all at once, sheltered within his indomitable embrace.

"Are you ready?" Atum asked, pulling back and searching my face like he might find visible scars from all the unpleasantness that happened at the Waset palace. But the only marks on my body were those I put on my hand during our remembrance ritual every morning at sunrise.

I flashed him a reassuring smile. "As I'll ever be."

E ACH STEP CLOSER TO the Waset palace dredged up more dread and anxiety—not because of what Inyotef did to me there, but because of what *I* had done. Because of the people *I* hurt. Not just those whose lives I ended, but those who lived on with a permanent void in their hearts.

My dread quadrupled when we crested the rise on the path leading to the palace and limestone walls came into view. The southwestern corner lay in ruins. My steps faltered at the sight, and I pressed my hands into my middle, like doing so might ease the knots tightening in my gut.

Atum continued for a few steps but stopped when he noticed I was no longer beside him. He turned toward me, concern softening his features.

"I didn't think it would be—" I gestured to the palace, my focus locked on the ruined corner. "I thought it would be fixed." I shook my head and clutched my hands together, compulsively rubbing the raised scars on the heel of my hand. "I know that doesn't make any sense. It's only been what—a month? And I thought they would have quarried stone and repaired the walls already? It's not like they don't have more important concerns, what with the mobilizing army and—"

"Tarset," Atum said, closing the distance between us. His large hands gripped my shoulders. "Can you do this?" There was genuine doubt in his worried stare. Did he fear I would lose control again and hurt more people?

I glanced down at my hands, double-checking to make sure there was no golden glow. I hadn't felt any welling power in my chest, which was usually the first sign that my soul was taking matters into its own hands, so to speak. But I felt more and more certain with each passing day that the only thing significant enough to push my *ba* or *sheut*—or whatever part of my soul it was that actually exploded—to rouse and take action was Atum.

I inhaled deeply, then blew the breath out and squared my shoulders. "I'm fine," I told Atum, forcing a practiced smile. "You don't need to worry about me." He had plenty else to worry about.

Atum shifted his hands toward my neck, and his thumbs traced lazy lines up and down the column of my throat. "If it becomes too difficult for you to be here—"

I raised my hands and curled my fingers around his wrists. "I'm fine," I repeated. "And if that changes, and I find myself *not so fine*, you'll just have to find some way to take my mind off my troubles." I smirked. "I'm sure you'll think of something."

Atum's serious expression remained despite my teasing. "You are too brave for your own good."

I coughed a laugh. "You do realize that I'm *literally* afraid of myself, right?"

"Bravery is not the absence of fear," Atum said. "But the fortitude to push onward *in spite* of fear. You chose life, my fallen star, despite everything you have been through. *That* is true bravery."

Tears welled in my eyes, and I sniffled and averted my gaze. "I don't feel brave," I said, my voice small.

"Neither do I," Atum admitted. He stepped backward and claimed my hand, pulling me into motion. "Neither do I."

37

MY HEART SANK INTO my stomach when a figure emerged from the front gates of the palace, his copper skin gleaming in the moonlight. Inyotef marched straight toward us, his expression thunderous.

I shrank back, angling myself behind Atum despite the logical part of my mind recalling Inyotef's death in vivid detail. Inyotef wasn't truly here; this was Atum's daughter, Tefnut, disguised as that despicable *dead* man.

Atum gripped my hand tighter, sensing my unease.

Another man followed Tefnut, larger and darker than her disguised appearance, his resemblance to Atum impossible to miss. I recognized him from my hazy memories following that fatal soul explosion here at the palace. This was Shu.

"By the gods," Tefnut said, wearing Inyotef's despised skin and speaking with his hated voice. "It took you long enough to return." She looked at me as she strode toward us, her sneer fitting all too well on Inyotef's face. Her cheek twitched when she glanced down at our joined hands. "Tarset," she said, both a greeting and a dismissal.

Atum gave my hand a squeeze before releasing it and stepping ahead to meet Tefnut first. "You will cease this childishness," he said, his voice low and threatening. "Or I will send you back to Rostau and deal with this dissonance without you."

Tefnut stopped dead in her tracks, her eyes opening wide and her lips parting. "You didn't." She looked past her father to me, her stare haunted.

Shu stopped a pace behind his sister, his curious gaze palpable as it roved over me.

"I did," Atum said, crossing his arms over his chest, which only broadened his shoulders and enhanced the weight of his presence.

Shu grinned broadly. "Congratulations, Father," he said, his voice deep and rich like Atum's. "May we all be so fortunate."

"Thank you, *Shu*," Atum said pointedly. He extended an arm back toward me, curving it around my waist when I stepped forward. "This is my bond-mate, Tarset."

Shu stepped forward as well, standing at his sister's side. "Delighted," he said, bowing his head. When he straightened, he added, "You bear a strong resemblance to your father."

"As do you," I noted. "So, you know my dad?"

"In another time, with another face," Shu said, gesturing to his incredibly handsome visage. "Not that he has any idea of who *I* really am." Mischief sparkled in his dark eyes. "Heru is a good man, though. A good leader and a reliable thread in the tapestry."

I nodded my agreement and reluctantly turned my attention to Tefnut, who still appeared dumbfounded by the news that Atum and I had bonded. "I want you to know that I considered everything you said very carefully," I told her, somewhat surprised by my incredible civility. "*But* as I stood in front of the portal . . ." My jaw worked, but no more words came out. I shook my head.

Tefnut studied me for a long moment, finally nodding her borrowed head once. "It is done." With that, her entire countenance changed, all hints of animosity vanishing.

She turned her attention back to Atum, leaving me with social whiplash. "We still have a few weeks until Nitocris reaches us, but her numbers grow with each passing day. Many of the refugees fleeing from the north have passed on troubling reports of forced conscription, and—" Tefnut hesitated, glancing my way. "Word of Inyotef's enslaved Nejeret has spread. A Nejeret retinue has joined forces with Nitocris."

"I saw," Atum bit out. "That's what convinced me to return."

My eyebrows rose. This was the first I was hearing of any Nejeret involvement.

"Yes, well . . ." Tefnut cleared her throat. "The ramifications of the conflict are causing the dissonance to grow exponentially, and I fear that waiting much longer to act will render correction impossible. Despite Nejeret involvement, Nitocris is still the linchpin of this invasion. If we remove her, the human forces will give up and return home. The Nejeret force is minor in comparison and will be relatively easy to deal with." Again, she looked pointedly at me. "Especially with her anomalous presence to loosen up their threads."

Atum drew in a deep breath, releasing it slowly. "What's your assessment of the situation?" he asked Shu.

Shu took his time in responding, giving me the impression he was far more cautious and conscientious than his opinionated sister. "At this point," he finally said, "removing Nitocris from the timeline early will cause far less damage than allowing her to continue to pursue this faulty course."

Atum nodded slowly. "I appreciate your input." He looked from Shu to Tefnut. "Both of you." His grip on my waist tightened, giving me the impression that he was far more bothered than his calm countenance suggested. "Give me the night to study the time tapestry," he said, sighing. "I'll decide the wayward queen's fate in the morning."

"As you say, Father," Shu said, while Tefnut nodded brusquely.

Tefnut stepped to the side, gesturing toward the palace gates beyond. "We have the tapestry queued up to the present situation in the nomarch's suite. I've been staying there, but the rooms are yours if you wish to reclaim the Inoytef identity." The way she said it gave me the impression she was *so over* being Inyotef. I couldn't blame her.

"If I must," Atum said, striding forward and releasing his hold on me. "So be it."

38

"A RE YOU IN LOVE with her?" I asked Atum as I watched him observe Nitocris on the time tapestry, dreading the answer but needing to know. To understand.

Did all corrections that required the taking of a life bother him so greatly? Or was this case unique? We had been in Inyotef's suite for hours, and Atum hadn't said a word. Not about Nitocris or the dissonance or the Nejerets who were now apparently involved. He just stared at the time tapestry patch and silently fretted. I probably should have asked about the Nejerets instead, but *this* was the question that stirred my soul.

He hadn't slept with her out of personal desire, but as a part of a bargain to convince her to leave Waset earlier—and to leave me behind—during her previous diplomatic visit. But there was always the chance that affection had developed anyway.

Atum tore his attention from the patch of the time tapestry on the wall in front of us to look at me, standing at his side. His gaze scoured my face, finally settling on my eyes, his expression baffled. "I'm in love with *you*."

I snorted a laugh. "I'm not naïve, Atum. The heart is fully capable of loving more than one person." I flashed him a sly grin, hoping to lighten the suffocating mood. "I, for one, once loved three people at the same time."

His eyes narrowed. "Emotionally, or physically?"

My grin widened. "Both," I said and turned my focus back to the time tapestry, though I could still feel Atum's gaze searing into the side of my face. Sure, I was his *now*, but it didn't hurt to remind him that he wasn't the only one with a past.

Within the time tapestry patch, Nitocris sat alone on a stool in her tent, her shoulders slumped and her head bowed. Atum had been switching between dozens of scenes relevant to this situation, some including various Nejerets—though none I recognized—but he always came back to this one of Nitocris, sad and alone. Why *this* scene?

"I respect her," Atum said, his own attention returning to the time tapestry. "She has a pure heart and a sound mind. In fact, she's one of the rare humans who refuses to bend to my influence. It's why I had to do what I did with her. Before Inyotef got his hands on her, she truly wanted what was best for this land and her people." Atum's jaw clenched, his hands fisting at his sides. "He has twisted her desires . . . warped her ambitions. I should have killed him when the dissonance in Waset first appeared, before you arrived."

I looked at Atum, studying his strong, dignified profile. "Can't you still do that?"

Atum shook his head. "My presence in Waset at that point in the timeline crystallizes that portion, closing it off to me completely." He glanced at me sideways. "A soul cannot exist in duplication. The overlapping matter would create a catastrophic paradox. It's why my father helped me to create Rostau to house the time tapestry in the first place—a realm apart, tethered to the timeline, but free of the flow of time."

I frowned, my mind spinning at the many significant implications of what he just shared. "What does that mean for my mom? If Rostau is free from the flow of time, will she continue to age? Or does everyone there live on indefinitely?"

The corner of his mouth tensed, rising minutely. It was the first hint of good humor I had seen on his face since we arrived at the palace. "So long as she is on Rostau, your mother will remain exactly as she is."

His words brought an unexpected relief. I hadn't considered I would get a relative eternity with my mom. After for so long believing I would never see her again, it was a dream come true.

Tears welled, and my chin trembled. I reached for Atum's hand, threading our fingers together. "Thank you," I said, my voice thick. "I can't tell you—" I sniffled and wiped under my eyes with my free hand. "And Kiya, too," I said, laughing so I wouldn't cry. "I know you didn't save them for me, but—" I shook my head, struggling to find the right words. "*Thank you.*"

Atum brought my hand up to his lips and pressed a gentle kiss to the back of my knuckles. "For you, anything."

The honesty in his statement struck me. He meant it. He really *would* do anything for me. Give me anything.

The least I could do was return the favor.

"**I**F YOU'RE SO CERTAIN that killing Nitocris is necessary to fix the dissonance, then why haven't you already done it?" I asked Tefnut and Shu as I approached them.

Atum remained in Inyotef's suite, staring at the time tapestry patch like he thought he could change the situation through sheer force of will alone, but I couldn't stand the stifling silence any longer. It hadn't taken me long to find Tefnut and Shu sitting together at the edge of the long, shallow pool in the courtyard Inyotef had favored, lush despite the decade-long drought ravaging the land.

Tefnut huffed out a breath as she watched me approach, once again wearing her own skin, though muted to appear human. "Because Father forbids lethal action on our part," she said. "He will not allow us to bloody our hands."

My eyes widened, but even though Tefnut's explanation came as a surprise, it made perfect sense. Of course Atum would try to protect them in this way. He had been forced into this life of ruthlessness and death by his father. He wasn't willing to do the same to his own children.

"What would he do if you disobeyed him?" I asked.

Tefnut let out a harsh bark of laughter. "Forbid us from assisting in further corrections," she said. "He would continue to police the timeline on his own." She eyed me and corrected her statement. "*The two of you* would be on your own."

I laughed under my breath and shook my head, expecting no less. I sighed, a plan forming in my mind. "I need to speak to Nitocris." I looked from Tefnut to Shu and back. "You can make spatial jumps?" I said, voicing my assumption. They were able to move about the land too quickly, just like Atum. It only made sense.

"You wish to *speak* with her?" Tefnut repeated back to me.

I gave Tefnut a look that said, *come on now, we're all grownups here.* Of course, I wasn't interested in a mere chat with Nitocris. I was offering to do what they couldn't. Atum wouldn't banish *me* over bloodied hands. He physically couldn't—his body was addicted to my bonding pheromones, and he had to keep me around to stay healthy.

"I see," Tefnut said. "My ability is limited in that regard," she admitted reluctantly and glanced at her brother. "But Shu is quite skilled." Tefnut and Shu shared a silent, secret conversation.

A moment later, Shu stood and brushed off his backside. "I can take you to see Nitocris."

"Good," I said with a nod. "Meet me here in an hour. I'd like to wash up and change." I flashed them a grim smile. "If I'm going to play emissary to a queen, I need to look the part."

39

SHU AND I EXPLODED back into reality in a shimmering cloud of iridescent mist. I had made spatial jumps enough times with Atum by now that the six Shu and I made in quick succession didn't leave me weak-kneed, though I was a little breathless.

We appeared atop a cliff overlooking the moonlit Nile Valley. I scanned the sprawling military camp set up just beyond the edge of the floodwaters in a wasted field. I had seen this scene on the time tapestry, but the size of Nitocris's force had far more impact when witnessed in person.

Unsettled, I turned to Shu. He stood tall, with the Eastern Desert spread out behind him. I frowned, surprised that teleporting seemed to be easier for him than it was for Atum.

"It doesn't exhaust you?" I asked Shu, my brows bunching together.

His handsome features, so like his father's, creased with confusion, but understanding quickly lit his eyes. "You have jumped only with my father," he said. "It is his weakest ability, of all his *sheut* powers." Shu smiled, looking a little ashamed. "Whereas it's my *only* power, aside from some trifling ability with illusion, but I can do little more than alter my appearance. Tefnut can't jump at all, but she has decent control over pulling At. Her real strength, however, is in illusion and mental coercion. It's why we usually work together."

"Oh," I said, taken aback. "I didn't realize." Since he literally *made* Tefnut and Shu from slivers of himself, I had assumed they all shared the same powers. "I'm sorry. I didn't mean to pry."

Shu offered me a lopsided grin. "Nothing to be sorry for," he said. He planted his hands on his hips, his focus shifting past me to the encampment in the valley below. "The queen's tent is the big one in the center of the camp." He looked at me again. "I'm going to jump you directly inside the tent, so we can avoid any prying Nejeret eyes."

Grim dread took root in my belly as I turned my back to him and once again gazed down at the encampment. "Is my dad down there?" I asked, hugging my middle. The universe couldn't afford for him to be caught up in all this.

"Not Heru, no," Shu said.

"But someone else important to me?" I asked, hearing what he *didn't* say.

"Aset is there," Shu said, his confirmation making the dread in my gut twist into knots. "And your grandfather."

"Osiris?" I asked, genuine fear in my voice. I didn't remember much about my grandfather beyond his formidable presence.

"I'm afraid so," Shu said.

"I am *definitely* in favor of avoiding him," I said, my pitch climbing higher.

"What are you going to say to Nitocris?" Shu asked from behind me. "Or will there even be any words?"

"There will be words." I turned my head slightly, glancing at Shu over my shoulder. "The queen owes me a debt. I'm here to collect."

"That must be some debt, if you think she'll agree to turn back her forces," he said.

I chewed on the inside of my cheek as I recalled the last conversation I had shared with Nitocris, the second time I found myself in a dungeon as Inyotef's prisoner. She hadn't offered to free me, but she had promised to end my pain if it ever became too much for me to bear. She had failed to fulfill that promise. While I was grateful to be alive *now*, she *had* broken her word.

"And if she attacks you?" Shu asked. "My father will not be pleased when he discovers I have brought you here, and he will repay me tenfold if I allow any harm to befall you."

I released a shaky laugh. "So long as I have breath to speak, Atum won't punish you. Not for this." I considered his question carefully, then exhaled heavily. "Do nothing to Nitocris," I finally said. "I'm more than capable of handling myself in a fight, *but* if you fear for my life, jump me away. *Do not* harm her, though. I won't have Atum accusing you of breaking your oath on my account."

"Understood," Shu said, bowing his head. He crossed his arms over his broad chest. "Let me know when you're ready."

I stared down at the encampment, watching the handful of soldiers in their white schenti kilts and woven leather cuirasses patrolling between the tents and around the perimeter. A cluster of larger tents along the eastern edge of the camp marked the Nejeret area. With any luck, none of them would even know I was there.

"I'm ready," I told Shu, not tearing my stare from the scene below. One way or another, by words or by blood, this misguided war was ending tonight.

40

S HU AND I BURST into Nitocris's tent in an explosion of iridescent mist.

The queen sat on the edge of her cot, looking exactly as she had appeared in the scene Atum had been watching endlessly on the time tapestry patch. Had he foreseen my interference or, considering I didn't appear on the time tapestry, *some* interference? Was that why he had been so drawn to this scene?

Nitocris slouched forward, her elbows planted on her thighs and her forehead resting in her open hands as she stared down at the woven reed mats lining the floor. Weariness wafted off her in waves. Watching her now, I suspected she didn't want war any more than we did. So why was she doing this?

"Nitocris," I said, stepping forward.

Her head snapped up, and her eyes opened wide. "Bek!" she exclaimed, using the name I had given Inyotef when I had been his captive. "How did you get free?" She shook her head in wonderment and stood, her wary gaze shifting past me to Shu, who followed behind me like a protective shadow.

I turned, holding a hand up to tell Shu to hang back, then continued forward to meet Nitocris.

She held out her hands to me, closing the distance between us. "I wondered if you still lived," she said, taking my hands in hers. Her gaze scoured my face, searching my eyes. "You look well." She smiled, disbelieving. "Far better than the last time I saw you." Her genuine joy at seeing me—alive and in good health—stunned me momentarily speechless. "What are you doing here?"

Regaining my wits, I squeezed her hands. "I needed to speak with you—urgently," I told her, locking gazes with her to make sure she heard what I was about to say. "I'm no longer Inyotef's prisoner because *he no longer lives.*"

Her jaw dropped, and her hands fell from mine. She took a step backward, stunned. "You killed him?" Nitocris asked, hope brightening her eyes.

"No," I told her, knowing she valued honesty above all things. "Someone else ended his life. A powerful Netjer-At, who now poses as Inyotef in Waset in an attempt to bring stability back to the region. So, you see—" I gestured toward the surrounding camp beyond the walls of her tent with a sweep of my hand. "This war isn't necessary. Inyotef won't move against you. He is *gone.*"

"I can't pull back," she said, looking sick to her stomach. She turned away from me, one arm across her middle, her other hand covering her mouth. "It's too late."

"What do you mean?" I asked, taking another small step toward her.

"They're already involved," she said, sounding wholly miserable. "And they won't let me stop."

"Who?" I asked, reaching for her arm. I turned her toward me. "The Nejerets?"

"I believe the mortal queen speaks of *me*," a deep male voice said from behind me.

I spun around to see a tall, distinguished copper-skinned Nejeret approaching Shu. He wore the same white linen kilt as all the other warriors in the camp, except gold embellishments lined his cuirass, and the pommels of his curved swords were gilded and bejeweled. It took my stunned brain long seconds to put a name to his distantly familiar face. This was Osiris, my grandfather.

Osiris moved blindingly fast, drawing and burying a long, gleaming iridescent blade into Shu's side before my companion could jump away.

"NO!" I exclaimed.

Osiris jerked the dagger sideways, then yanked it free. Shu clutched his middle, holding his insides *inside*, and took two stumbling steps toward me before his knees gave out.

I rushed toward Shu, reaching him as he dropped to his knees.

"Fetch Aset," Osiris ordered. "I'd rather this one didn't die."

PRESENT DAY

41

NIK

"LET'S GO AGAIN," KAT said between panting breaths as she raised her *At* Katana, Mercy, and widened her stance. The evening sun shone behind her, creeping ever closer to the desert horizon.

I held out a hand to stave her off as I worked to catch my breath. "Let's take a break," I told her. "I want to wait and see what my mom says about how your *ba* looks after using so much power."

Kat glowered at me, lowering her sword until the tip of the gleaming opalescent blade touched the sand. "Aset cleared me for exercise. She *told* me to use my powers."

I guffawed. "I was there, Kat," I reminded her. "She told you to *take it easy* and to *go slow*." I raised one eyebrow, then smirked, knowing the eyebrow trick would piss her off since she couldn't do it herself.

With a growl of frustration, Kat reached over her shoulder to sheath her sword on her back. Now that her hands were free, she planted her fists on her hips. "You're such an ass."

"Hmmm," I murmured and stalked toward her. "You know I can't resist you when you get all huffy."

She backed away even as she fought a smile.

I lurched forward and caught her, twisting her around so her back was to my front, and I wrapped my arms around her. Her sheathed sword poked into my upper thigh, and I pulled her closer, held her tighter, making the blunted blade dig in painfully. My body responded to the pain instantly, and I breathed her in, her intoxicating scent more potent after the exertion. I had to have her. Right here. Right now.

I shifted one hand up to her neck and slid the other down her taut abdomen until it dipped between her thighs.

Kat gasped as I worked her through her workout leggings, using the center seam to my advantage. "We're out in the open," she exclaimed even as she widened her stance and tilted her hips to give me easier access.

With a focused thought, I willed thick opaque *At* walls to form a circle around us, shielding us from any prying eyes back at the oasis. "Not anymore," I said, gripping her jaw and angling her face toward mine so I could steal a kiss.

I willed vines of *At* into existence and directed them to undress Kat while I continued to tease her between her legs. "Any other protests?"

She turned even as the vines removed her sneakers and yanked my T-shirt off over my head, then unbuckled my belt. "Let's go again," she said, a dangerous, promising gleam in her rich, brown eyes. She pushed my jeans down, and I toed off my shoes so I could step out of the pants completely.

Kat lifted one leg, then the other, as the vines removed her pants and underwear. She shrugged out of her sword harness herself but let the vines pull her shirt off over her head. Once she was fully, deliciously naked, she bent down and drew her sword, leaving the sheath and harness on the sand.

"Kat..."

"Just one more time, Nik," she said, twirling her sword. At her direction, more *At* and *anti-At* vines sprang up from the surrounding sand, weaving slowly like snakes preparing to strike. At me.

I groaned, resisting the urge to give in. Fuck, I wanted to, but she was still recovering, and she'd already drawn on her *sheut* more in this sparring session than she had the last few months combined.

"I think we should stop," I said, hating myself for uttering those cautious words even as I spoke them.

Kat grinned wickedly. "Make me," she said a moment before her vines struck.

NIK

I WATCHED KAT'S NIMBLE fingers as she shuffled her tarot cards. We sat on stools beside one another at one of the worktables in my mom's lab, waiting for her to come down and assess Kat's *ba*. My body was exhausted from the exertion in the desert. Even my *sheut* felt spent, and that was really saying something. My blood thrummed with echoes of the pleasure Kat had wrung from not just my body, but from my soul.

Kat's cheeks reddened, and she glanced at me out of the corner of her eye. "Get your mind out of the gutter."

I leaned in closer and repeated her words from earlier. "Make me."

She snorted her amusement and elbowed me in the gut. "I can't concentrate when you're so close."

"I know," I murmured. I loved that about her. Even so, I straightened, giving her some space. "Tarset again?" I asked, looking pointedly at the cards.

Kat nodded as she shuffled one last time, then flipped the top card.

The Eight of Swords, according to the label at the bottom of the card. It depicted a woman who was clearly Tarset, dressed in a white linen shift. She was shown gagged and bound to a post in the middle of an encampment filled with white tents, and she was surrounded by eight gleaming bronze swords that had been planted in the dry earth.

Holding her breath, Kat flipped the next card and set it down beside the first.

The Five of Swords. Tarset was featured on this card as well, again in a white dress, except this time instead of being imprisoned by swords, she held three while two more lay on the ground. Behind her, two men walked away, looking defeated. I was fairly certain the darker figure was Atum, based on Kat's description of him. The other wasn't so easily identifiable, but something about him was definitely familiar.

She flipped one more card, and the breath whooshed from her lungs. I stiffened when I saw who appeared on the Emperor card with Tarset.

My grandfather was easy enough to identify, even when the card was upside down. Now I knew who the other figure on the Five of Swords was. He had been gone for so long; I hadn't thought seeing a likeness of him would affect me any longer, but as I stared down at him sitting on his gilded throne, a shiver ran down my spine.

"That's Osiris," I said, my voice tight.

Kat looked at me curiously. "You didn't like him?" she asked, her brow furrowing. "I thought he was this amazing leader."

I blew out a laugh. "Heru is a good leader," I said. "He listens to his people and puts their needs first." I shook my head and clenched my jaw. "Osiris was—" I exhaled heavily. "I suppose you would call him an authoritarian, or possibly even a dictator. It was his way or the highway, and he viewed the people around him as tools, which he used—and punished—as he saw fit."

Kat frowned. "People . . . like Aset?"

I nodded, recalling how difficult it had been for me to conceal my gifts around him when he bullied and belittled my mom. She had been terrified of him discovering what I could do, knowing he would find some way to use me, just as he had always used her. If not for the fact that he was *her father*, I would have ripped his head off for the way he treated her. But she made me promise not to hurt him.

"So you really don't mind that he didn't get resurrected with the rest of our people," Kat commented.

"Fuck that guy," I said, shaking my head. I was more concerned with the dozens of others who had cropped up, reported missing by their loved ones. "It is weird, though."

Kat nodded thoughtfully. "Were you there when he died?"

I shook my head again. "My mom was, though," I told her, then forewarned, "but she doesn't like to talk about it."

"Hmmm..." Kat gathered her cards with a sweep of her hand and shuffled again. She laid out three cards in quick succession.

King of Swords, upside down. Again, Osiris was shown, sitting on his gilded throne, holding what appeared to be an *At* cuff bracelet on his open palm.

The Moon, also upside down. The scene depicted was strange, almost certainly laden with symbols and meaning I didn't understand. The full moon hung bloated in the sky and two women stood in profile, their faces angled up toward the moon—Tarset and my mom. A pool of blood filled the bottom edge of the scene, almost touching their bare feet.

The Nine of Swords. The scene on the card displayed my mom, perched on the edge of a bedroll, tears streaming down her cheeks. A dark-skinned man who I hadn't thought of in at least a thousand years lay in the bedroll, his eyes closed and his face relaxed.

"That's weird," Kat muttered. She pointed to the card on the left. "There should be a sword in the king's hand on this card, but instead he's holding, like, a bracelet or something—which makes me think it must be a weapon of some sort?" She pointed to the middle card. "And this one should include a scorpion or *something* crawling out of the pool."

I leaned forward, placing my forearms on the table, and studied the images. "But your cards change all the time."

"Yeah, but the symbols don't," Kat said, shaking her head. "Each card has symbols that are linked to that card's meaning. When the designs on my cards change, the symbols always remain." She fell quiet, studying the cards. "I was thinking about your mom and Osiris and his death when I pulled these cards, wondering what exactly happened." She planted her index finger on the middle card. "It's like the universe is telling me that pieces are missing." Kat looked at me.

I narrowed my eyes. "Missing from where?"

She tapped the depiction of my mom on the leftmost card. "From Aset's memory."

⁺ASET

"YOU LOOK BETTER," I told Kat, releasing the golden, glowing hand to let her incorporeal arm settle back into her physical body.

Kat held her hand up in front of her face and turned it back and forth, like she was trying to see what I could. "Even better than yesterday?" she asked, looking past her hand to me.

I smiled and nodded, folding my hands together on my lap.

"Can we do another, uh, *therapy* session?" Kat asked, her cheeks flushing pink.

"If you two are up for it." I glanced from Kat to Nik and back. "Why the rush?"

"She wants to talk to Isfet," Nik said, nodding toward Kat. "But to do that, she has to enter *Duat*, and Anapa warned her that reentering *Duat* when her *ba* is still healing could have dire consequences, so we agreed she would hold off until he gave her the all clear."

"Ah," I said, pursing my lips. I returned my attention to Kat, who had slumped beside Nik, clearly sulking. "Well, you're definitely still healing. I wouldn't bother Anapa to check your *ba* just yet. But I'm happy to head upstairs and get you settled for another *therapy* session to help speed things along."

Kat pressed her lips together like she was trying to hold something in.

Again, I looked from Kat to Nik and back. "Unless there's something else?"

"I wanted to ask you about Osiris," Kat blurted. "Specifically about his death," she added, looking slightly ill.

"Oh." I stiffened. "I—" I cleared my throat and straightened my shoulders. "I would prefer not to discuss my father."

"I know," Kat said. "And I'm sorry, but I think it's important." Her words continued in a rush. "I did a reading for Tarset, and Osiris showed up on the cards. Nik doesn't have the best things to say about him, and, well, I'm worried about her—again—and after finding her note, then realizing Osiris never resurrected . . . well, it just feels important." She shrugged. "I've learned to trust my gut when it comes to these feelings." She offered me a weak smile. "Do you think it's possible your memories of Osiris's death have been tampered with?"

"What?" The feet of my stool screeched as I stood. "No, of course not," I said, crossing my arms over my chest. "How dare you suggest such a thing!"

Both Kat and Nik watched me with eyes widened in surprise. Belatedly, I understood their reaction. Mainly because *my* reaction had been so extreme. Possibly because someone had inserted something into my mind, some sort of failsafe to prevent me from examining that specific memory too closely.

Taking a deep breath, I relaxed my arms and eased back down to sit on the stool. "I'm sorry," I said with forced calm, though my heart still raced. "That was uncalled for. I'm not sure why that upset me so much." I focused on Nik. "Can you tell if a memory has been altered?" I asked him. He had some minor skill in that area, after all.

"Yeah, of course," he said, standing. He walked around the corner of the worktable and stood behind me, touching the fingertips of both hands to my temples. "Close your eyes and draw that memory to the forefront of your mind."

I squeezed my eyes shut and recalled that ancient time. I pictured the flooded Nile valley. I pictured a war encampment and my father marching toward me, a thundercloud of authority, his hand raised to strike me down with a sword, and I saw another step in front of me. A man whose name had taken up residence in my heart thousands of years ago: Shu. In my mind's eye, I watched Shu gut my father to prevent him from killing me. I recalled watching the funeral pyre as my father's body burned.

Nik pulled his fingers away, and only then did I realize my cheeks were wet with tears. I sniffled and wiped them away with both hands, but oddly enough, I didn't think the tears were for my father. They were tied to Shu and the bittersweet ending to our relationship.

"There's no other sensory information—just what you saw and heard," Nik said, returning to his stool. "A true memory would have included smell, at least. The stink of punctured viscera, the scent of smoke from the fire." He leaned forward, planting his elbows on the table and lacing his fingers together. "I don't know how Osiris died, but that wasn't it. Someone planted that memory in your mind."

"And the rest of my memories of Shu?" I asked, afraid of the answer.

"No," Nik said, shaking his head. "I remember him, and memory tricks don't work on me. Shu was real, and he definitely loved you."

I sniffled again and pulled a tissue from the pocket of my lab coat to wipe under my nose. "Well, that's something, at least." I took a deep, steadying breath. "Can you remove the false memory?"

Nik shook his head. "Not without messing up the surrounding memories," he said. "It's woven into the surrounding events too seamlessly. I would end up damaging part of your mind." He shrugged one shoulder. "The only person who can remove it is the one who put it there in the first place." He fell quiet, but I could see on his face that he had more to say.

"What are you thinking?" I asked.

"Shu had a *sheut*," he ventured. "We know that now, even if we didn't know it then. It's possible he was capable of—"

"No," I said, punctuating that single word with an adamant shake of my head. "I may not have known exactly who he was, but he wouldn't have violated me like that." My chin trembled, and my nostrils flared. "He *wouldn't* have."

Nik's stare remained unwavering. "Then maybe his father. If Atum planted that memory in your mind, that would explain why I can't break through it."

"So it all leads back to Atum," Kat said sullenly. "Just like everything else."

Nik crossed his arms over his chest. "All the more reason we should figure out what's going on with that island."

44

⁺ASET

"OH!" I SAID, STALLING in the doorway to the lab after setting up Nik and Kat upstairs. A man stood near the counters on one side of the room, squinting as he held up a slide to read the label written in Neffe's tiny, precise handwriting. "Hello."

The Nejeret turned to face me, a bright smile on his handsome face. "You must be Aset," he said, not a question. He strode toward me and thrust out his hand. "I'm Dorman, an old friend of your brother's."

I stepped into the lab and placed my hand in his. "I've heard a lot about you," I told him, though I was more familiar with his long and complicated history with my brother from watching on the periphery than from anything Heru had told me about him. After a firm shake, he released my hand. "What are you doing here?"

"Neffe sent me here," he said. "I'm visiting from the Olympic safe haven, and I'm interested in assisting with your research."

My eyebrows rose. "Do you have experience in a lab or working on a research team?" I asked.

"Ah, no." His disarming smile returned, dimples and all, and he averted his gaze to the floor. His charming, awe-shucks demeanor quickly put me at ease. "I'd like to volunteer as a subject."

"Oh!" I laughed under my breath. "Sorry, I misunderstood." I glanced around the empty lab. "Wishful thinking, I suppose."

Dorman looked around as well. "Do you need a hand in the lab?" he asked. "I'm happy to offer myself up as a grunt. I'm a fast learner, and this is important work."

"Maybe," I said, smiling. "We have many helpers filter through, but most are in a hurry to return to their loved ones. It seems the sense of immortality so many wore like a second skin for so long has faded, and there's a general joie de vivre that interferes with most Nejerets' willingness to commit to the team long term."

"Ah yes," Dorman said, nodding slowly. "I've noticed this as well. Inopportune for you, but it is nice to see our people finally learning to seize the day."

I nodded along with him and felt like I was grinning like a fool, but there was just something about Dorman that made me smile. "It is nice, isn't it?" I gestured to my preferred worktable, where my closed notebook, pen, and a folder filled with data awaited me. "Sit, please," I told him. "Tell me about your explosive episodes."

"That's just it," he said, his expression serious for once. "I've felt the stirring, but I've been able to avoid actually exploding."

My eyes widened. "Truly?" I shook my head, fighting disbelief. "All of my subjects have detonated at least once. I'd love to examine your *ba*."

"Offer to buy a guy dinner first," he teased.

I laughed. "Sorry, that was a bit forward coming from a relative stranger," I admitted. Most of the people I had examined out of body so far were family or close friends. "Let me start over," I said. "I'm able to pull Nejeret souls from their physical bodies, and we've started a new phase of experiments that draws on this ability."

"Intriguing," Dorman drawled.

"We're testing the capabilities of disembodied Nejeret souls," I told him. "And since you seem to have a heretofore unseen amount of control over your soul's volatility, I would very much appreciate the chance to examine your *ba*."

"Well, when you put it like that," Dorman said. "How could I refuse?"

45

NIK

K AT AND I STOPPED in the doorway to the lab and exchanged a look when we noticed the compact Nejeret man organizing paperwork into files spread out across several worktables.

Kat's brow furrowed. "Is that *Dorman*?"

I nodded. "Hey, man," I said, striding forward. "How the hell are you?" I extended a hand toward him.

Dorman turned and slapped his palm against mine. The faintest tingle danced over my skin, confirming my suspicions from the last time we met that Dorman had a secret *sheut*. "Nice to see you again, Nik," he said and looked past me. "Kat."

I released his hand and glanced over my shoulder to see Kat nod a greeting before meandering over to my mom's worktable for her post-*therapy* assessment.

"What are you doing here?" I asked Dorman. "Get bored of the rain?"

"Never!" he laughed, though his expression quickly sobered. "Neffe called the other day, asking about Nejerets who were missing after the big resurrection." He glanced at Kat, the one responsible for bringing us all back to life. "I asked around and gave her a few names, but then she mentioned this new phase of your mom's research, and I was intrigued."

"The out-of-body trials?" I said.

Dorman nodded a confirmation. "I was just helping with some filing while we waited for a bed to free up upstairs." He eyed me, then Kat, who now sat with my mom, her golden forearm once again separated from her body. "You two were just incorporeal?"

I nodded. "Kat's *ba* was damaged during the battle," I told him.

"I heard," he said.

I sniffed bitterly, not surprised he had heard about Kat's injuries when so many of our people had pinned their hopes on her to fix our broken world and repair relations with the now hostile humans. "Yeah, well, going incorporeal together has been helping her heal," I said. "She's been champing at the bit to get out there and help. Pretty soon, she might be able to do some real good again."

"I don't doubt it," Dorman said, again eyeing Kat. "She is one formidable Nejeret."

I nodded my agreement. "You have no idea."

My mom stood and started toward us, and Kat followed. "Are you ready, Dorman?"

"As I'll ever be," he said and caught my eye again. "See you around, Nik." He nodded to Kat. "Glad to hear you're on the mend."

"Thanks," she said, her smile genuine. She came to stand beside me, and we watched my mom leave the lab with Dorman. "Still think he has a *sheut*?" she asked once they were out of sight, her voice pitched low, for my ears alone.

"Abso-fucking-lutely."

ANCIENT TIMES

TARSET

46

"Y OU'RE MAKING A MISTAKE," I told Osiris as I struggled against my bindings.

I sat on the floor of Nitocris's tent, my bound wrists tied behind my back to one of the sturdy tent posts and my ankles tied together. I split my attention between Shu, who lay bleeding and unconscious on Nitocris's cot while we waited for Nitocris to fetch Aset to tend to his wounds, and Osiris, standing sentry with his back to me in the tent doorway, one arm extended to hold the tent flap open.

"You don't want to do this," I proclaimed, grasping for anything that might sway him. "You don't understand. I'm not the enemy. I'm your—" I caught myself before admitting to Osiris that I was his granddaughter. The same granddaughter he had to have heard had died some twenty years ago. Here was a brand-new way I could screw up the timeline.

Osiris turned toward me, his expression curious. He let the tent flap fall back to cover the opening. "I am the son of the Great Father," he said, approaching sedately. He clasped his hands behind his back. "Every

Nejeret is my *something*." He glanced at Shu. "He is my nephew, the son of Atum, as you are most certainly aware." Osiris's attention returned to me. "But I'm more interested in *your* relation to Atum. You are his . . ." Osiris crouched and narrowed his eyes, studying me. "Consort? Does he love you?"

"He will rip you to pieces if you harm me," I snarled.

"I have no doubt he would kill for you. That's part of the problem," Osiris said. "But would he *die* for you?"

My mouth opened and closed as I floundered for words. "I would never let him."

Warmth swelled in my chest, my soul rousing at the threat posed by Osiris. I reminded myself that Atum wasn't here. Osiris couldn't hurt him. For the time being, he was safe.

I glanced at Shu, grateful as the stirring power calmed, settling down but not going completely dormant. If I detonated here in this tent, everyone within would be destroyed.

I took a deep breath, hoping it would calm and steady me. "If you touch Atum," I told Osiris. "If you so much as mention his name in a way that I don't like, *I* will tear you to shreds."

"Ah," Osiris said, flashing me a brief, close-mouthed smile. "Bond-mate, then?" he asked, raising his eyebrows. He was incredibly perceptive, which was probably the quality that had made him the leader of our people instead of one of Nuin's many, *many* other children. Osiris held his forearm up, studying the goose bumps pebbling his skin. "And you have a *sheut*." He lowered his arm, his eyes locking on mine once more. "No doubt you make a powerful ally for my brother."

I pressed my lips together, annoyed with myself for giving so much away, however unintentionally.

"What powers does your *sheut* afford you?" Osiris wondered aloud.

"You don't want to find out," I ground out.

He frowned, considering my warning. "I don't doubt that," he said, standing.

Motion at the tent flap drew our attention that way as Aset strode into the tent. She stopped just inside the threshold and surveyed the scene, skimming over Osiris and me until she found Shu, her patient, bleeding out on the cot.

"Aset!" I blurted before I could stop myself.

Her attention returned to me, and she studied me more closely, though no recognition lit her stare. Atum or Tefnut must have concealed her memory of our recent encounter in Men-nefer and of her help in healing Atum.

"Daughter," Osiris said. "Do you know this woman?"

Aset gave a delicate shake of her head. "No," she said, her brow remaining furrowed. "I can't say that I do."

My shoulders slumped, protestations dying on my tongue. What good would it do to claim a shared history she couldn't remember? I feared it would only push her further away from helping me.

Osiris looked from Aset to me and back. "Well, she certainly seems to know you," he noted. "Perhaps you just don't recall your encounter. I know my brother is capable of twisting memories and warping minds." His focus dropped to the pendant dangling from a gold chain around her neck. Even I could see the winged scarab stamped into the quarter-sized disk of At.

Aset swallowed roughly. I wondered if Atum hadn't completely removed the memory of her saving him.

Osiris's gaze flicked to Shu's unconscious form. "We will discuss it later," he said ominously. "Tend to him, but ensure he remains unconscious. He's *slippery*."

Aset bowed her head, displaying a meek side I had never witnessed from her, and hurried across the tent to the cot.

I studied Osiris, hiding my scrutiny behind an easy glare. His smug expression and haughty attitude made him all too easy to dislike.

I didn't recall much about my grandfather from my childhood—nothing beyond a memory of his grand appearance and a vague sense of equal parts awe and terror—and my dad hadn't spoken of him much by the time I was revived thousands of years in the future. By then, Osiris was little more than a distant memory for all Nejerets, including his own offspring, and I couldn't help but think that was a good thing. Aset, for one, had certainly blossomed when she emerged from her father's shadow. I wondered if it had been the same for my dad.

The more I considered what little I knew about Osiris's life—and death—the more certain I was that his death happened within the current era. That realization soothed me, reinforcing my spine with something stronger than steel. With *At*.

My lips curved into a cruel smile. "This won't end well for you, Osiris," I vowed. Because I knew. Whether it was the coming confrontation with Atum or something shortly after, he wasn't long for this world.

Something in my tone gave him pause. He seemed to reassess me, like he sensed I wasn't making an empty threat, but a prophetic promise.

Osiris retrieved a small wooden stool that was tucked against the wall of the tent and carried it closer to me. He sat, draping the loose fabric of his kilt between his legs, and leaned forward, resting his forearms on his thighs. His eyes met mine, the irises like molten liquid gold.

"I'd like to tell you a story," he said, then paused, like he was waiting for my acceptance of his offer.

"I'm not really in the mood for stories," I said, raising my chin and looking toward the bed. Aset was bent over Shu, meticulously cleaning his abdominal wound.

"Indulge me," Osiris said.

I glared at him out of the corner of my eye. "I can't stop you."

"Such fire," he said, chuckling. "If I didn't keep such close tabs on my offspring, I'd guess you were one of my own children."

I looked at him dead on, struck by a sudden idea. "I'm your grand-daughter," I said. "My mother hid me from you." I eyed him, my gaze traveling down to his sandals and back up to his face, my lip curling in distaste. "For obvious reasons."

He sighed and shook his head. "Impossible. But a commendable effort." He rubbed his hands together and inhaled deeply. "Where to begin . . ." His brow furrowed and his stare grew distant.

I rested my head back against the wooden post behind me.

"There once was a pair of boys—brothers—the younger born, the older made," he began, and despite my dislike of Osiris, I listened. Because this story was clearly about Atum, a boy who had been *made*. "The younger boy was one of their father's countless children, while the older boy—their father's first child—was absolutely unique. He stood out in the father's eyes, earning the father's attention and love far beyond what his other children received, while the younger boy learned early on that the father had no room left in his heart for him. So, the younger boy instead set his sights on his eldest brother, aiming to earn *his* love in place of the father's."

Though I tried to harden my heart against Osiris, I could already feel his tale of a neglected child softening me up.

"The younger boy idolized his eldest brother, following him everywhere, assisting in the tasks assigned by the father," Osiris went on. "And the eldest brother opened his heart to the younger boy, confessing his fears about the future and his reluctance to fulfill the duty their father had already assigned to him. The eldest brother loved the younger like he was his own child."

Aset stood and quietly made her way to Osiris's side, waiting until Osiris finished speaking and we both looked up at her.

"Will he live?" Osiris asked, sounding curious if not *too* concerned.

"Most likely," she said. "I've cleaned and stitched the wound. He's in a regenerative sleep now, but I must make a draught to keep his mind muddled when he wakes." Her eyes met mine but quickly darted away. "I'll return in a few hours to check on him," she said, and when Osiris nodded, she strode away.

I watched her depart, wishing desperately that I could follow.

"Where was I?" Osiris mused, drawing my attention back to him. He pursed his lips in thought. "Ah, yes—the eldest loved the younger brother. He taught the boy all he knew, and for many years, they were inseparable."

Sensing a *but* coming, I held my breath.

"Until, one day, the eldest emerged from a private lesson with their father in a foul mood," Osiris said. "He raged quietly in private until the younger boy worked up the nerve to check on him, and the eldest confessed that it was time for him to leave to fulfill his duty to their father." Osiris's voice thickened with dredged up emotions. "The younger boy wanted to accompany his brother, but the eldest warned him not to follow—to *never* seek him out. And then, much to the younger boy's horror, the eldest swore he would kill the boy if he ever saw him again."

I shook my head, tears welling in my eyes.

Osiris flashed a self-pitying smile. "I'm sure you've surmised that I was the younger of the boys, and that your bond-mate was the eldest."

DARKNESS BETWEEN THE STARS   279

"He wouldn't—" I cleared my throat, steadying my voice. "I don't believe it. Atum would never be so cruel."

Osiris let out a hollow laugh. "Since the day he left, I have followed every lead—every whisper. This is the closest I have come to seeing my brother in thousands of years. It has been so long that I've lost count."

Again, I shook my head. "Why do you want to find him? Do you *want* to die?"

"On the contrary," Osiris said. "I want to live. But shortly after Atum departed that last time, my father finally took notice of me. Since I had been so close with Atum, I knew better than anyone else what Atum could do." His lips curved into a tight-lipped smile. "My father taught me how to defeat Atum, and he made me promise to keep my brother's powers in check." Osiris fell quiet, studying me. "He's been neglecting the timeline. Of course, now that I'm aware of your relationship, I suspect I know why."

I shook my head. "He's sacrificed so much," I said. "Can't you let him have this one thing?"

Osiris sighed. "The pattern has grown too unstable as of late," he said. "Proof of Atum's neglect." Osiris exhaled heavily, seeming to deflate as the breath left his body until he appeared incredibly weary. "Unfortunately, he is no longer a trustworthy guardian of the timeline, and it is time for *me* to step in and fulfill *my* duty to our father." He turned his head, glancing at Shu. "There are others who can take his place. The timeline will be better off in the end."

"What do you mean?" I asked, my words hushed. "Speak plainly."

Osiris hung his head. "I have to kill my brother before *he* destroys everything and everyone."

Dread took root in my gut. "Why are you telling me this?" I asked, a slight tremor in my voice.

Osiris raised his head just enough that he could look at me. "You already know the answer to that."

I gulped, swallowing my rising fear. "You want to kill him—" I drew in a shuddering breath—"through me." Because of our bond, if I died, Atum would soon follow.

"I want you to know that it's not personal," Osiris said. "I bear you no ill will. It is merely a matter of what must be."

I shook my head, desperation rising within me. "But it *is* personal," I blurted. "I truly *am* your granddaughter."

47

OSIRIS SCOFFED. "THAT IS not possible," he said dismissively. "I keep a close watch over all of my descendants."

"My name is Tarset," I told him. "You probably remember me as a little girl who died twenty years ago, the same day as Nuin." I raised my chin defiantly. "Except *I* didn't die." With that last word, I held my breath.

The amused disbelief faded from Osiris's expression, and he stared at me for a long moment, his gaze roving over my features. Slowly, he narrowed his eyes. "Explain," he said, sitting up straighter on the stool. "I'm not saying I believe you, but I'm listening."

I relaxed a little. At least I had bought myself some time. He wouldn't kill me—yet. I wagered that so long as my tale intrigued him, I would stay alive.

I inhaled deeply, preparing to share my story with him. "On the day that Nuin died," I started, "I was playing in the oasis with my siblings." I knew Lex had altered everyone's memories of what actually happened that day, erasing herself from their minds as best she could. "There was no illness," I revealed. Lex had made everyone who was present in the oasis believe that I, along with the dozens of others who perished that day, died from a lethal illness—a pure fabrication, of course. "It was poison in the water. Poison that would have killed me if I hadn't been transformed into *At*."

Osiris hissed in a breath. "My brother—"

I shook my head. "Not Atum." A small smile touched my lips. "I was saved by someone even more powerful than your brother," I told him. "Her name is Lex, and she carried Nuin's power within her."

"She stole it from him," Osiris accused.

I shook my head. "Nuin gave it to her—for safekeeping," I corrected him. "And she didn't just save my life. She saved yours, as well." My smile broadened. "She saved the entire universe, and you didn't even notice." I tilted my head to the side. "Or did you?"

Osiris's brow furrowed. "Perhaps I noticed something was off. The story everyone shared was too similar." He shook his head minutely. "Too rehearsed."

"Should I keep going?" I lifted my chin, baring my neck to him. "Or would you rather get this over with and slit my throat now?"

Osiris leaned forward again. "Continue."

"**H**ERU HAS A BOND-MATE," Osiris said, a disbelieving smile on his face as he shook his head. "I never thought I would live to see the day."

I raised my eyebrows and pressed my lips together, forcing a smile instead of telling him he *wouldn't* live to see the day but was long dead by the time Heru and Lex finally bonded.

Osiris's gaze sharpened. "I don't, do I?" he guessed. "I don't live to see the day." Not a question, but an observation.

"I suppose that's up to you," I told him. "Change course." A plea entered my voice. "Give up this vendetta against your brother. Even if you kill me now, the bonding withdrawals won't reach a lethal level for days, possibly weeks."

I recalled Atum's savage vengeance when he witnessed what Inyotef had intended to do to me in the courtyard of the royal palace in Men-ne-fer, and I knew that his reaction to discovering his own brother had killed me would be exponentially more brutal.

"You cannot run away fast enough. He will catch you, and he *will* destroy you," I said, pausing to let those words sink in. "Kill me, and you will ensure your own death. It is a self-fulfilling prophecy. His warning drove you down a path of fear and hatred, and your father capitalized on that. Can't you see that?"

Osiris chuckled and shook his head. "My brother is powerful, but I am not as helpless as you think," he said. "Nor as blind. I have had thousands of years to consider his warning. But whether cruelty or prophecy fueled his words, I cannot turn a blind eye to the threat he now poses to the timeline." Osiris sat up straighter on the stool and clapped his hands to-gether. "But you are correct about one thing. I cannot—I *will* not—kill you, granddaughter. I bear you no ill will."

It was the first time he acknowledged our relationship, and I felt some of the tension ease from my muscles. Perhaps there was hope yet. I wanted to point out that if he killed Atum, he would end my life as well, by way of the bonding withdrawals, but I didn't want to push him and lose all the progress we had made. Atum and I weren't out of the woods yet, but I had bought us some time to find our way.

"And this future that is beyond the reach of the time tapestry," Osiris said, his expression troubled. "My line continues with you, obviously, but what of Heru and Aset and my other children? Do they survive this great battle with the godlike Netjers?"

I nodded. "I'm not sure how it all played out, but so far as I know, everyone is alive." Considering what Kat had said about the destruction of *Aaru* and resurrection of all the Nejerets when I saw her in *Duat*, I supposed there was a chance that Osiris himself once again walked the earth.

"Even my father?" Osiris asked.

I shrugged, uncertain. "I think so," I said, figuring Nuin—or Re, Nuin's true Netjer name—technically counted among *everyone*.

Osiris's features relaxed, and a curious smile curved his lips. His eyes lit up with an idea. "Perhaps we all come back in this strange and mysterious future you describe," he said. "What happens here and now need not be a true ending for any of us, but merely a pause."

Belatedly, I realized the mistake I had just made—unintentionally offering him absolution. He intended to go through with his ill-fated plan to kill Atum, likely by killing me first. I closed my eyes and bowed my head. He was a fanatic, a zealot, and attempting to reason with him was as fruitful as banging my head against a wall of *At*. Considering the headache throbbing at the base of my skull, I thought arguing with Osiris was *exactly* like banging my head against a wall.

"It doesn't have to be like this," I said softly. "You are not his enemy."

Osiris's voice was gentle when he responded. "But he is mine."

I USED TO SNOWBOARD, much to my dad's chagrin. Before I manifested and my regenerative Nejeret traits became active, he was always
reminding me of my fragile mortal body. *After* I manifested, he was like
a broken record stating that Nejerets weren't truly immortal, merely
long-lived and hard to kill.

I wasn't sure if I would ever hit the slopes again. It wasn't that I
couldn't—snowboarding existed in the final decades contained within
the boundaries of Atum's timeline—and even in earlier eras, I supposed
I could always ask Atum to create a snowboard out of *At*. But I didn't
really *want* to snowboard. Looking back, I became fairly certain that my
dad's disapproval was a big part of what made it so appealing.

At the moment, looking into the face of my grandfather—the man
who intended to kill me, however indirectly—I wished I could take back
every rebellious act from my past, including every miserable trip to a ski
resort.

There were many things I disliked about snowboarding, like the feeling of being out of control and the height of the chairlifts. I didn't like the cold, which was kind of a requirement for snow sports. And I didn't like the fuzzy feeling in the air on the runs that crossed under high-voltage power lines.

That was what it felt like when Atum arrived.

Static charged the air, making the tiny hairs on my arms and the back of my neck stand on end, and a faint hum touched my ears. I sat up as straight as I could with my ankles bound and my wrists tied together around the post at my back.

Osiris glanced at me from the front of the tent, where he had been posted the past thirty minutes, periodically peering out through the door flap. "You feel that, too?" he asked me.

I nodded. "He's here."

"Well, then." Osiris strode across the tent, heading straight for me. "It's time," he said as he withdrew a small, stoppered copper vial from a hidden pocket in his kilt and pulled out the tiny cork. "Open up," he ordered, crouching before me.

Eyeing the vial dubiously, I pressed my lips together as firmly as I could and turned my face away from him.

"Don't be so tiresome," Osiris grumbled, gripping my jaw tightly enough that tears welled in my eyes, then squeezing even harder.

I held out for as long as I could, but even after all the torture I had endured, I hadn't grown immune to pain. I whimpered, cracking my jaw open to relieve the agonizing pressure. Osiris capitalized on my moment of weakness by dumping the contents of the vial into my barely open mouth, then forcing my jaw shut and sealing his palm over my lips.

The liquid was foul tasting, and I pushed what I could out through my compressed lips and resolved to hold the rest in my mouth until Atum arrived and Osiris found himself otherwise occupied.

"You're actually helping me by resisting," Osiris said. "The toxin enters the bloodstream much faster when held in the mouth than when swallowed."

I searched his eyes but found no hint of deception. Despite his twisted logic, Osiris had only ever been honest with me. Trusting my gut, I gulped down the horrid liquid.

"What was that?" I asked, gasping for air when he finally removed his hand.

Osiris held the empty vial pinched between his thumb and forefinger. "A curious poison Aset developed for me," he said, eyeing the vial. "There *is* an antidote, but again, Aset created it, so it is not something Atum could find elsewhere." He flashed me a devilish smile. "Don't worry, though. I have a dose hidden nearby. Assuming Atum is amenable and values your life more than his own..."

I ground my teeth together. "Your plan is flawed," I gritted out. "You'll still be killing me when you take Atum's life. It won't matter to him that I'll get to live for another week or two." My volume increased as I grew more frantic. "The moment you kill him, my fate is sealed. He *won't* go for it." My chest heaved with each breath, and tears welled in my eyes. "Please, Grandfather," I pleaded, "you don't have to do this."

But my words fell on deaf ears. His stare remained bright with anticipation, and a small, secretive smile curved his lips. He had been on this path for too long. It was a part of him. He couldn't turn back now.

"If he hurt her . . ." Atum's words floated into the tent from outside, little more than a harsh growl.

"She's fine, I swear," Nitocris said in a rush.

My attention snapped to the tent flap. I could hear Atum's footsteps drawing closer, and my heart beat faster.

"Tell him about the poison," Osiris urged, standing. "If he kills me, there will be no antidote, and both of you *will* die."

"It won't matter!" I exclaimed, exasperated.

Osiris reached for me, wrapping his fingers around my arm, and hoisted me up to my feet. "Tell him," he hissed, drawing a dagger from a sheath at his belt and pressing the blade to my throat. "Or I will end this, and none of us will survive."

Jaw clenched, I glare into Osiris's manic stare. The sharp edge of the dagger bit into my skin when I swallowed. "Fine," I spat. "Remove your knife from my throat."

His eyes narrowed, but a moment later, he lowered the dagger.

I cleared my throat, then drew in a deep breath. "I'm in here," I called out to Atum, raising my voice. "And I'm fine. Don't hurt Osiris."

Atum pushed through the tent flap, Nitocris and Tefnut following close behind him. Tefnut shoved Nitocris forward, and the queen stumbled, sprawling on her hands and knees on the overlapping woven reed mats that made up the floor of the tent. She didn't bother getting up, merely knelt with her head bowed, her shoulders shaking.

"I'm sorry," Nitocris whimpered softly. "I didn't want this. I didn't—" Her words died in quiet sobs.

Atum scanned me, his stare lingering on the stinging cut on my neck. A moment later, *At* vines burst from the ground, exploding through the reed mats. They wound around Osiris's legs, quickly working their way up his body until his arms were bound against his sides and only his head was free to move.

"*Why*, little brother?" Atum said, his raw emotions turning his voice ragged. He glanced at me, agony in his stare. "Why would you do this?"

Osiris pushed his shoulders back and held his head high. "Because I can no longer live with your threat looming over me," he said, as calm and dignified as one could be while bound in otherworldly restraints. "Every day of my life has been overshadowed by fear, and I cannot live like this anymore. I cannot wake even one more time, wondering if I'll live to see sunset."

"That is life!" Atum boomed. "Death is inevitable for all of us. You cannot outrun it. You cannot hide from it. Death comes for all of us."

"Even you, Temu?" Osiris asked, shocking me by speaking the name Atum had used when disguised as a human in Inyotef's court. I had thought of *Temu* as something akin to a stage name; I hadn't realized it had a deeper meaning for Atum.

Atum raised one hand and reached for me, resting his palm on my cheek. "Especially me," he said.

I felt a tug on the rope twisted around my wrists and craned my neck to see that Tefnut was behind me, slicing through the bindings with an *At* knife. Atum crouched and cut through the rope tied around my ankles.

"I should kill you now and be done with it," Atum told Osiris, standing.

Out of the corner of my eye, I watched Tefnut hurry to her brother's bedside as I rubbed my sore wrists. "You can't kill him," I told Atum, glaring daggers at my grandfather. "He poisoned me."

Atum's body tensed, his neck tendons standing out as he drew in a breath to speak.

"There's an antidote," I blurted before he could say anything.

Osiris turned his attention back to Atum. "Which I will gladly administer the moment *your* heart has stopped beating." Out of the hidden pocket in his schenti, Osiris managed to pull a hinged wrist cuff that appeared to be made of At, except ribbons of glowing crimson cut through the opalescent material. He displayed it in his open hand. "And put this on. We can't have you changing your mind at the last moment and lashing out with your powers, now can we?"

Atum eyed the cuff dubiously. "Father made that?"

"He did," Osiris said with a dip of his chin. "He came to me shortly after you left and gave it to me. He said it was the only thing that could suppress your powers, should you grow lax in your duties and need to be *retired*." Osiris glanced at the cot, where Tefnut knelt, gripping her brother's hand and watching us, mute horror warping her beautiful features. "Your children are more than capable of carrying the mantle. Be comforted by the knowledge that you trained them well, and that the timeline will be safe in their hands."

Osiris looked at me, his gaze filled with pity. "Safer, I dare say, than it would be in your hands, now that you're so distracted by your bond-mate."

Atum closed his eyes, and a tear snuck free, streaking down his dark, chiseled cheek. "Why are you forcing this?"

"For the greater good! It is what *must be*!" Osiris shouted, coming momentarily unhinged. "I *loved* you, Temu. You were the father Nuin could never be, and when you swore to kill me—" He shook his head, seeming to regather his composure. "You practically groomed me for this role yourself when you told me to stay away from you, threatened to kill me, then abandoned me."

"I was trying to save your life," Atum said, his voice low and even. "That day—" He paused, breathing in deeply. "Father showed me a scene on the time tapestry. I saw myself ending your life, and I couldn't bear confessing to you what I had seen—" Again, Atum paused, caught up in the old emotions. "I was trying to spare your feelings, little brother. The truth was too awful—"

"What truth?" Osiris snapped.

"Father wanted me to kill you," Atum confessed. "Our threads were too entangled, and you were destined to cause my death, regardless of how the pattern changed—and in doing so, you would doom the time-line Father was grooming me to protect." Atum inhaled shakily. "Father only agreed to let you live if I made sure our paths would never cross again."

Osiris stared at his older brother, sagging in his unyielding restraints. "Father told me none of this," he said. "You could be making it all up. You would say anything to save your bond-mate."

Atum sighed, and his shoulders slumped. "Give Tarset the antidote," he said. "Please, little brother."

Osiris's expression seemed torn, but after a long moment, he shook his head. "Only after you block the bond," he said, straightening. "She is innocent in all of this. She need not suffer merely because fate has twisted our threads so unfairly."

"What?" I blurted, looking from Osiris to Atum. "What does he mean—block the bond?" My brows bunched together. I knew Lex had done something similar to my dad during her vast leaps through time, but I had never considered that Atum might be able to do the same thing. He had certainly never mentioned being able to create such a block. "You can do that?" I asked him, searching his dark gaze.

"I can," Atum said, nodding once. "And I will." He leaned in and pressed his lips to my forehead. I gripped his sides, digging my fingers into his flesh. He pulled away, his heartbroken stare lingering on my face. "I'm sorry," he whispered before he turned to Osiris. "It is done."

The *At* vines binding Osiris dissolved into a glittering mist that quickly dissipated.

"Much appreciated, Temu," Osiris said, rolling his shoulders. "Now put this on." He held the cuff out to Atum. "And tell me, how would you like to die?"

49

M Y SOUL AWAKENED THE moment Atum snapped the mystical
cuff around his wrist. He now had no power beyond that of a
normal Nejeret. The threat posed by Osiris had felt insufficient until this
moment. Until Atum gave up.

Muted by shock at what was happening, I shook my head in silent
protest. He couldn't seriously be considering this—letting Osiris kill him
to save me. It was ludicrous. We were supposed to *be together*. Our souls
were bound. We should have had forever.

"Perhaps it's for the best," Atum said, his usually deep and resonant
voice sounding hollow.

"Don't be ridiculous!" Tefnut barked. She stood and took a single
lunging step toward us. "Father—"

Atum held his hand up, stopping her with the gesture alone. "Look
at the mess I've made of the timeline. I've tangled the threads until the
pattern is barely salvageable."

Breaths coming faster, I focused on the swelling heat in my chest. The silently mounting power burned away my fear and anger, fueled by the hatred I now felt for my grandfather and his attempt to separate me from Atum. He couldn't. I wouldn't let him. Atum was *mine*.

I didn't just love him. We had merged, body and soul. He was a part of me now, as our mixed eye color suggested. The way we had come together during that last boundary crossing had fused our beings together deeper than the soul bond that connected our eternal *bas*. Our *sheuts* had melded, leaving behind slivers of the other embedded deep within either of us.

I realized I could feel him, even now. Even with his powers suppressed by Nuin's cuff. Even with the supposed bonding block he had planted within me. I could *still* feel him. I sensed his intent, and it had nothing to do with giving up, however compliant he may have seemed to Osiris and Tefnut.

Either Atum had lied about the bonding block, or our souls were so entangled that it hadn't worked.

"Father . . ." Tefnut was no longer looking at Osiris or Atum. Her wide-eyed stare was locked on me. Likely because my skin shimmered with that telltale golden glow that suggested my soul was mere moments from exploding out of my body and ripping apart everything within reach.

Atum turned his attention to me, a knowing glint in his eyes and the hint of a smirk tensing the corners of his full lips. He hadn't planned this, but he *had* hoped it would happen.

"Get out of here, Tefnut," I said between heaving breaths. "Take Shu and run."

Tefnut didn't hesitate for even a moment. She spun around and dragged her brother's limp body over her shoulders into a fireman's carry, demonstrating the enhanced physical abilities of a Nejeret. Grunting, she stood and marched toward the door flap, her features locked in a fierce mask of determination. Nitocris fled from the tent behind her.

"What's happening?" Osiris asked warily, taking a backward step toward the exit.

"No," I gritted out as Atum grabbed his brother's arm, just above the elbow and held him in a vice-like grip. Osiris wouldn't be running away from this. I was practically panting with the effort to hold in my soul, and the golden light shining through my pores brightened with each pounding beat of my heart. "The bond is too strong," I told my grandfather. "It can't be blocked."

"If I die," Atum said, dragging Osiris closer. "She dies." He jerked his brother close enough to embrace. "And I will watch the world burn before I let you kill her." His chest heaved with each breath. "Give Tarset the antidote *now*."

Osiris's focus shifted back and forth as he searched Atum's rage-filled glare, inches from his own confused face. "I can't." He licked his lips, his throat bobbing. "I *won't*. I swore an oath to Father. You have your duty, Temu, and I have mine. You're a danger to the timeline—to the entire universe." His attention slipped past Atum, landing on me. "I'm truly sorry, Tarset. If there was a way to spare you, I would, but the timeline . . ."

"I can't say I feel the same," I panted, losing my grip on the surging power within me. Any sense of self-preservation abandoned me. Atum and I were already dead. This wasn't about survival anymore; it was about revenge. "If you're determined to take us down . . ."

Bolts of blinding golden light broke through the physical shell of my body and shot out of me. Cracks formed in my skin, linking the points of light, and I felt myself coming undone.

Atum squinted against my brilliance, and Osiris raised a hand, shielding his eyes.

"I'm dragging you down with us," I vowed, tendrils of my soul lashing out from the cracks in my skin like solar flares.

I dragged in a ragged breath, and then I let go, surrendering to the explosive power roaring within me. Golden light exploded out of me, consuming Atum, Osiris, and the tent and everything within it until there was only that ethereal fire born of my rage.

That, and Osiris's screams.

I came to lying on my side, my ears ringing and my skull throbbing with a splitting headache. A tickling sensation touched the side of my face and the exposed outside of my bare arm. I peeled my eyes open to find snowflakes fluttering down around me through a thick fog. Except they weren't cold against my skin.

Flickers of memory returned. Osiris threatening me, and through me, Atum. Atum refusing to surrender. Tefnut fleeing with Shu. My soul expanding and detonating. Osiris's screams.

The flakes weren't snow, I realized, but ash. They were the tent and everything in it. They were Osiris.

They were Atum.

"No," I breathed, my heart lurching. I pushed myself up until I was sitting on my hip. A layer of ash slid off me, settling atop what had already accumulated on the ground.

I stared around, refusing to believe I had killed Atum. That I had, in my blind rage, accomplished Osiris's grisly task for him. But the dust and ash were so thick, I couldn't see more than a foot away in any direction.

"Atum?" My voice was nonexistent, coming out as a choked whimper.

I shifted to my hands and knees and crawled in one direction, feeling the ground for anything but ash. When I found nothing, I turned, searching in another random direction. Again and again, I turned, feeling my way through the destruction, but all I found were chunks of debris that could fit in the palm of my hand and an endless blanket of ash.

I coughed, choking on the ash, and blood sprayed the backs of my hands. I stared at it, confused. Had inhaling the ash and dust damaged my lungs?

But then horror crept in, replacing the confusion. The poison. Osiris had poisoned me.

Atum was gone, and I was dying.

I coughed again, spraying more blood. Dark spots danced around the edges of my vision, slowly closing in. My arms gave out, and I collapsed on the ground, curling into a ball and hugging my knees to my chest.

At least I wouldn't have to live long without him. Soon enough, we would be reunited in *Aaru*. We would still have our forever, just not in the way we had intended.

With that comforting thought, I let my eyelids drift shut and surrendered to the darkness.

I GROANED, MY HEADACHE threatening to split my skull in two, and dragged my eyelids open. The beautiful, copper face of an angel swam in front of my blurred vision. I tried to sit up, but the pressure on my shoulders and chest kept me on my back.

"Be calm," the angel said, and there was something familiar about her voice. She looked away. "Can you help? Soothe her mind with your *sheut*? Her heart rate must not elevate, or the poison will win."

"Tarset," another woman said, her voice also tickling my memories. "Be still, Tarset."

And then another face was there beside the angel's, darker and more beautiful still. This was the face of a goddess.

She touched her fingertips to my temples, and my eyelids grew impossibly heavy. They drifted shut despite my best efforts, and my awareness faded away.

"**S**HE IS ROUSING," A woman said, her voice hushed. "Nitocris, Fetch Aset."

"But she's sleeping." The second woman's voice was huskier and somewhat drab compared to the first.

"Then wake her!" the first woman barked, her harsh tone rousing my awareness enough to give her a name: Tefnut.

My eyelids fluttered as I lifted them. "Was it a dream?" I asked, my voice breaking. "A nightmare?"

"Shhh," Tefnut said, leaning closer. "You must not excite yourself until the healer has looked at you." She pressed her fingertips to my temple, and a calm lethargy washed over me, slowing my breathing and heartbeat but not knocking me out completely. My eyelids drifted shut, and I floated in that state of partial awareness for some indefinite period of time.

"She is awake?" another woman asked, her voice quiet but brusque. "I didn't expect her to rouse for hours yet."

"She is strong," Tefnut said, and I imagined her raising her stubborn chin. "She can survive what others cannot, like my father. She is *more*."

"Be that as it may, she is still gravely ill," the other woman said, and a name drifted up from my lulled mind: Aset. "We dosed her with the antidote too late. She *should* be dead."

"Lucky for us all, she isn't," Tefnut said.

For long, tense seconds, neither woman said anything. "How long has she been awake?" Aset finally asked.

"Only a few minutes," Tefnut said. "I subdued her, but she's still conscious."

"Was that necessary?" Aset asked, a sharp edge to her question.

"Yes," Tefnut said. "She was getting herself worked up, and I didn't think you would want her to see . . ." She trailed off meaningfully, and in the furthest edges of my mind, I wondered what, exactly, they didn't want me to see. "At least not until she's more clear-headed and can understand."

"Yes, well," Aset said, exhaling a sigh. "That's probably for the best, then. If you don't mind . . ."

There was the sound of rustling clothing and shuffling feet. Gentle fingers pressed against the side of my neck, then my chest and abdomen. Aset's touch was pure agony. My eyelids were lifted and then lowered, and my mouth was opened and then shut again a moment later.

"The poison's grip is loosening," Aset said. "Sedate her fully again."

"Shouldn't we feed her?" Tefnut asked, her concern audible. "Some broth or—"

"Her organs are still severely inflamed," Aset said. "Introducing anything foreign at this point will only aggravate the damage faster than the energy can be transformed into healing. She will be the worse for it. Sedate her, and hopefully the forced sleep will trigger regeneration."

"She's wasting away," Tefnut said, sounding defeated. "Will she survive another round of regenerative sleep?"

"I don't know," Aset said. "Only time will tell."

I FLOATED THROUGH A dark cloud of needles. Voices faded into and out of my awareness, echoing and blurring together. Boiling acid was poured into my mouth, searing my throat as it trickled down to my stomach. I coughed and spluttered, too weak to fight. Too tired to cry.

But then it was over, and I was left alone to drift away again.

"TARSET?" IT WAS A woman. Aset. I felt her cool hand pressed against my cheek, then against my forehead. "Can you hear me, Tarset?"

I cracked my jaw open, parting my dry lips, and I tried to speak, but all that came out of my cottony mouth was a breathy moan. My eyelids fluttered, resisting lifting, but finally I dragged them open.

Aset knelt on the floor beside my bedroll. "Here," she said, dipping a thick cloth into a large bowl and holding it over my mouth.

Cool water dripped onto my lips, and I opened my mouth further, letting the liquid land on my tacky tongue. Aset twisted the cloth, and a thin stream poured into my mouth. I gulped it down greedily.

"Thank you," I whispered when she dunked the cloth back into the bowl.

Aset smiled, bringing the saturated cloth back to my lips. "You are dangerously dehydrated and malnourished," she said, squeezing the water into my mouth. "I'd like to try propping you up so you can drink more quickly." She returned the cloth to the bowl, this time draping it over the side. "Do you think you could do that?"

I nodded, finding the gesture took far more effort than usual, like the resistance offered by the air was quadruple what it should have been.

"Cris," Aset said, waving someone over. I was surprised when the queen of the northern portion of Egypt stepped into view. "I'm going to lift her shoulders, and I need you to wedge your knees in behind her back to prop her up. Can you do that?"

"Of course, my lady," Nitocris said, bowing her head as she sank down onto her knees beside Aset.

Aset leaned forward and slipped an arm behind my shoulders, then lifted me off the bedroll. Nitocris scooted closer until I was resting on her lap.

"How do you feel?" Aset asked, studying my face closely. "Dizzy? Nauseated? Do you have a headache?"

As soon as she mentioned a headache, my brain throbbed. "Headache," I whispered. "Bad headache."

Aset frowned, clearly not liking that answer. "Hopefully this will help," she said, dipping a small ceramic cup into the bowl and lifting it to my lips. I drank every drop, but it only seemed to make me thirstier. She fed me another cupful of water, then dropped the cup into the bowl and pushed both away.

I whimpered, wanting nothing more than for Aset to hold the bowl up to my lips so I could drain it dry.

"We must wait and let what you've already had settle, or we risk upsetting your stomach and having it all come back up," she said, clasping her hands together on her lap.

"Tefnut was here before," I said, my voice raspy, but at least it was there. "Or did I make that up?"

Aset shook her head. "Tefnut has rarely left your side," she said. "She seems to believe she can heal you through sheer will alone." Aset nodded to one side, the corners of her mouth lifting. "Perhaps she is right. You should not be alive, and yet, here you are."

I smiled weakly. "I died once before," I told her. "Went into *Aaru* and everything."

Her eyebrows rose. "Truly?"

I shrugged one shoulder. "Atum believes that's how I ended up with a *sheut*." As soon as I said his name, my throat seemed to close up and my eyes stung with the threat of tears. My chin trembled, and I stared at Aset's face. "Did I kill him?" As an afterthought, I added, "And Osiris?"

"My father is gone, but Atum lives on," she said, but her expression was far less reassuring than her words. "In fact, he is in far better shape than you."

"I'm sorry," I whispered. "About Osiris." I rushed to add. "I didn't want this to happen."

Aset inhaled deeply, staring up at the white cloth ceiling as she released the breath. Only then did I realize I was in a large, white tent, with a floor of layered woven reed mats.

"My father was good for our people, I think, but he wasn't good for me," she said, closing her eyes. A tear snuck between her lashes and stuttered down her cheek. "Part of me hates you for what you did, but another part of me owes you my life." Her lids lifted, and she swiped the tear away, sniffling softly. "Because of you, I have a future that is *my own*."

I nodded, unsure what else to say. "Where's Atum?" I asked, looking around. "Why isn't he here?"

Aset reached for a waterskin and held it out, angling the opening toward my mouth. "Let's try some broth."

I raised one hand to push the waterskin away, but I was too weak to move the heavy bag of liquid even an inch. "Answer my question," I demanded.

"After you drink," she countered.

I pressed my lips together, but the rich scent of the broth made saliva pool in my mouth. My stomach groaned, and it was impossible to pretend I could hold out for long. Exhaling a sigh, I parted my lips and angled my face up toward the roof of the tent. Aset dribbled a little of the broth into my mouth at a time, slowly increasing the amount she fed me until I was taking full mouthfuls.

"He is in regenerative sleep in another tent," Aset finally said when she lowered the empty skin and set it aside by the bowl. She picked up another waterskin, this one near to bursting. "But I don't like your headache, so I'll have him moved in here. Exposure to the residual bonding pheromones should alleviate the worst of it." She held the fresh waterskin up to my lips. "Sweetened cream. Your body needs the fat to fuel your next round of regenerative sleep."

I let her pour the thick liquid into me, grateful for the sustenance. After all, this wasn't my first time being force fed for the sake of healing.

"Why have you been keeping us separated?" I asked when that skin was empty as well. A heavy lethargy fogged my mind, and I knew from experience that I didn't have long until regenerative sleep dragged me away.

Aset filled the small cup with water again and handed it to me, allowing me to drink at my own pace. "You have been battling for your life," she said, refilling the cup after I drained it and handed it back to her. "You are skin and bones, and he—he was gravely injured. It would have been too distressing for either of you to see the other so ... damaged. The stress would have hindered the healing process."

"And now?" I asked, my eyelids drooping.

Aset gestured for Nitocris to move away with a shift of her chin. "Let her lie down. She's ready to rest." Aset waited until I was flat on my back, then leaned closer. "I am sure you both will live. *Now*, keeping you separated will hinder the healing process." She rested a hand on my shoulder and smiled gently. "Sleep now, Tarset. When next you wake, Atum will be with you, and your soul will be whole."

52

I WOKE UP ON my side, the front of me pressed against a solid, warm
body. I didn't need to raise my heavy lids to know the powerful
arms wrapped around me belonged to Atum. The throbbing headache
had dulled somewhat in his presence, but it was very much still there. I
figured it wouldn't ease until we did something to intentionally boost
our bodies' output of bonding pheromones. Even half asleep, however,
I could tell my body wasn't ready for any kind of exertion—not even the
fun kind.

Atum's lips found mine, and he kissed me gently, then pulled back
once more. "How's your head?"

"Achy, but not as bad as before." I admitted, dragging my eyelids open.
New fractal scars branched across his skin like copper lightning bolts. My
eyes widened, and I sucked in a breath to ask about the new markings,
but Atum spoke first.

"I would attempt to ease your pains further, but you're still too weak,
and we have a limited amount of time before your body's regenerative

instincts take over." He sat up slowly, pulling me up with him. "Eat, so that you may return to the healing sleep. Perhaps next time . . ." He trailed off, promise glittering like stars in his midnight irises as he lightly skimmed his fingertips over my belly, causing me to suck in a shuddering breath.

Convinced that I was sufficiently motivated to heal, Atum arranged himself behind me like a living backrest and handed me a waterskin. "Broth," he said when I took hold of the skin.

His assessment of my physical state proved accurate when I attempted to lift the waterskin but found it too heavy. He helped, nuzzling my hair as I attempted to guzzle the broth without making gross gulping or slurping sounds. When I had drained the broth, he replaced the waterskin with another, filled with sweetened cream.

After I finished that one as well, Atum dragged a linen wrapped bundle about the size of a football closer, then lifted it and set it on my lap. My salivary glands tingled with anticipation as he unknotted the wrappings. Was I really going to get to chew *actual food*?

I suppressed a groan when the corners of the linen bundle fell open, revealing a pile of small sandwiches. Fig, soft white cheese, and honey squished between two thin pieces of flatbread. I lifted one of the scrumptious delicacies to my mouth and bit into it reverently. The rich, sweet, and tart flavors exploded across my tongue, and that time I *did* groan.

I savored that first bite, then scarfed the rest of the sandwiches in an embarrassingly short amount of time. I had dozens of questions for Atum—about his new scars and how he had survived my soul explosion—but I couldn't push past my body's need for sustenance for long enough to ask any of them.

I finished my feast with a third waterskin, this one filled with clear, crisp water. My eyelids were drooping before I had drained even half of the skin, my body relaxing back against Atum. My tongue felt leaden, and I whined, annoyed at my weakness. My questions would have to wait.

"That's enough," Atum murmured, when I drifted off for a moment, letting water dribble out from the corners of my mouth. He set the waterskin aside and eased back down onto our shared bedroll, laying me on my back and tucking in close against my side.

"Rest now, Tarset," he said, his voice a quiet rumble. He pressed his lips to my forehead, and I sighed as a deep, dreamless sleep carried me away.

53

"**T**ELL ME WHAT HAPPENED," I said between bites of stew, my gaze lingering on the copper scars branching across Atum's neck and up the sides of his face. The broth was thick and savory, and the chunks of meat and vegetables melted in my mouth before I even had the chance to chew. It was delicious, but not even regeneration-fueled hunger could distract me from digging for the truth.

Atum's gaze was steady on mine from across the corner of the squat table. He swallowed the nuts he had been chewing, then raised his hand to his mouth, pouring in some more.

I gritted my teeth together, forcing a slow inhale and exhale. Some things would never change, it seemed. Apparently, Atum's non-answers were something I was going to have to live with—and pry out of him—for the rest of eternity.

"It was me, wasn't it?" I said, setting down my spoon, which seems like a simple task, but was actually quite difficult with my unnatural hunger. "*I* gave you those scars."

Atum swallowed again, then raised a cup to sip some wine. "When you unleashed your soul on Osiris, it didn't tear through me as it did him, but I wasn't untouched, either."

Appeased that he was finally talking about what happened, I continued to eat.

Atum touched the fingertips of one hand to the new scars along the side of his jaw. They reminded me of the intricate, temporary markings that appeared on a person's skin after they were struck by lightning.

"Your soul wrapped around me," he explained, "shielding me in a cage of golden fire." His gaze grew distant. He was still looking at me, but it was clear that he wasn't seeing me. At least, not me *right now*. "I watched the world burn all around me. I watched my brother—" Atum closed his eyes, like he was trying to block out the mental image.

I set down my spoon, unsettled by what I had done to Osiris. Atum's brother. My grandfather. I killed him. I willingly ripped him apart, body and soul. And I didn't even have self-defense as an excuse. I was already dying, and through me, Atum was as well. Pure vengeance had fueled my attack on Osiris.

"You had no choice," Atum said, his voice rougher than before. He opened his eyes, fully present once more, and focused on me. "I'm sad that it came to that, but Osiris forced your hand. I wish he had seen reason, but he was so blinded by the wounds I inflicted when I left. Our father used that, twisted him into a man who would die for his so-called duty. I will never forgive Nuin for that."

I pretended Atum's words appeased my troubled heart, and I reclaimed my spoon, but the next bite of stew tasted like ash on my tongue. I wasn't as deeply disturbed by intentionally killing Osiris as I had been by accidentally ending the lives of those innocent people at the Waset palace. Osiris hadn't been innocent. He had wanted us dead. He had been actively killing us. That knowledge was a balm on my guilt, even if it didn't erase it completely.

"Tarset," Atum said, his stare cutting me open. "I can sense your disquiet." He exhaled heavily. "Tell me what is troubling you so."

I choked down the unpalatable bite of stew and set down my spoon beside the bowl. "I'm sorry I killed Osiris," I said, then rushed to add, "I don't regret it, especially not considering the outcome, but I'm disturbed about *why* I did it."

Atum tilted his head to the side, listening carefully.

"I was dying from his poison, which meant you were dying, as well," I said. "He wasn't going to let you live, no matter what. And that made me *so angry*. I've never felt such rage before." I took a deep breath, reorganizing my next words. "I didn't think we would survive. I wasn't trying to save us. We were dying, and all I wanted was to destroy him for what he was doing to us—to *you*. It wasn't fair that we were dying, and he was going to live on." I let out a despondent laugh. "Who does that? Who thinks like that? Who craves such unnecessary destruction?"

Atum was quiet for a long time, but finally he drew in a deep breath to speak. "I believe your soul knew exactly what it was doing, even if you did not." I shook my head, but before I could respond, he continued, "Your soul has proven it has a mind of its own, time and again. Perhaps what we need to focus on is figuring out a way to merge those two separate awarenesses. Then, I believe, you will feel more settled with what happened here."

My brows bunched together as I considered his words. "You're not upset—about what I did to you?" With my gaze, I traced the overall flow of the coppery scars climbing up the right side of his neck and curving along the edge of his face.

Atum shook his head, a small smile curving his full lips. "Am I upset that I now carry a visual marker of your love for me?" Heat entered his dark stare. "Not in the slightest. Unless. . ." He narrowed his eyes, just a little. "Do you find the markings unsightly?"

My eyelids opened wider, and my lips parted. "No," I said automatically. "Not at all." And I meant it. The markings were really quite beautiful and only added to his unique, otherworldly appeal. "Though they'll make you more memorable to others," I noted. "It won't be quite so easy for you to blend in."

"I have ways around that," he said, the heat in his gaze lighting a fire within me.

I reached across the corner of the table and trailed my fingertips over the curling path of one branch of the markings as it wound down and around his torso, over the older, familiar pattern of his self-inflicted scars. Ghosts of sensation danced along my nerve endings where I touched him, like the markings weren't so much scars but a part of me transposed onto him, similar to what had happened with our eyes during that pivotal boundary crossing.

"Where do they end?" I asked, leaning forward to plant my elbow on the table as my hand neared the knot on his waistband holding his schenti in place. "Do they continue down here?" I asked, dipping my fingers into his waistband.

His abdominal muscles flexed involuntarily, bunching under my touch.

I pushed my hand deeper into his kilt, finding him hot, hard, and ready. "Here?" I asked, curling my fingers around him and letting out a low, pleased moan. Again, I could feel that ghostly touch on my own body, in my most intimate of places. I was touching him, but it was as though I was touching myself as well.

Atum hissed in a breath, pulsing in my tight grip. "I cannot recall," he said, his voice husky.

"Perhaps I should take a look," I said, rising onto my knees and scooting closer as I stroked him. The sensation that I was pleasuring myself intensified with his increasing desire, and my legs trembled.

"Perhaps you should," he said, sliding a hand under my skirt and up my thigh.

I glided my thumb over his bulging head, collecting a drop of his arousal. A jolt of pleasure shot through my core, and I gasped, my fingers clenching around him.

Atum's hand froze on my inner thigh, close to my sex but not yet touching me. "Tarset?" he asked, his expression one of bafflement.

"I can feel them," I said, my hips rocking against the ghostly touch. "The markings," I added, my voice shaky.

I released him and quickly untied the knot on his schenti, revealing his proud length. Sure enough, the branching copper markings extended along his shaft all the way to the tip.

As I studied him, a bead of his arousal leaked out and crept down his length, following the path of the delicate scars. A light sensation mirrored the path on my own body, almost like Atum was teasing me with a feather between my legs.

I traced the branching scar up from the base of his shaft to its head and shuddered as the direct contact echoed through me. "When I touch the markings, it's like I'm also touching myself."

A slow smile curled Atum's lips. "So, if I touched myself," he said, gripping the base of his shaft, "it would be like I was touching you, as well?" He stroked himself, pushing my hand away. The firm, deliberate motion rocketed through me, more intense than before because he was the one eliciting the sensations, not me.

"Yes," I moaned, gripping his shoulder to steady myself as he continued to stroke himself. Our bodies were different, obviously, and mine seemed to interpret the translated sensations in new and unique ways. The pleasure I felt now was different from anything I had ever felt before.

Atum's hand on my thigh continued its journey upward. My eyelids fluttered when he trailed a fingertip along my slit, and my breaths came faster. "And this? Can you feel both of us now?" he asked, circling my needy, swollen apex with that clever fingertip.

"Yes," I hissed, my whole body trembling from the overwhelming sensations.

"Hmmm . . ." Atum removed his hand from between my legs, using it to push my skirt up and over my hips, exposing me to him completely. He curved his arm around my backside and pulled me closer.

Instinctively understanding what he wanted—it was what I wanted, too—I straddled his lap. I clutched his shoulders as he guided himself toward my entrance, and I shifted my hips forward. He sank into me, and my body shuddered, already on the cusp of release.

Atum wrapped his arms around me, pulling me closer, until he was buried to the hilt within me. "And this?" he asked, searching my face like he was memorizing my response. "How does this feel?"

"Insane," I breathed, practically panting against him. "And incredible." I rocked my hips, freezing as our dual pleasure coursed through me. "I can't—it's too much," I said between gasping breaths. "Atum . . ." His name was a plea on my tongue, except I didn't know what I was asking him to do. "Please," I begged. "I can't . . ."

A low, rough growl rumbled through his chest. He turned us away from the table in a swift, graceful motion and laid me on my back, wasting no time to pull out, then thrust back into me.

Pleasure-like starlight danced across my vision, and I groaned and dug my nails into his shoulders. This was the kind of ecstasy that usually only lasted a few seconds, during the moment of climax, but now, his every movement within me sent me floating through an ocean of bliss.

Atum froze above me. "Should I stop?" he asked, concern tensing his features.

"Don't you dare," I gasped, and his worries evaporated.

Atum pulled out, then pushed back into me, slower this time, his gaze roving over my face. On his next thrust, he leaned in, claiming my lips. My eyelids fluttered closed, and I sank into the sensations, letting the mounting pleasure pull me higher and higher toward an impossible peak.

My breath caught. My heart stopped. For a brief eternity, white-hot ecstasy flooded my nerve endings, becoming my entire existence.

Ever so slowly, I floated back to earth, spent and sated. My muscles hummed with remnants of the climax, little electric bolts of pleasure making my fingers and toes spasm. Atum nuzzled my neck, and I could feel him softening within me. His own limbs trembled, exhausted. We had both pushed our still healing bodies to their limits.

Atum kissed his way up my throat, over my chin, and found my lips. His kiss was slow and sensual. A promise of more to come later, when we had recovered. I wrapped my arms and legs around him, holding him close. This man. This god. He was mine. Until the end of time.

And after.

A TUM AND I WATCHED Shu and Aset walk away, heading up the gradual slope of the field toward the high road beyond the reach of the floodwaters, to join the troops marching north. Evening sunlight reflected off the water's surface, turning it into liquid gold. For weeks, they would march through the cooler nights until they reached Men-nefer.

Tefnut was somewhere near the head of the caravan with Nitocris, tasked with keeping the cowed queen in line until the end of her reign. According to the original pattern on the time tapestry, before I showed up and carpet-bombed the entire area with chaos, she was marked for death within the next few years. If it didn't happen naturally, Atum and I would return to Men-nefer to ensure it happened *at all*.

Aset walked arm in arm with Shu, the two having bonded while she doctored his stab wound. They made a striking couple, and he clearly adored her. But even as my aunt's evident happiness brought a small smile to my lips, I couldn't help but think back to the future I had left behind. He certainly wasn't with her then, and she had never mentioned him. I didn't think this relationship was fated to last.

I sensed Atum's worry as he watched them go, and I turned my head to look at him. "What troubles you?" I asked. "The memory block? Are you worried it wasn't enough?"

Aset's was the most complex of all the memory modifications Atum and Tefnut had carried out over the past few days, including Nitocris and all of her soldiers. He had excised me and the explosion from her recollection completely, as well as altering the details surrounding Osiris's death. He removed himself but left Shu and Tefnut, only minimally altered.

Atum shook his head, his brow furrowing. "I took my time on hers," he said. "It will hold."

"Then what are you so worried about?" I asked.

He sighed heavily, adjusting his hold on the small box that held Osiris's ashes. Tefnut had burned what little remained of him after the explosion. "They have the potential to bond," Atum admitted. "If they do—"

"They don't," I said, feeling confident in my presumption.

"But how can you be certain?" Atum asked, finally tearing his stare from Aset and Shu to look at me. "Their relationship wasn't a part of the original pattern, and the time tapestry has yet to resettle around their entangled threads." He shook his head. "The way they took an immediate liking to one another—it's like they were drawn together by some stronger force than simple attraction." His midnight gaze searched mine. "We both know how *that* feels."

"Some people just click," I told him, linking my arm with his and pulling him closer. "Like me and Kiya. And we don't share a soul bond."

Atum pressed his lips together, unconvinced.

"I've seen the future that lies beyond your reach," I reminded him. "Aset was there, and Shu was not."

"But the pattern—"

"They've already met," I said, interrupting him. "Their relationship has already started." I gestured to the world around us with a sweep of my arm. "And the universe has yet to unravel." I raised my eyebrows for emphasis. "If they were to alter the pattern enough that it changed the future I left behind—a *fixed* future—then I think we would notice." I shrugged. "We would probably already have unraveled."

"Perhaps you're right," Atum said, his features relaxing and some of the tension leaving his shoulders. "But I'll feel better once I can examine the time tapestry, to be sure."

"Well then," I said, turning to face him fully and wrapping my arms around him, linking my hands behind his lower back. "Whisk me away to one of your secret lairs so we might check on your precious pattern."

Atum's arms slipped around me, and he pulled me closer, bending his neck to press his lips against mine. A colorful mist surrounded us, followed by the dizzying sensation of being yanked across a vast distance between one heartbeat and the next.

I gasped, breaking the kiss as the world reformed around us, and clutched onto Atum for stability. "A little warning would have been nice," I said breathily, closing my eyes against the temporary motion sickness that seemed to make the world bob and sway around me.

Atum kissed my forehead. "Next time, I promise."

I breathed deeply, waiting for the world to stabilize. It didn't take long. Exhaling my relief, I lifted my lids and locked eyes with Atum. We were in another of his *At* caverns, the slight differences in shape and the arrangement of the faux fire pit and low table telling me this wasn't the Waset cavern. That one was too far away for him to reach in a single jump, anyway.

"Better?" Atum asked.

I nodded, then looked past him to the glowing rectangular patch on the wall behind him. The window to the time tapestry had a distinctly rosy hue, but it wasn't nearly as red as it had been when we first arrived in Waset. "It looks better," I said.

Atum turned toward the time tapestry patch. "It does," he agreed. His arms slipped away, and he took hold of my hand, linking our fingers together. He approached the glowing patch on the wall, pulling me along beside him. "See how the threads are straightening out?" he said, raising his free hand to point to the outer parts of the visible portion of the time tapestry. "They're resettling, pulled back to their original pattern—or as close as they can get."

I scanned the patch, my eyes moving constantly. The fainter the rosy glow, the smoother the threads appeared. "The time tapestry does this all by itself?"

Atum nodded sagely. "Indeed, it does," he said. "The lifethreads *want* to retain their usual, comfortable pattern. So long as we correct the more disruptive disturbances, the pattern will continually self-correct."

"Why?" I asked, looking at him.

"I think it's because of me," Atum said. "Well, Shu and Tefnut, too. Not because we're so proficient at tending the timeline, but because every time we enter the timeline, we create a fixed point or period. The era solidifies, locking us out from ever visiting again but also locking *in* the pattern formed by the lifethreads during that specific period of time. It's why we try to limit our visits to the bare minimum and rarely overlap when we enter the timeline, to keep as much of the pattern available to each of us as possible in case we're needed for a correction."

Shaking my head, I faced him fully. "You should be doing the opposite," I said, feeling the truth of the statement in my bones. In my soul. I was no theoretical physicist—or whatever discipline claimed theories of time travel as one of their areas of expertise—but even I could see the error in his logic.

Atum pulled back, his brows drawing together.

"Why don't you just live through the timeline?" I asked. "What if the thing that makes it malleable and open to disruption is the fact that you and Tefnut and Shu *live outside* of the timeline?" The more I voiced the theory, the more certain I felt I was correct. "What if it's the absence of your threads that *creates* the instability that allows for dissonances?"

Atum narrowed his eyes thoughtfully.

"If you went back to the beginning—to the first moment you stepped out of the timeline—and *lived* it, wouldn't the entire thing be set in stone? No more possibility of dissonances? No more need for you and Tefnut and Shu to devote your eternal lives to tending to the timeline? You would be free to live your own lives."

I could feel Atum's internal struggle. He shook his head slowly, pushing against my logic. "But my father—"

"Was a manipulative dick," I said.

Atum's eyebrows climbed up his forehead.

I rolled my eyes. "I *know* he's the Great Father and we wouldn't exist without him and all that, but over and over again, Nuin—or Re or whatever you want to call him—has proven himself to be highly fallible and generally not the best guy—at least where individuals are concerned." I laughed bitterly. "*Especially* in the future. Some of the shit he pulled with Kat and Nik . . ." I scoffed and shook my head. "He sees the big picture—he's blinded by it—and he's not the least bit concerned with the lives that are destroyed along the way, so long as his end game is achieved."

I could sense Atum's resolve wavering.

"What did he tell you to do, exactly?" I asked.

"To guard the timeline and ensure the pattern allowed for Heru and Alexandra to bond at the far, future edge," he said, his stare unfocusing as his thoughts turned inward. "To remove any obstacles to that end. That's it." He shook his head, laughing under his breath. "It sounds simple enough, doesn't it?" His brow furrowed. "I don't know how it became so complicated. Over time, it just—" He looked at the time tapestry patch. "I overcomplicated it, didn't I?"

"Maybe?" I said, shrugging one shoulder. "Maybe I'm wrong. Who am I to question the will of a god?" I laughed. "I'm just a singer."

Atum turned to me. "Obviously, I'm not the only one who doesn't see things clearly." He said, leaning in and pressing his forehead against mine. "You are so much more than that."

"You mean—I'm a chaos bomb as well?" I asked, my lips curving into a teasing smile.

"As you have just so expertly proven," he said and kissed me soundly, silencing any further banter for a delightfully long time.

Maybe I was right about the timeline. Maybe I was wrong. I honestly didn't know. But of one thing, I was certain—Atum and I would find out. Together.

EPILOGUE

TARSET

A TUM AND I LAZED on our narrow bed platform in Inyotef's sleeping chamber on a pillowy mattress of *At* he created every night to make me more comfortable—the thin pads that passed for mattresses nowabouts just weren't cutting it anymore. My head rested on his shoulder, and I traced the branched copper markings cutting through his dark skin with a gentle fingertip as he slowly trailed his hand up and down the side of my body.

We had been in Waset for a few weeks, overseeing the repairs to the damaged portion of the palace and gradually restoring a sense of normalcy to the land. One day, when the near war was a distant memory and the drought had released its death grip on the land, the people would blossom with innovation and art, but right now they were focused on surviving. Atum and I assisted in any way we could, but even he didn't have the power to hydrate the parched river valley.

"Are you decent?" Kiya asked from the other side of the curtain blocking the doorway. She snickered, like she was laughing at her own personal inside joke.

"Give us a moment," I called out to her, kissing Atum's shoulder before sitting up.

I reached for the shift hanging on a stubby peg in the wall beyond the foot of the bed and pulled it on over my head. I retrieved the schenti hanging on the next peg over and tossed it to Atum.

"All right," I called to Kiya a minute later, as Atum tightened the knot on his linen kilt. We would both have to undergo a more drastic transformation than merely getting dressed—turning into Inyotef and his new human wife, Nebeth—before we actually left the room.

Kiya pushed the curtain aside and strode into the room, her face bright with excitement. "We found him," she said. "The boy."

My eyes widened. "Mentuhotep's ancestor?" I asked, looking from Atum to Kiya and back.

Kiya nodded. "Tefnut confirmed it on the time tapestry," she said eagerly. "It's him."

"Where is he now?" Atum asked, planting his hands on his hips.

"He's an orphan," she said. "A neighboring farm took him in when his parents perished the year before last, but they're struggling—too many mouths to feed, not enough of anything."

Atum nodded, his eyes narrowing. "Bring him here," he said. "Offer the family positions at the palace, so it seems more natural. I want to keep a close eye on the boy."

I looked at Atum sharply, my eyebrows rising. "You want to keep a close eye on him—*yourself*?" I clarified.

Atum shrugged one shoulder. "Your theory about the timeline intrigues me. I think we should test it out."

"You want to live *in* the timeline?" I asked, my brows climbing higher.

"Only if you're willing," he said.

My mouth opened and closed as I floundered for words. Finally, I nodded. "Yes," I said, a slow smile curving my lips. "If it means you might one day gain your freedom, then absolutely *yes*."

Thanks for reading! You've reached the end of *Darkness Between the Stars*, but Tarset's adventure is still far from over. The Fateless Trilogy continues with *Uncross the Stars*, available for pre-order in Lindsey's bookshop.

lindseysparksbookshop.com

Don't want to wait? You can read the serialized version of *Uncross the Stars* on Lindsey's Patreon, with new episodes released every month as she writes them! There are also loads of bonus stories and other serials, some of which are free to the public. :)

https://www.patreon.com/lindseysparks

Sign up for Lindsey's newsletter to receive updates on the Fateless Trilogy as well as to gain access to her FREE subscriber library, including four full novels (ebook and audiobook), two exclusive novellas, and more!

www.authorlindseysparks.com/join-newsletter

About
Lindsey Sparks

Lindsey Sparks lives her life with one foot in a book—so long as that book transports her to a magical world or bends the rules of science. Her novels, from Post-apocalyptic (writing as Lindsey Fairleigh) to Time Travel Romance, always offer up a hearty dose of unreality, along with plenty of history, intrigue, adventure, and romance.

When she's not working on her next novel, Lindsey spends her time hanging out with her two little boys, working in her garden, or playing board games with her husband. She lives in the Pacific Northwest with her family and their small pack of cats and dogs.

www.authorlindseysparks.com

SIGNED COPIES & MERCH: lindseysparksbook-shop.com

PATREON: www.patreon.com/lindseysparks

MAIN SOCIAL MEDIA
Instagram: @authorlindseysparks
TikTok: @authorlindseysparks
YouTube: Author Lindsey Sparks
Discord: discord.gg/smTeDHQBhT

www.authorlindseysparks.com/join-newsletter

CPSIA information can be obtained
at www.ICGtesting.com
Printed in the USA
LVHW041642250623
750732LV00034B/430